FIGHTING DESTINY

Forsaken Sinners MC Series: Book Two

By Shelly Morgan

FIGHTING DESTINY

Limitless Publishing, LLC
Kailua, HI 96734
www.limitlesspublishing.com

Formatting: Limitless Publishing

ISBN-13: 978-1-68058-539-1
ISBN-10: 1-68058-539-8

DEDICATION

This book is for my girls; Debbie, Sara, and Mary.

Thank you for those late night chats, for keeping my head on straight, and for always telling me how it is. I wouldn't be where I am right now if it weren't for you girls.

You all are not only my beta readers, but have become my friends—my sisters.

You girls are the best!

So here's to more late night chats (even those that turn into talking about flab, pears, and meatballs LOL), to always sharing those sexy guy photos that make our days seem better (even for a couple of minutes), and to more books that rock peoples' world!

I love you three to pieces. <3 <3 <3

CHAPTER 1

A Month Earlier

Toby

I don't see anyone as I walk into the gym, so after dropping my bag off in the locker room, I head over to the treadmill to start my warm-up. I hope someone comes in soon that can spar with me because I've been itching for a fight. Things with the club haven't been too rough lately—not that I'm complaining because it's nice not having a situation that needs to be taken care of—but I need to release this pent-up energy somehow. And since I can't do it at the club and I haven't been scheduling any fights lately, I need to find someone here that will help me work this out of my system.

Ten minutes later, I'm rewarded when I see Dani walk in. This girl is something else. She's like me in a lot of ways, but there is a softer side to her too that she doesn't show to most. When she started working for Mack, I knew something bad had

1

SHELLY MORGAN

happened to her. She had this beaten, broken-down-by-life look to her, but I never pushed for information. Instead, I showed her how to channel her anger and pain, taught her ways to make sure she was never in a situation she couldn't control again. I taught her to *fight*.

"Yo, Dani! What brings you in this early? Blaze not fuckin' ya enough? Ya need me to wear your ass out?" This has her flipping me off as she walks into the locker room, but I see the smile on her face so I know she's all right. Dani is like a sister to me. I'm always acting like her big, overprotective brother, which drives her fucking crazy, but that's what makes it so much fun.

After she's changed, she heads straight to the ring and I follow, knowing that we're here for the same reasons.

We start out slow, each taking our time before going full throttle, but this won't last long. I used to take it easy on her in the ring, not wanting to hurt her or give her more than she could handle. But after years of working with her, I know she can take what I throw at her. That doesn't mean that I fight her like I would in an actual fight or if one of the guys was in the ring with me, but I don't take it easy on her, either. I learned the hard way that if she feels you aren't giving her everything you've got, you're going to feel her wrath and let me tell you this—Dani is one tough bitch, and I mean that in the most sincerest way. I've seen her take men down that are three times her size.

She's the first to take our sparring to the next level. She fakes a right cross and catches me off

2

guard with a left uppercut. *Fuck, that hurt!* Shaking it off, I smile at her. *Game on.*

An hour later, we've both had enough. It still amazes me that sometimes I can get a better workout with her than some of the guys around here, but what can I say, she learned from the best.

Throwing a towel in my face, she plops down to stretch out her body. Out of the corner of my eye, I can see some of the guys checking her out. Catching my glare, they quickly look away. I'm not blind, I know that she's fucking hot, but I've never had an attraction toward her. The only feeling I got when I first met her was that she needed someone to protect her, not fuck her. I took on a guardian role and it's been that way ever since.

When she's done, she gets up and comes over to me, rubbing my shaved head. "Lovin' the new do, Toby. Or should I start calling you Mr. Clean?" I've always kept my hair short, liking the buzz cut I've had since joining the Marines, but a couple nights ago I shaved it all off, leaving only my facial hair. I'm still getting used to it but it's working for me.

I look up and give her a smile, which takes her by surprise. I guess you could say that I don't smile much, but she's one of the few select people that get to see that side of me. I'm not used to showing or expressing emotions, but since she's come into my life, it's come more easily to me. There's something about her that makes people feel comfortable and at ease around her, or at least the people who really know her. If she doesn't know you, she may seem to come off cold and if she doesn't like you, you'll know it.

"Get the fuck outta here before I call Blaze and have him drag your ass home." Standing up, I head over to the heavy bag. Even after that workout, I still feel that itch. I won't be able to concentrate on anything until I beat it out of my system.

When she walks past me to head into the locker room, she pinches my ass, causing me to jump a little out of surprise. "Don't tease me with a good time. There's nothing I love more than my old man going caveman on me." She throws a wink over her shoulder and then she's gone.

When I finish with the heavy bag, I lift weights for a bit and then decide to run until I can't feel my legs anymore. I have nothing that I need to do today so working myself into exhaustion isn't going to be a problem.

I'm in the middle of my run when I see Wes walking my way. Wes runs the gym and he was my coach when I first started fighting in the cage. He's also the one that helped me start my MMA career, knowing a guy who knew a guy, or some shit like that. They came and watched one of my fights and from that day on, I was fighting professionally and the money started rolling in. I didn't fight for the money though. I didn't need it because I make a good living with the business I do for the club. It was the thrill of the fight and a means to an end with all the anger I had rolling around inside my head.

He stops by my treadmill and leans against it. Powering the machine down, I walk over to grab my water bottle and towel. "What's up?" I ask, out of breath. Fuck, maybe I pushed myself a little too

4

hard.

"I've gotta head out of town for a couple of weeks. My sister's not doing too well. I need you to take over my classes till I get back." Wes not only runs the gym and helps train fighters, but he also holds a couple self-defense classes a few times a week.

I've run the classes a couple of times for him, and even though I don't want to add anything else to my plate right now, I can't say no. "Yeah, man. I got you." He nods his head in thanks and walks away. I grab my shit and head outside to my bike. I want to get home for a shower and relax for the rest of the day before I do Wes's class tomorrow.

***

The class today is a beginner's course in self-defense for women. I get everything set up and wait for the students to arrive. This class will only have five women in it, but I prefer it that way. It allows me to work with them one-on-one. Most of the women who take this class have been abused at one time in their lives, so I want to do everything I can to make sure they know how to protect themselves if it ever happens again.

Growing up the way I did, I find it important that everyone knows how to get out of a sticky situation—man or woman. My mother was a junkie whore and would do anything for her next fix—she even tried to pimp me out once, but I put a stop to that quick. I don't want anyone to ever feel the way I felt when I was growing up, helpless, alone, and afraid.

I hear the bell over the door chime. Looking up, I'm taken back by who I see. I've never seen this chick before, but there's something about her that seems familiar. She reminds me of Dani when I first met her—the same beaten down look that is screaming for help.

She's not wearing any makeup, which you would think is normal for women when they come to a gym to work out, but you'd be surprised what women will do these days to catch a man's attention, especially at a gym. I'm not gonna lie, I've had my fair share of hook-ups with those same types of women I've met here, but I'm sick of the monotony. I don't want to spend my whole life with random women every night or die alone. I want a woman who is just mine; one to ride on the back of my bike, be waiting for me at home, and who loves me for me—not what I do for a living or who I'm associated with.

I wait to see what she does, but when she just stands there, looking around like she has no idea what she's looking for, I decide to help her out. "Can I help you with something?" I have no idea if she's one of the five for the class today or if she's just checking the place out, but a part of me is hoping she'll be in my class. It seems she could use it too.

She looks cautious and scared. I've been known to scare people away with just my looks, but to be honest, I don't think I've ever scared a *woman* away. But the way she's looking at me, I can see a glimmer of fear that she's trying hard to hide. It pisses me off that there is any kind of fear in her eyes when she looks at me.

The anger must show on my face because she gasps and takes a step back from me, but she doesn't look away. Fuck, someone really did a number on this girl. "Are you okay?" I have this overwhelming need to protect this woman. The only woman who has ever made me feel this protective need is Dani, but this stranger has me wanting to keep her safe from the world.

"I, uh, I was just..." she doesn't finish, but continues to back up even more. *Fuck, Toby, think!* I cannot let her walk out of here afraid of me. Holding my hands up, I crouch down a little to catch her eyes.

"I'm not gonna hurt you, doll. You're safe here, I promise."

She must see the sincerity in my eyes. Her shoulders drop and she stands taller. "I saw a flyer about a class that's held here." She doesn't say anything else, but that's all I need to hear.

I step to the side and motion for her to follow me. "Right this way. You're the first one here this morning." Walking ahead of her, I glance over my shoulder to make sure she's following and catch her checking out my ass. The lustful look that radiates off of her makes me want to turn around and show her that the feeling is mutual, but I know that's not a good idea. At least, not yet. She's here for a reason and looks like she really needs this class.

I stop and clear my throat. When she looks up, I wink at her, letting her know she's been caught and it doesn't bother me one bit. She blushes slightly and starts to walk ahead of me, which gives me the chance to return the favor.

I leave her to her own thoughts as she does some stretches to prepare for class and I try like hell not to stare at her. It's been a long time since a woman has caught my attention with just one look. I can't help but think there is so much more to this woman. I can tell she's been through something, but the fact that she's here, wanting to learn to protect herself, shows that she's ready to take control of whatever traumatic event happened to her, and that shit does something to me. She's strong, and I know if I can get her to relax around me, she will probably surprise me even more. One way or another, I'm going to figure her out.

Fifteen minutes later, the rest of the girls show up. "All right, ladies. We're going to start with the basics. Then, I'll show you some easy, but effective moves to ward off a predator," I say as I look around the room. "Always stay in groups when you are out at night. If you have to go out alone, stay in well-lit areas, and always carry your keys in your hand—they make a great weapon. And always go with your gut. If something doesn't feel or look right, it's probably not." I pause again to make sure everyone is on the same page. "Okay. Now that we have that covered, if you spot someone, what is the first thing you do?"

All the girls raise their hand, except *her*. I realize that I don't even know her name, so I walk over to her. She'll be my first volunteer. "What's your name?" I whisper so no one else can hear. She blushes a beautiful shade of red before raising her

8

eyes to mine.

"Sara." A beautiful name for a beautiful woman.

"Sara, what would you do if you spot someone that looks like they're up to no good?" I say louder so the whole class can hear as I stand in front of her, giving her my full attention. She hesitates for only a moment before answering me.

"I would study my surroundings first. If there are people close by, I would move toward them. If I was alone, I would try to get away quickly." She's on the right path, but I want more from her.

"And if that doesn't work, what do you do?"

"I'd scream." I nod and smile. Walking back to the front of the room again, I address the class. "That's right, Sara. But if that *still* doesn't work and he gets a hold of you, I'm going to show you what to do. Would you please come up front to help me demonstrate?" I've made it sound like a question, but I don't expect an answer. She holds her head up high and walks right up to me. Atta girl!

I turn her around to face the class so her back is to my front. I hope I can control myself enough so she doesn't feel how much her mere presence affects me. "First, I'll show you what to do if you get attacked from behind."

***

After class, I notice that Sara is at the front desk. I hope she's signing up for more classes, or maybe even a membership. I want to see more of her and hopefully work up to being able to see her outside of the gym.

Walking over to her, I place my hand lightly on her shoulder. I feel her stiffen, which makes me even more motivated to teach her self-defense, though I hope she never has to use it. I want to be the one to protect her, but if it *does* come down to her having to fight back, I want her to have knowledge and skills to do so. "Sorry, I just wanted to come over and see if I could help get you signed up for our next class," I say softly. She looks up at me with a look I can't quite place, but before I can examine it further, she looks away.

"I'm not sure when I'll be able to do another class yet, but thank you. You were a great instructor." She hands Katherine some paperwork she filled out and walks out the door. I watch her go, hoping she turns around to grace me with her beautiful green eyes, but I get nothing.

I look at Katherine quick to see if she's noticed anything about our exchange, but she's busy typing away on the computer. Relief washes over me. Katherine is the type of girl that would talk about things that aren't her business. I hate that about people—they don't know when to mind their own business or realize that if I wanted their opinion, I'd ask for it.

Walking over to the speed bag, I can't get her out of my head. The way she looked when she first came in compared to how she looked after the class. The difference was astounding. She seemed more comfortable around me by the end of the class.

I can also tell from the time I spent with her that before whatever happened to her, she was a strong-willed woman who wasn't afraid of anything, and that just makes me more determined to figure out what caused that change and help bring her back to the way she used to be. And once she's strong again, I will do whatever I can to make sure no harm comes to her—ever.

Needing to get away from here and the image of her, I decide to head home for a shower and stop by the clubhouse. I may as well do something to try to keep my mind off of Sara since I don't have to worry about the other class now that Wes is back. And who knows, maybe I can get into some trouble there and pass the time till I can see Sara again. I hope it isn't long, otherwise I may have to take matters into my own hands.

***

Once I'm at the clubhouse, I notice Louie at the bar so I head in his direction, but I'm stopped before I make it there. "Hey, baby. I've missed you," Trixie, one of the club whores I hook up with when I need a release, says. Not wanting anything to do with her tonight, well, not wanting anything to do with her anymore period, I brush her off.

"Not tonight, Trix." Walking past her toward Louie, I hear her huff and stomp away, probably to someone else with a dick. Good luck to that, brother, whoever the unlucky bastard is.

"Yo, Toby. What the fuck was that about?" Louie doesn't look toward Trixie, but motions toward her with his thumb. I'm usually better at turning away pussy so my brothers don't give me shit about it, but I'm just not in the mood to deal with this shit tonight.

"I don't know, man. Bitch needs to learn her place, though," I say, avoiding the subject. Louie is usually pretty good at not pressing me, and he doesn't disappoint tonight.

"You see Dani lately?" he asks. Louie and Dani used to have a thing a couple years back, but for him it was different. He wanted to make her his old lady, but it wasn't like that for her. She wasn't using him, but he was a part of her healing process, I guess you could say. That's my take on it, anyway. I don't get into other people's shit unless I need to. Now, he and Dani are back to normal, or as normal as could be expected. Things were touchy at first when Blaze came back into her life, but I think Louie sees the way they are together. Those two are meant to be.

"Yeah, she came by the gym yesterday. Why, what's up?" I ask, knowing he would only ask for a reason.

"Nothing. Just wanted to talk with her is all." Taking a page out of my own book, I don't push for answers. When he wants to talk, he will.

The rest of the night is uneventful. I sit and drink with my brothers, keeping to myself and watching the others as I usually do. No one gives me shit anymore because they're used to my brooding attitude and watchful eyes by now.

Heading home that night, I can't get Sara out of my head. Since that day, she's filled my thoughts, day and night.

CHAPTER 2

Present Day

Sara

I cringe as I pull into the parking lot of Club Sin. I hate that I have to work here, but it's the first place that hired me. At least I don't have to be up on the stage taking my clothes off. No, I just have to wear these ridiculous outfits while tending the bar. Oh well, it could be worse. I could be back in New York with Rick…no. I'd definitely take up stripping before ever going back there again. This is the lesser of the two evils.

Stepping out of my car, I pull down my leather mini skirt, and then I pull up my tight-as-fuck tank top as much as I can so my ass and tits are at least *marginally* covered before I walk into the club.

I give Lyle a genuine smile as he lets me through the door. He's actually a really nice man, and one of the few reasons I don't leave this place. Having him here makes me feel safe—or saf*er*. I've only been working here for a little over a week, but there hasn't been a night that he hasn't been here. When I'm tending bar and start to get a little freaked out over a customer that's a little too touchy, I look to where he's standing by the door and see him watching me. All it would take is one signal and he'd be over to take care of the problem.

After putting my purse under the bar, I do a quick inventory of what we need to stock for the night. It's not too busy yet, but I know within the hour the bar will be so packed that even the waitresses will have a hard time walking around. Getting everything I need now is key to making the night go as smooth as possible.

JR walks behind the bar just as I finish stocking the beer. "S'up, Sara?" JR is a couple years older than me. I'm guessing thirty to my twenty-eight. He's not bad on the eyes, but he's a little too arrogant for my liking, though he is funny to hang around with. I greet him, then turn back around to finish stocking.

My boss, Burke, walks over and calls out my name as he plops down on a stool. "I need you to work the floor tonight. Trixie can't come in so I had to pull one of the girls off the floor and onto the stage." I know I should be grateful for this because I'll make more money waitressing than bartending, but I'm not in the mood to strut around all night, taking drink orders and having men grab my ass. At least behind the bar, there's that extra barrier and I have a direct line of sight to Lyle if I need him. Being on the floor will make it harder for him to keep an eye on me.

"Me? I'm not sure if that's a good idea, Burke. Shouldn't you have Tasha do it instead?" There's gotta be someone else that can do it.

He levels me with a hard stare and points at me. "You either do what I tell ya, or you're fired. Ya hear me?" Without waiting for my reply, he picks up the stack of bills he was counting and walks down the hall toward his office. Fuck. I guess I don't really have a choice now, do I?

Tossing my dishtowel down on the bar, I turn around to walk out and run right into JR. "Fuck! Shit, I'm sorry, Sara. You all right?" he asks as he grabs me by my shoulders to steady me.

"I'm fine. Looks like you're on your own back here tonight," I tell him as I step out of his reach.

Heading into the bathroom, to try to calm down and prepare myself for the job that needs to be done. Reaching into my bag, I take out my red lipstick, hoping it will give me the confidence I so desperately need. Once my makeup is touched up, I look down at my outfit. I guess if I'm going to do this, I may as well do it right. With that in mind, I fix my skirt so it sits lower on my hips and then roll the bottom of my tank top up to show a little more skin. Giving my boobs a little lift, I take one last calming breath before walking back out into the bar.

***

Two hours later, my feet are killing me. The place is at maximum capacity, but Burke is still letting people in—anything to make an extra buck. Idiot. I shouldn't be complaining. I'll make enough tonight to add to my savings and should be able to get out of the hotel room I've been staying in for the past month.

Walking up to the bar to fill my order, I trip over some asshole who's stumbling around. "Whoa there, sweet cheeks," the guy says as he grabs my hips to stop me from falling on my face, but even when I'm steady, he doesn't let go.

"Thanks, but you can let go now," I say as I try to wiggle out of his grasp. Instead, he tightens his hold.

"What's the rush?" he asks as he leans down, placing his face in the crook of my neck and…sniffs? Did he just smell me? I try to break his hold on me again, but he releases one hip and clamps his fingers around my arm to the point of pain.

"Let go of me!" I say a little louder this time, but he just smiles and reaches into his pocket for what looks like a wad of money. Taking a ten-dollar bill out, he pushes it into the waist of my skirt.

"How about you and me go into one of those back rooms for a private dance, huh?" Instead of waiting for my reply, he jerks on my arm and practically drags me toward the back.

I try to pull my arm free but it's no use, so I try another way. "Look, I appreciate the offer, but I'm not a dancer. I'd be happy to grab one of the other girls for you, though," I tell him, still trying to pull my arm free. I look around, trying to see if I can find Lyle for help, but he's nowhere to be seen. Fuck, what am I supposed to do?

I can see that we're almost to the back, and if I

don't do something about this guy now, there's no telling what he'll do to me when he gets me in a room alone. Remembering the self-defense moves I learned last month, I use force to get away from this guy. With my free arm, I move it in a hard downward motion to try and dislodge his hold. It works. I'm free from his hold, but it also pisses him off. Before I can turn around and head back to the bar and completely away from him, he has me by my throat. "You little *bitch*!" he screams in my face.

I can literally feel my face turning red and my airflow being cut off by the tight grip he has on my neck. I'll probably have bruises tomorrow if I survive the night.

I reach up with both hands, scratching at his, trying to get him to release me but he just bats my weak attempts away with his free hand. "You are nothing but a fucking whore, so you'll get your tight ass into that back room and give me what I want. Do you hear me?" he spits. I can't do anything but shake my head, and even that is difficult. There's no way in hell I'm going into that room with him.

He doesn't let me go, but he does loosen his grip enough to allow me a small breath so I don't pass out. He starts to drag me toward the back room again, this time by my neck. I'm still lightheaded, even with his hold slightly loosened. My struggles are pitiful, my strength gone from fighting to breathe. We're almost to the hall that leads to the private rooms and I've lost all hope of getting out of this.

Suddenly, out of nowhere, I'm ripped out of his

hold and pushed behind someone's back. Gasping for air, the first thing I notice is that it's not Lyle who has saved me. The man in front of me is too tall to be Lyle. The second thing I notice is that he's wearing a black motorcycle vest kind of like the one Lyle wears with **'Forsaken Sinners MC'** written across the back and a picture of a skull with guns and flames on it. Even though I've seen a few guys wearing vests like this around the club, I don't know much about them. But if I'm going by just the look of the vest and the way this guy was able to pull that scumbag off of me, they're not people to be messed with.

"We got a problem here?" the man asks. His voice sounds familiar, but I can't place it. I've probably served him at the bar, which makes sense.

"Nah, man. This pretty little thing just offered to give me a lap dance, so I was taking her in the back to collect." *What. The. Fuck.* Is this guy for real? In what universe did he take what just happened as me offering him a lap dance?

"The hell I did!" I yell back at him as I peek around the man with the vest. My voice is a little scratchy from being choked, but I press on. It pisses me off that this guy is lying and thinks it's okay to treat women like they are nothing. "You fucking dragged me over here after I told you no, you piece of shit!" I'm done being treated like trash. If I didn't need this job so much, I'd even tell Burke where to shove it.

"You hear that, shit-for-brains? The lady didn't offer you jack shit, and sure as fuck didn't go with you willingly. So, I'll say this one time and one time only. If I catch you even *looking* in her direction, you're a dead man. You got me?" he growls. Judging by the sound of his voice, it's not a threat, but a promise. Too bad for the dipshit in front of him, he doesn't heed the warning.

"The fuck you say to me, asshole?" he sneers, but before he can say anything else or even take a step toward us, vest guy levels him with a solid hit to the face. I jump back in surprise, not fear, and feel my panties dampen. Since when does violence turn me on?

I wait for the guy to get back up and try to retaliate, but he's out cold on the floor. I've never seen someone get knocked out with just one hit before. It's actually kind of amazing. Shit, Sara, get your head on straight.

I back up even further from the man who saved me, but it's more out of self-preservation than fear. I have no idea what's going on with me, but this guy is bad news. If what he just did to that fuckstick shows what type of person he is, then it's something he must do often. Okay, that was a harsh assumption considering he just saved me from God knows what, but can you blame me? After everything I've been through, harsh assumptions are better than blindly trusting a man that will end up beating me on a daily basis, or worse.

When he turns around, I stop my retreat. He looks so familiar. "You okay, doll?" he says quietly, but with enough volume that I can hear him over the music. I look into his eyes, looking for any remains of the anger he just displayed, but I see only compassion. I'm used to seeing a lot of different emotions when a guy looks at me, but compassion is a new one to me.

"I-I'm fine, thanks," I whisper, hoping he hears me.

Out of the corner of my eye, I see Lyle heading our way. I should be angry he didn't keep an eye on me and prevent this from happening in the first place, but I can't. This place is packed tonight and being on the floor makes it difficult to follow my every move. Plus, he has other things to do besides watching me every second of the night.

I open my mouth to tell him that I'm fine and explain what just happened, but the guy in the vest beats me to it. "Hey, brother. Sorry about the mess, but this son-of-a-bitch was dragging her down the hall by her throat."

Lyle pats him on the back and looks down to the guy who's still out cold on the floor and kicks him in the gut. "No worries, man. I'll take it from here." They start murmuring to each other, but the conversation is too low for me to hear. I just stare at them in shock, trying to piece together what just happened. I'm so ready for tonight to be over.

I turn around to head back to the bar. I want to see if I can spot Burke to tell him what just happened to me and that I'm going home. My throat is starting to throb and burn and my head is pounding. I just want to soak in a nice hot bath and go to sleep. Too bad I'll have to do that at the hotel.

I'm just about to the bar when I feel someone gently grab my elbow, causing my whole body to stiffen. Turning around, I see it's the man in the vest. "I'm sorry, I didn't catch your name," I say hoarsely. Fuck, my throat is killing me. He gives me a sweet smile and pulls me closer.

"It's Toby. You don't remember me?" I know he looks familiar, but I just can't place him. I feel kind of bad, but after the night I've had, my mind is coming up blank. I can't concentrate on anything but getting out of here.

"You attended a self-defense class I was teaching a couple of weeks ago." Shit, it's *him*. I can't believe I didn't recognize him right away since he's the hottie from the gym that I've been pleasuring myself to since our first meeting. Fuck, just thinking about it makes me blush. I hope he can't tell what I'm thinking.

"Oh, I remember you now. God, I'm sorry. It's been a long night." I know my face is still red with embarrassment because he smiles seductively. I know he can read my thoughts. Fuck, just what I need right now. I take a step back, suddenly needing distance between us, and smile back at him shyly. "Well, I better get back to work." I know I need to walk away, but for some reason, my feet won't move and I can't look away from him.

He lets out a small laugh but it sounds foreign, like he doesn't laugh often, if at all. He takes me by the hand, then says, "Come on, I'm taking you home." He leads me to the door and before I know it, we're outside.

I pull on his arm, just enough to get his attention, but not to dislodge myself. I love the way my skin tingles when he touches me but I shouldn't like it. It should frighten me. "Wait. I can't just leave. I need to tell my boss about what happened and I don't even have my purse." Just as I finish that sentence, I hear the door open and see Lyle walk out, holding my purse.

"Thought you might need this," he says as he hands it over.

I'm not sure if I should leave with Toby or not. I mean, I don't even know him, but Lyle does, apparently. My gut is telling me he's not going to hurt me, but my gut has been wrong before. "And I'm sorry about tonight, Sara. I should've kept a closer eye on you." I can hear the regret in his voice and I feel bad that in a way, I'm responsible for him feeling this way.

I wave his apology off. "You have nothing to be sorry for, Lyle. It wasn't your fault he did what he did and you have a lot of girls to look out for. I'm just thankful it didn't turn out worse." I hate to see Lyle blaming himself, and hopefully my words give him some sort of comfort.

He gives me a smile and turns to Toby. "Make sure she makes it home safe, will ya? And call me if you have any problems." Yeah, they must know each other pretty well for Lyle to let me go off with him. That's good to know. I trust Lyle and his judgment, but I'm still not one hundred percent sure I should leave with him. I think it's more because I want to jump his bones though, not because I think he'll hurt me.

"Will do, brother. I'll catch you later," Toby says, then does some sort of fist bump with Lyle before taking my hand and leading me away from the club.

"Lyle is your brother?" I ask. That's the second

time I've heard him call Lyle that. They don't look alike, but I suppose that doesn't mean anything.

Toby lets out a small chuckle, this time it comes out easier, and shakes his head. "Not by blood, but yeah, he's my brother in all the ways that count." I just nod, not wanting to ask too many questions. If he wants to share more, he will.

I stop short when I notice he's leading me toward a motorcycle. I've never been on one before. "Oh, I think I'd rather take my car."

"You aren't driving by yourself right now. I promise, I won't let anything happen to you and I'll even bring you back in the morning to pick your car up." Damn, he looks sexy as he lifts his leg to straddle the bike. I don't want him to think I'm easy though, so I stand my ground.

"That's a fair point, but you could drive my car and I could drop *you* off in the morning to pick up *your* bike." I try but fail to hide the smirk that appears on my face. I can't help it, even to my ears it sounds funny. He doesn't look like the type of man that would allow a woman to drive him around. Not like it's a bad thing though. With him, it just seems right that he'd be that way.

Getting off his bike, he stalks toward me with a swagger that has my panties wet again. "Nice try, doll." He stops in front of me and literally picks me up and places me on the back of his bike before he gets back on. I should complain or argue, but I'm speechless.

Handing me the helmet, he starts the bike and waits until I have it on, then grabs my hands and places them around his waist. "Hold on tight." He revs the engine and takes off out of the parking lot. The forward movement has me gripping the bottom of his shirt for dear life. I think I almost fell off back there.

He places a hand over the top of mine, giving them a squeeze before reaching back and placing it on my thigh. It's feels natural the way he does it, like we've been riding together for years. It's comforting in a way and causes me to loosen my hold on him and relax. It's not so bad once you get over the initial shock.

After being on the road for a couple of minutes, I realize I never told him where I lived. Not like I really want to tell him that I'm currently residing in a hotel, but at this point I have no choice. It's not till then that I notice we've been going the opposite way of my hotel. I tap him on the shoulder and yell over the sound of the bike, "You're going the wrong way!" He briefly glances over his shoulder at me and shakes his head, then turns back around. Not wanting to be ignored and pissed that he's not taking me home, I hit his shoulder again, this time harder. "You need to turn around!" He doesn't say anything, but a minute later, he turns down a residential street. I think he's going to listen and head back the other way, but instead he pulls into a driveway and shuts the engine off.

I don't move as he gets off the bike, waiting for him to tell me what we're doing here. "You gonna sit there all night or come in?" I don't answer and level him with a hard glare. If he thinks I'm getting off this bike, he's sadly mistaken.

I don't move, so he takes a few steps in my

direction and lifts me off the bike, carrying me toward the front door. "Put me down!" I yell, and when that doesn't work, I start banging my fists into his back. Do I look like I need to be manhandled by two men tonight?

Once we're through the door, he walks into a kitchen and deposits me onto the countertop. "What the fuck do you think you're doing? Take me home right now." I try to jump down, but he steps in between my legs, stopping me.

"Look, I just thought that you'd be better off here for the night than alone." He's looking me in the eyes and I can see in his eyes that he means me no harm, but I still don't think this is a good idea. He's hot as fuck and it's been so long since I've been with a man I'm attracted to and wholeheartedly want to sleep with willingly.

"How do you know I'd be home alone? What if I'm married and my husband is waiting up for me?"

He shakes his head, obviously calling my bluff. "Well, if you did have someone waiting for you at home, I don't think you'd be looking at me the way you are right now." Fuck. Surely I can keep my hands to myself for one night, right?

Sighing, I relent. He's right anyway; I'd rather not be alone right now, and I don't have anyone waiting for me.

CHAPTER 3

Toby

I had some business to discuss with Burke, the manager of Club Sin. He's been managing the place for almost a year for my MC, but the books just haven't been adding up since he took the position. We've been keeping an eye on him for the past couple months to see if we can catch him red-handed, but the asshole is sneaky, so I'm here to ask some questions.

Once I walk through the door, I take a quick look around and what I see has my head spinning. I spot her right away, walking toward the bar in a tight ass tank top and a leather mini skirt that leaves little to the imagination. Even though I'm pissed that she's in a place like this, I'm also happy as fuck I've found her. Now I can finally talk to her, see what she's been up to and why she hasn't come by the gym.

I try to figure out why she's in a place like this, but I come up empty, until I see the tray she's carrying around. She fucking works here? That's about to change real fast.

I see Lyle over by the side door so I head his way to have words. I don't know why I wasn't informed of her working here. I get papers on every new employee at the club but I haven't received anything in a while.

Before I make it to Lyle, I hear someone yell. I can tell right away it's her. I turn around and instantly see red. Some asshole has his hand around my woman's throat. That motherfucker just signed his fucking death certificate.

Charging through the crowd, not caring about who I'm knocking over, I keep my eye on Sara. My only thought is getting to my girl; killing the fucker is second. I don't waste a minute once I reach them, grabbing Sara and placing her protectively behind my back before I glare at the piece of shit in front of me. "We got a problem here?" I snarl at him.

The scumbag didn't know when to quit, forcing me to knock his ass out. I hate that Sara was there to witness me doing it, but hopefully it will prove to her that she's safe with me; that I'll protect her.

She didn't remember who I was—which I'm not gonna lie, it stung my ego a bit—but once I jogged her memory, I saw the lust in her eyes, just like at the gym. I wish I could take her in my arms and show her exactly how I feel, but after everything she went through tonight, I can't. She was just manhandled by someone and almost violated, I don't want to push my luck with her. Especially since I know she's been through something possibly worse before tonight.

27

Since I wasn't going to let her stay here and I couldn't stand to leave her tonight, I decided to take her home. After a brief fight over her riding on my bike, I was able to get her home quick, though she was pissed I didn't take her to *her* house. She even tried arguing the fact that she had someone waiting for her, but I knew right away that was a lie. And even if she did, I didn't care. I needed her with me, to know that she was alright.

I snap out of my thoughts and look at Sara, still sitting on my counter where I placed her. She's giving me a look I can't quite comprehend; it's almost wistful. I turn toward the cupboard where I keep my bourbon and pour two fingers full into two glasses, handing one over to her.

She takes it hesitantly and just looks at me. I down my shot then wait for her to follow, but she looks confused.

Filling my glass once more, I nod at her full one. "I figured you could use something after what happened at the club." She visibly winces and I want to kick myself.

Looking down at her drink, she slowly brings it to her lips before taking a small sip. As soon as she swallows it, she goes into a coughing fit and I have to hide my smile. "It's better if you take it all at once, doll." She looks at me with watery eyes, but there's also a spark there. Sweet Jesus, this woman is going to be the death of me; one sassy look from her and I feel like I'm going to burst.

Keeping her eyes locked on mine, she downs the rest of her drink. She doesn't cough or even flinch from the burn. My eyes drop to her throat as I watch her swallow the bourbon. It's a little red from where that piece of shit's hand was, but the slender curve of her neck makes my cock harden. I never thought a woman's neck would be sexy, but I'm finding that everything about this girl in front of me surprises me and turns me on at the same time.

Clearing her throat, she looks around my kitchen before her eyes finally land on mine. "So, uh…is this your house?" she asks nervously. I nod, afraid that if I speak, I may say something that will give away how bad I want her, and I don't want to scare her away.

I turn around to clear my head of thoughts of her naked and in my bed. She's been through enough tonight and doesn't need me hitting on her. "Let me show you where you can sleep." I hear her jump off the counter and then feel her behind me. It takes everything in me not to turn around and shove her against the wall and take her mouth with my own.

When we reach my room, I turn to the side and motion to the open door. "Here ya go." She walks in and sits down on the bed. Fuck, the sight of her on my bed has me lightheaded with want.

"Where are you going to sleep?"

"I don't sleep much, but I'll be in the living room if you need anything."

Not giving her a chance to respond, I turn around and walk down the hallway before I storm in there and strip off her clothes and make her mine. I stop when I hear her say, "Thank you."

I don't turn around. "You're welcome."

***

I must have fallen asleep on the couch after my fourth glass of bourbon when I'm jolted awake by the floorboards creaking. Someone is in my house.

Before I have time to even make a grab for my knife under my pillow, I feel someone touch my arm. Without hesitating, I grab them around the wrist, ready to twist it hard when a female screams, making me stop. Sara.

I sit up and loosen my grip before I pull her down onto my lap. "Shit, I'm sorry, doll. You caught me off guard." I hold her close and rub my hands up and down her arms to calm her. "I'm sorry, babe. I'm sorry," I whisper in her ear.

After a few minutes, I feel her rigid body relax into my arms as she lets out a long sigh. Neither of us says anything as I hold her, letting her rest against my chest, and that's when I feel a sense of peace settle over me. I've never truly felt peace until this moment. I've always been on guard, always fighting, so this is a foreign, but welcome feeling. How is it possible that a stranger, whom I've only met once, has this effect on me? I don't understand it, but I'm not willing to let it go. I like the way she makes me feel.

I don't know how long we sit here, or even why she came to me, but I hear her breathing even out and I know she's asleep. It warms my cold heart to know that she's comfortable enough with me to fall asleep in my arms, especially since I'm a stranger to her. It's the best fucking feeling ever.

Closing my eyes, I fall back asleep, holding her with a smile on my face.

***

I've never slept so well for as long as I can remember. I barely ever sleep for more than a couple hours each night, and that's on and off, but with Sara in my arms, I slept like a baby.

We're still on the couch, me lying on my back and Sara lying on top of me, her face pressed against my bare chest. Lying like this, it's like she was made for me. She fits so perfectly in my arms.

I barely have time to bask in the feeling when she starts wiggling around. Fuck, if she keeps that up, she'll be in for a surprise. "If you keep moving around like that, you're going to wind up on your back with me between your legs," I growl when her leg brushes against my hard cock.

She gasps and stills her body. She's probably scared shitless, trying to figure out how to get away from me as we speak.

I'm surprised and shocked as fuck when the little vixen starts to move again, and it's not to get away, either. Her hand slowly moves up my chest and back down. When she reaches the waistband of my pants, I grab her wrist. "Not that I don't want your hand on me, but if you continue, I won't be able to stop once you start."

She pauses for only a moment before she brings her legs up on both sides of my hips so she's straddling me, then she sits up straight. My hands move on their own to her hips, holding her to me so she doesn't change her mind and move away. "Sara?" I need to know what she wants. I'll do whatever it is she needs.

31

Looking into her eyes, I see that spark that drives me insane. "I want you, Toby," she whispers as she rocks her hips once. I clench my jaw and groan.

"Fuck. You have no idea how bad I want to fuck you right now, but I'm not sure if this is a good idea." That was the wrong thing to say. I realize it as soon as that spark leaves her eyes. She looks away from me and moves to get up.

"I get it," she whispers sadly.

The fuck she does! Tightening my grip on her waist so she can't go, I wait until she looks at me before speaking. "Sara, it has nothing to do with not wanting you because I want you more than my next breath." To put meaning to those words, I grind myself up against her pussy so she can feel how hard I am for her, "But I don't want to do anything that you'll regret later." When she looks away again, I know she isn't listening. Fuck this.

I sit up so fast she doesn't have time to react as I take her mouth. She lets out a gasp, which I take advantage of by pushing my tongue past her lips. Damn, she tastes even better than I thought she would.

She only hesitates for a moment before she starts kissing me back, and that's all it takes for me to know she's all in. Grinding my hips up into her barely covered pussy, I feel her heat all the way through my jeans. Sliding my hand up her shirt, I run my thumb over her bare breast, teasing her. She moans into my mouth when I pinch her nipple as she grinds down on my cock. I thrust up against her.

Wrapping my arms around her waist, I stand up without breaking our kiss. Walking down the hall and into my room, I lay her on my bed. Lifting my head, I look down at the halo of blonde hair that surrounds her beautiful face. Fuck, she's perfect.

"You sure about this? Once I bury my cock inside of you, there's no going back." I need to know for sure. If we do this, she'll be mine. I won't let her go.

She nods her head with her eyes half closed, but I need more. "Answer me, Sara. I want your words. Are you sure?" I repeat. This time, the spark in her eyes comes to life as she replies.

"Yes, Toby, I'm sure. I want you to fuck me."

The words are barely out of her mouth before I grab the bottom of her shirt and tear it right up the middle, then I'm on her, taking her lips with a desperation I've never felt before; like if I don't have her lips on mine right now, I will cease to exist.

Her hands start to travel up my chest to wrap around my neck, but I quickly grab them and pin them above her head. Holding her hands in one of mine, I move my other hand over her breasts, down her stomach, and stop at the top of her panties.

She tries to wiggle her arms free, but I squeeze them tighter and tear my mouth from hers. "Stop. Moving," I growl. Her eyes snap open in fear and I instantly regret my tone. If I didn't know it when she first walked into the gym that day, I know it now; something really bad happened to her. Someone took advantage of her while she was helpless to stop it. The fear I see directed toward me cuts me to the core. Looking away from me, she starts to shake.

Panic seizes me. I need to erase that fear. I need her to know I would never hurt her. "Look at me, doll," I say as I release her hands. I should probably roll off her too, but I just can't bring myself to move.

Each second that passes adds to my own fear and growing panic, but she finally looks at me. The fear that was there before has now been replaced with uncertainty and embarrassment. I place my hand to her cheek to reassure her that everything's okay, but I stop when she flinches. God fucking dammit! I want to jump off this bed and run my fist through a wall. I want to shout and scream at the world for allowing something so bad to happen to her that would cause her to flinch away from my touch. I want to scream and tell her that I would never hurt her, but I don't do any of these things.

Pushing my anger and panic aside, I move my hand toward her face again, but slower so she can see my intentions. "It's okay. I don't know what happened to make you react that way to me, but I shouldn't have done it. Not till we've gotten to know one another better. I'm sorry. I will never hurt you, Sara. Please tell me you believe me."

She hesitates a second before nodding her head, but I need to hear her say it. I need to know without a doubt that she really believes me; that she trusts me. "Tell me. Tell me you believe me." She looks deep into my eyes and I let her. I don't close myself off, but I let her see me. I hold her gaze, willing her to understand how I feel.

Finally, after what feels like hours later, she gives me what I so desperately want. "I believe you." Leaning forward slowly, I gently kiss her lips.

I roll her over, letting her straddle my hips like she did on the couch. I want her to know that she's in control of what does or doesn't happen between us.

She leans down, kissing me tentatively at first, but once I open my mouth for her, she deepens the kiss.

I fist the sheets to keep my hands off of her. I don't want to move them until I know she's ready for me to take control again—until she knows without a doubt that I would never hurt her or force her to do something she doesn't want to do.

"Touch me, Toby. Please touch me," she murmurs against my lips.

"Not yet."

A small growl emanates from her throat, then she moves her hands down my chest to the waistband of my jeans. Without hesitation, she unbuttons my pants and I lift my hips as she shimmies them down my legs, taking my boxer briefs with her.

My cock springs free and almost hits her in the face.

Once she removes my clothes and throws them behind her, she stands and slides her panties off her hips, tossing them and the ripped shirt to the floor.

Standing there completely naked, I take in the sight before me. Smooth, tanned legs meet the apex of her thighs and lead me to her shaved pussy. I can see her arousal glistening from here.

Wanting to get the full view, I reluctantly move my eyes up to her full breasts before locking onto her eyes. Once she knows she has my full attention, she slowly climbs back onto the bed and brings herself down on top of me again. "Like what you see?" she asks boldly. I don't know where this confidence is coming from, but I love that it's there and the fear from only moments ago is forgotten.

"You have no fucking idea."

Leaning up on my elbows, I kiss her neck and groan when I feel her rub her bare pussy against my cock.

"Do you have condoms?"

I reach over to my bedside table and pull one out. Before I can rip it open, she takes it from me and brings it to her mouth, tearing it open with her teeth. "Fuck," I whisper. Watching her take charge is even sexier than I thought it would be, though I can't wait for the day she allows me to take control.

I watch her slide the condom on slowly, and without wasting another second, she lifts herself up and slides down, both of us letting out a tortured moan as she fully seats herself on my cock.

She starts slowly, moving up and down before picking up the pace. I stay focused on everything she's doing, from her sliding up and down on my cock, to her breasts bouncing with each movement. She has me close to coming already, but I hold on. Needing to get some control back, I grab both her wrists and pin them behind her back while she keeps her rhythm. I make sure to look her in the eyes so she knows what I'm doing, but the only thing I see from her is pure pleasure.

I start pounding into her from below, which has her arching her back, causing my cock to slide in deeper with each thrust. "That's it, take my cock deep in your tight pussy," I manage to say between clenched teeth, thrusting harder and faster. Feeling her start to tighten around me, I know she's close to coming. "Don't come until I tell you to."

"Please, Toby. I'm ready to come. I *need* to come!" she yells, closing her eyes.

"Open your eyes, Sara. You will look at me when I make you come, dammit."

Moving both her hands into one of my own behind her back, I move my free hand around and start to rub small, tight circles over her clit, then I release her wrists and grip her hip tightly. Lifting my hips off the bed for better leverage, I power into her over and over again. "Come for me. Come all over my cock." She looks into my eyes as she comes hard, squeezing my cock so hard that I feel my eyes roll into the back of my head. It's feels so fucking amazing.

I pump myself into her twice before falling over the cliff with her. "Fuck!" I slow my thrusts until I no longer feel her walls contracting around me, then I pull her down to me and kiss her.

When our breathing slows, I pull her head back so I can look at her when I say, "That was un-fucking-believable, doll." This causes her to smile, but what I say next wipes the smile off her face, replacing it with a look of what I can only describe as panic. "You're mine now, Sara. I'm never letting you go."

CHAPTER 4

Sara

"You're mine now, Sara. I'm never letting you go." Never letting you go. Jumping up, I grab the ripped shirt lying on the floor and run out of the room to the bathroom. *I'm never letting you go, Sara.* Slamming the door behind me, I sink down onto the floor. *You're mine.*

Shaking my head, I feel the first tear fall. I can't go through this again. I will not become someone's property like I was with Rick.

The first time Rick said that I was his, I thought it was kind of hot—sweet even—that he wanted me so much he was claiming me. I never thought for a second that he was messed up in the head, even when he started telling me what to wear, who I could or couldn't hang out with. He hid my car keys from me so I would have to depend on him to take me wherever I needed to go.

I lived that way for a year before the abuse started. It was a slap here and there, but then he became more violent. He beat me whenever he felt like it. When he wanted to have sex, he would get rough, and it was during those times that he would tell me that I was his, a possession, and he would never let me go. I can't go back to that—I won't.

I jump when Toby starts to pound on the door, shaking the whole frame. "Sara! Sara, are you okay? Let me in!" I take a deep breath and stand up. After a quick glimpse in the mirror to wipe my face clear of any tears, I open the door to see Toby rubbing his shaved head and pacing back and forth.

When he notices me, he reaches out and grabs my face. I flinch, which makes him remove his hands like I've burned him. "What happened back there, doll?" Not knowing what to say, I just shake my head, hoping he doesn't push me on this. I don't want to tell him about Rick or how I fear he's just like him. Why did I let this happen? I don't know this man, but I wanted him. I am such a mess. "Sara, talk to me." He's getting upset and I can't handle this. I have no idea if he gets violent when angry or how he's going to react. I need to calm him down and get him to take me back to my car.

I sidestep him and walk back into his bedroom so I can get dressed. "Look, Toby. It was nothing, really. I just had a moment." Pulling off his torn shirt, I fake being confident in my nakedness and don't rush to put my clothes on from last night. I hate knowing I'll be seen wearing the same outfit as yesterday when Toby drops me off, but I have more important things to worry about, like getting away from Toby and this attraction I have to him.

Once I have my clothes back on, I turn toward

the door and see him standing there with his arms crossed. He doesn't look happy, but he doesn't look pissed, either. That could work in my favor.

When I walk up to him, he doesn't move to let me pass. We stare at each other, neither of us wanting to break the hold first.

After what feels like an eternity, I finally blink, but I don't look away. "It's been a while since I've been with someone intimately like that. I guess the attraction I have for you hit me a little harder than I thought it would. I wanted it and you didn't do anything wrong. I just wigged out a little, but I'll get over it, I promise." I can tell he wants to push me for more, but the sound of his phone ringing interrupts what he was going to say.

"Don't move. We aren't done talking about this," he says before walking into the living room to answer his phone.

"Yes we are," I whisper low enough that he won't hear me.

"Yeah?" he barks into the phone as I follow him. He watches me put my shoes on as he listens to whoever is on the other line. "Yeah, I'll be right there." He hangs up and walks over to where I'm sitting. Rubbing the back of his neck, he looks torn between wanting to sit next to me and continue our talk, or going wherever it is he needs to be. I really hope it's the latter.

Blowing out a long sigh, he reaches down for my hand and pulls me to my feet. My emotions are being pulled in two separate directions; a part of me wanting to move away from him so he can't touch me, and the other part wants to collapse into his arms and beg him to hold me forever.

"I have to make a quick stop, but then I'll take you to your car. That okay with you, doll?" He sounds defeated, like he doesn't want to leave without figuring out what's going on between us, but knowing he doesn't have a choice. If I were in a better situation or even state of mind, I would feel guilty, or even a little heartbroken by that look, but I don't. I can't afford to. I silently thank whoever called for giving me the escape I needed.

"Yeah, that's fine," I say as I grab my purse and walk outside to his bike.

***

After riding on the back of Toby's bike for the last ten minutes and wondering where he's taking me, we finally pull up outside of a tattoo shop I've never seen before. The sign says **'Sinners Ink,'** and I'm curious whether it's connected to the motorcycle group he rides with, or if it's just a coincidence that the name has Sinners in it. I'm assuming it's the former, considering I'm pretty sure his group owns the strip club I work at as well. That's gonna suck for me, but hopefully I'll find another job soon so I can quit there and not have to see Toby unless I *want* to see him. I want a different job anyway. I don't want to bartend at a strip club for much longer, especially after what happened last night.

When he turns the bike off and puts the kickstand down, he takes my hand to help me off the bike. "I just have to run in and talk with Dani quick, then I'll take you to your car and follow you to your house so we can finish our conversation." He turns toward the door, but I grab his hand to stop him.

"You don't have to follow me to my place. We can just talk later, can't we?" He looks at me like I just spoke in gibberish.

"No, we can't talk later, Sara. Something happened back there and you're going to tell me what it was. The truth this time." Shit. He didn't believe what I told him back at his house.

He turns back in the direction of the shop, but I pull on his arm again. "I don't want you coming to my place. I barely know you." I'm starting to get pissed. This domineering act he has going on is getting old. Just because we had sex doesn't give him the right to invite himself over.

Turning himself completely around so he's facing me, he levels me with a hard look. "I didn't hear you complain that you barely knew me when I was balls deep inside of your tight little pussy," he growls.

I step back like he slapped me. I can't believe he just said that, like I'm some whore who just put out for him for the hell of it. "You're an asshole!" I yell and storm off down the street. I'll fucking walk to my car. He can go fuck himself.

Barely making it three steps, I'm lifted up and thrown over his shoulder. "Put me down! Put me down right now!" I yell while kicking my feet. I hope I connect with his balls!

He puts me down so I'm sitting sideways on his bike and places his hands on my shoulders so I can't get away. "I'm sorry. I shouldn't have said that, but you need to understand that I've wanted you since I first saw you, and when you told me you wanted me too and we fucked, you became mine. You gave yourself to me and I'm giving myself to you. I'm not going to let you walk away from this. So, we are going to go to your place when I'm finished here, and we are going to figure this shit out. End of fucking discussion."

I drop my head, feeling defeated. I'm not going to win this fight, and now he'll know that I don't even have a place of my own. For fuck's sake, I live in a fucking hotel room.

Toby gently places his finger under my chin so I have no choice but to look at him. "What's going on inside that beautiful head of yours?" he whispers. I may as well just tell him before he finds out.

"I don't have my own place," I whisper, but I know he hears me.

"So you have a roommate? That's okay. Nothing to be ashamed about, and I'm sure they won't mind us talking for a bit." I wish that were the case, but it's not.

"You don't understand. I don't have a house or an apartment. I've been staying in a hotel until I have enough money to get a place of my own." I look away, not wanting to see the pity in his eyes.

Taking my hands in his, he pulls me to my feet and waits for me to look at him, and when I do, I don't see pity. The only thing I can see in his eyes is compassion. "Is that why you didn't want me to follow you home? Because you've been staying at a hotel?" He makes it sound like it's no big deal, but it is. I'm embarrassed that he knows I didn't have enough money to get an apartment as soon as I got into town, but I'm not going to tell him that I had to leave with barely enough money for gas to drive here and have nothing besides the clothes I could fit into a small suitcase.

"Well, that's the main reason, yes. It's also because I have to get ready for work tonight and I'm not prepared to talk about what's going on with us. Can you just give me some time to process what you're saying? I wasn't expecting this, and with everything else on my plate, I don't want to feel pressured into something without thinking it through. Can you give me that, please?" I don't think I should jump into a relationship right away, especially one with a guy that's as alpha male as Toby. I just got out of a controlling relationship, and I'm not looking to go there again.

I give Toby a pleading look to just drop it for now, and he does. "Come on. Let's see what Dani wants, then we can figure the rest out." He takes my hand in his and we walk into the tattoo shop to see this Dani guy.

The bell over the door rings, signaling our entrance. I spot a guy behind the desk who I assume is Dani. He looks frantic and pissed off at the same time. I don't know what happened to make him that way, but I would guess the reason is why he called Toby here.

Toby walks up to him, still holding my hand tightly in his. "Hey, brother, what's going on?" Only releasing my hand long enough to shake hands with Dani, he then pulls me against his side, wrapping his arm around me tightly. I've seen this move done enough times to know he's staking his claim, though I'm not sure why he would feel the need to do this in front of someone he calls "brother."

"She's gone, Toby. I got in this morning to find this note saying that she had to leave town and she didn't know how long she'd be gone." I don't want to get in the way of them talking, so I try to wiggle out of Toby's hold, but it's no use. He looks down at me and shakes his head, silently telling me that he doesn't want me to go anywhere.

Once he sees that I've given up, he looks back at Dani. "Does the note say why she left? Did something happen that we need to be aware of?" Toby is looking at Dani almost accusingly; like he thinks that he did something to this girl to make her leave.

Dani literally growls and bares his teeth. "The fuck? You think I did something to make her leave?" Not wanting them to start a fight, I decide to step in to diffuse the situation. I have no idea who left, or why. I don't know Dani and what he may or may not have done to her. I don't know if he's even with this girl, but I've dealt with enough confrontations to know how to steer it in the right direction to figure out what's going on and what needs to be done to fix it. It's been awhile since I've had the confidence to intervene, but I know I can do this. I'm at least comfortable enough with Toby to know it'll be okay. I don't know Dani, but if he doesn't take too kindly to what I'm doing, Toby will keep me safe.

"Now, children, we won't get anything figured out if you boys insist on having a pissing contest. Now, Dani, why don't you tell us what the letter said—specifically?" Dani looks at me with what I can only describe as shock at my words. I know how he feels because I sometimes shock myself with what comes out of my mouth, or how bold I can be. I actually miss that part about myself. It's been so long since I felt like my old self.

"Well, I'd be happy to tell you about the letter. All you needed to do was ask," a feminine voice says from behind me.

Spinning around, I see a woman who looks like she should be on the cover of one of those badass biker magazines. You know, the ones with a sexy chick sitting on an even sexier bike. Yeah, one of those. She has long, dark hair with red and blonde highlights, high cheekbones, full lips, and a lot of tattoos covering her toned body. Who is this girl?

She must see my confusion because she walks up to me with a smirk on her face while reaching out her hand to shake mine. "Hi, I'm Dani. He's Louie, and you must be Sara," she says as I take her hand into mine, then she looks over at Toby and winks. I'm flabbergasted and completely speechless. *This* is Dani? "I can see you're confused," she says with a laugh. When I still don't say anything, she continues, "My full name is Danielle, but everyone calls me Dani." I feel my cheeks redden with embarrassment. I look at Toby and the guy I thought was Dani, but now know is named Louie.

"I'm so sorry," I whisper. He just shakes his head, but I think I see a smile on his face.

"No worries, babe. It's not the first time someone mistook me for her and I'm sure it won't be the last." I can tell Louie is trying to put me at ease, but his heart just isn't in it. It's probably because of the girl who left, which brings us back to why we're here.

Dani notices where my thoughts have gone. "Harlow left a note here sometime in the night, saying that she had to go home and didn't know how long she would be gone. I'm sure it's nothing to worry about, but Louie thinks something is wrong," she says as she rolls her eyes. She's one brave woman. I don't think I would have the courage to do that to men that look like Toby and Louie.

"Well, if it's no big deal, why call me here, Dani?" Toby asks. Instead of answering right away, she walks behind the desk and sits down in the chair.

"Well, it's not because I think Harlow went missing, that's for sure." Looking up, I know she sees the same look of impatience that I see written all over his face. "I'm left without an office assistant now, and with Zane being extra *protective* since we found out about the baby, he insists that I need to get someone ASAP, so I was thinking that maybe you could help me out. If you could come in until I can find someone to fill in, or maybe even know someone else who could start immediately?"

"I have the perfect person for the job, actually. She just quit her old job last night."

Dani looks at him in annoyance when he doesn't go any further. "You gonna tell me who she is so I can get in touch with her, or are you just gonna stand there all day looking like the smug son-of-a-bitch you think you are?" I barely know this girl, but I like her already. She has a "take no prisoners" attitude and an air about her that says "don't fuck with me." I should take notes because that's exactly the type of woman I want to be.

A chuckle escapes my lips, which makes Toby look at me in amusement. At least he isn't pissed about being called out by Dani or that I'm laughing at his expense.

Looking back over to Dani, he continues, "You don't have to try and get in touch with her because she's right here." Wait, what? He wants me to work here?

Dani looks between the two of us before smiling at me. "Great. Since that's all settled, when can you start?" My head is spinning by this rapid turn of events. I have no idea what is going on around me, but apparently I just quit a job I hate and now I'm being offered another.

All eyes are on me as I'm still trying to process this. "Well, um…" I look at Toby for help since he's the one who got me into this mess in the first place.

"How about she starts tomorrow morning? That will give us some time to stop by her place, pick up her things, and get her set up at my house for the time being."

They continue working out the details of my life without my input, and I won't have that, so I turn my anger to Toby. "Now hold on just one goddamn minute. First of all, I didn't quit my job last night.

Second, I would love to work for you, Dani, but I'd like to sit down with you, *alone*, to discuss it further. And third, I'm not moving into your house, Toby. You've got to be out of your fucking mind if you think that's going to happen." I'm fuming by the time my last words are spoken. This is exactly why I don't want to be in a relationship with another alpha male; they make decisions for me and never ask what I want or think. Well, fuck you very much, but I'll decide what is best for me.

Out of the corner of my eye, I see Louie smirk. It barely reaches his eyes, but it makes me happy I was able to put it there.

Just as Toby opens his mouth to say something else, Dani comes up and puts her arm around my shoulders. "You're right, Sara. Let's go talk about this…alone." The last part is directed at Toby. Without looking to see if he approves or not, I follow her into a room that must be her work studio. It has a chair for clients, a stool, a work station that looks like a big toolbox that probably holds all her supplies, and a drawing easel that's set up in the corner.

Taking the seat that Dani offers me, which happens to be the client chair, she then crosses her arms and looks intently at me. I'm not sure what she wants me to say, so I wait her out. She stares at me for what feels like an eternity, trying to read my mind, I suppose, before she speaks. "So…you and Toby, huh?" she asks with a smile on her face. Even though I don't know her at all, I actually feel like I can tell her stuff and she wouldn't judge me or my situation. Not like I'd tell her everything, but I want someone to confide in, and it's been so long since I had a true friend.

"To be honest, I'm not sure what we are. The only thing I know is that he's sexy, we have a lot of sexual chemistry, and he's an asshole." That makes her laugh, which in turn has me smiling.

"I'm going to like you. You got spunk, which you'll need to deal with these dipshits." I have a feeling she doesn't just mean Toby and Louie, though I don't know of anyone else.

She rolls her chair closer to me and levels me with a serious look. "Okay, here's the deal. I don't know what you got going on for work, but there must have been a reason Toby said you quit your job last night, but you say you didn't, so I'm guessing he doesn't approve of the place." She pauses only for a second, just long enough to see if I'll add to her statement, which I don't. "As you know, I'm in need of someone to run the desk for me and do a few other tasks as needed. I don't know how long Harlow will be gone, but I can promise you that if or when she gets back, you won't be out of a job. I will be able to schedule you and Harlow to share the schedule and as my pregnancy progresses, there will be more I'll need help with. You with me on this so far?" I just nod because honestly, I would do anything to not have to work at the strip club.

"Now, on to your living arrangements. Again, there must have been a reason Toby wanted to move you in with him too, but I have another option for you if you're interested." I don't even have to think about that either. I know I need to get out of the hotel, but I won't allow Toby to strong-arm me into moving in with him so he can control me that way, either.

"I moved here about a month ago from New York. I don't want to go into specifics, but I left there in a hurry and was only able to bring enough money for gas to get here with a little extra to spare and some of my clothes. I've been staying in a hotel and working at a strip club in town, trying to save up money to get my own place, so, I would accept any position you would offer me and I'd like to hear about this living arrangement, if that's okay with you?" I end on a question because I don't want her to think I'm being pushy or demanding. Honestly, offering me a job is good enough.

Dani gives me a genuine smile, then reaches out for my hand. "You and I have a lot in common. When I moved here four years ago, I left in a hurry and stayed in a hotel too." Knowing that we have that in common makes me feel a little bit better, though I doubt her situation was anything like mine is now.

She continues on, "I saw a sign in this shop window saying they had an apartment for rent, so I came in and met Mack. He's the president of the same MC Toby is a part of. Anyway, he offered me the apartment and a job, and the rest is history. These guys became my family and helped me get back on my feet. I'd like to offer you the same." I don't move or say anything, afraid this is too good to be true. I also don't want to assume anything either and make an ass out of myself, so I just wait for her to continue.

"The apartment upstairs is open, though I still have some stuff up there from when I was here late and didn't want to drive home. Now that Zane and I are together, he doesn't like me staying here anymore, so if you'd be interested, you can move in upstairs as soon as today and stay as long as you need to." I feel a tear slip down my cheek, but make no move to wipe it away. I can't believe she's offering me not only a job, but a place to live too.

Dani is patient enough to wait for me to calm down so I can speak. "I would love that, Dani. You have no idea what this means to me. Whatever you need me to do in the shop, I'll get it done. If I don't know how to do it, I promise I'll learn. And I have some money saved up from bartending at the strip club, so I can give you some of the first month's rent now and the rest when I get paid, if that's okay?" God, I hope she's okay with that. I really want this to work out. I don't even know what the apartment looks like, but I don't care. It's better than what I currently have, I'm sure, so I'll take it no matter what condition it's in.

Squeezing my hand, she says, "Actually, the rent is free. As long as you help out around the shop, the apartment is yours." My mouth pops open and I'm speechless. *Free?* I open my mouth to argue, but she holds her hand up to stop me. "Listen, I don't know your story or why you left New York, but I want to help. I was offered the same deal when I walked into this shop all those years ago, now I'm doing the same for you. Now, let's go upstairs so I can show you your new place." Without waiting for my reply, she gets up and heads out the door.

I follow in a haze, still not really believing this is happening. We walk outside from the back of the shop and up a set of stairs. By the time I make it to the top, I've come to terms with what I've been offered and I couldn't wipe the smile off my face if my life depended on it.

When I'm standing beside Dani, she opens the door and lets me walk into the apartment first. My only thought is that I love it. It's one hundred percent perfect. "Am I dreaming?" I whisper to myself. Dani laughs and comes up behind me.

"No, babe, you are most definitely not dreaming." Looking around, I start to picture what I want to buy and imagine myself relaxing on the couch, reading a book.

By the time I do a full circle inside, I'm facing Dani again and she has a serious look on her face. My smile drops, along with my heart. I knew this was too good to be true. She probably just realized what she offered me, a complete stranger, and wants to take it back. I open my mouth to tell her it's okay, but she speaks before I can get anything out.

"You don't have to tell me anything specific, but I need to know one thing. Are you in any sort of trouble, Sara?" I stare at her with what I hope is a blank expression, not wanting to go into the details of my past, especially now. "Look, I can't help you if I don't know what you're up against. I meant what I said, you don't have to tell me specifics, at least not yet, but you to tell me if we need to be looking out for anyone. You can trust us. You're one of us now and we protect our own." The tears are back, and even though I know I won't be able to get the words out, she deserves an answer.

I nod once before dropping to the floor on a sob. Dani follows me down and takes me into her arms. "It's okay, Sara. I've got you. I won't let anything happen to you, I promise. I've got you."

CHAPTER 5

Toby

Dani and Sara have been upstairs for almost an hour now and I'm starting to get twitchy. I still can't believe that I offered for her to come and stay with me at my house. I barely know her, but ever since she walked into the gym that day, I haven't been able to get her off my mind. I can't explain it, but there is just something about her, something that draws me in. Whenever I'm around her, I lose my shit in every sense of the word.

Not able to sit still any longer, I stand up and start pacing. I don't know what's taking the girls this long to talk, but not having her close to me, or being able to see that she's all right, is driving me nuts. I hate feeling like this; like I want to tear this place apart until I have her in my arms, but wanting to beat my own ass at the same time because it's insane of me to be thinking like this.

Finally having enough, I head toward the back to find out what's taking them so long when Louie walks into the room. "You good, brother?" he asks while looking at me like I've grown two heads. Not wanting to think too hard about his motivation, I just push past him when Dani comes walking through the door, alone.

"Where the hell is Sara?" My voice booms louder than I intend it to, but I don't care.

Louie looks at me like I've lost my mind and Dani looks about ready to deck me. "She's upstairs in her new apartment, asshole." Her new apartment? What the fuck? Before I can say anything about it though, Dani turns toward Louie. "I need you to watch the shop for a couple hours. I'm going to take Sara to get her stuff and then I'm going to take her shopping for things she'll need for the apartment. Text me if you need anything." Without even waiting to see if I'm going to comment on what she just said, she turns around and walks back outside.

I want to march up those stairs and drag Sara out and lock her away at my house, but I know this is the best thing for her, the most logical thing for her. And me too it seems. I need to get my shit together and stop thinking of her as mine. I mean, this can't be normal, the shit I'm feeling for her. I just met her for fuck's sake. Why do I feel this connection, this pull, toward her?

All I know is that it's not right. I need to put some distance between us until I can figure out what I really feel. Is it a real interest in her or something else, 'cause right now it feels a lot like an obsession.

At least there's one good thing about her working here at the shop—I'll know she's safe, and

I'll be able to stop by to check on her whenever I need to.

***

It's been three weeks since Sara moved out of that hotel and into the apartment above Sinners Ink. I haven't spoken to her since she went into the back room with Dani that day to discuss the job and apartment, but I've spoken with Dani to see how things are working out and she seems to be adjusting well.

I told Dani to let her know that her resignation had already been submitted at the strip club the day I brought her to the shop and that she didn't need to worry about going back to pick up her check. From what I heard, she wasn't happy about it, but she didn't put up a fight, either.

I've driven by the shop more times than I'd like to admit, but never got the balls to actually go in and talk to her. I still can't get her out of my head and every time I think about her and that morning at my house, in my bed, my cock gets so hard that I think it will bust through my jeans.

Things at the club are still quiet. Ever since shit went down with Dani and Blaze a couple months ago, we've been keeping our eyes out for trouble, but since there has been no sign of things going to shit, Mack pulled everyone back last week.

I've been spending a lot of time at the gym. It's fucked up, but I think a part of me keeps hoping that Sara will come back for another self-defense class, but she hasn't.

I don't have any fights scheduled since the club is my main priority and will always come first, but sometimes I'll take them on last minute if someone failed their drug test or got injured before the fight. Of course, it always depends on what's going on with the club too.

I've still been training hard, trying to keep my mind off of Sara, but it's not working One minute I feel like my obsession with her is going to drive me crazy, and the next I'm picking up my phone to call Dani to see how she is.

I'm forcing myself to find things to concentrate on, so I've been putting my name out there for upcoming fights. I've always thrived from the release it offers me and the power I feel inside the cage. However, since Sara came into my life, nothing feels the same anymore and I can't help but feel like there's something missing.

It might be time to stop fighting and just work at the gym, training new fighters. I wasn't planning on doing that for at least a couple of years, but maybe now's the time. I'm just not as focused on it anymore. Since I held Sara in my arms and I had that feeling of peace wash over me, I've been longing for that feeling again, but nothing works, Not even fighting in the cage. She's turned my world upside down and I fucking hate it. Nothing is simple anymore.

Grabbing my gym bag from my room, I head out to my bike. I'm doing a training session this morning before I need to head to the club, and I'm hoping it will be enough to get my mind off on straight.

Just as I'm mounting my bike, my phone vibrates in my pocket. Without even looking at the screen to see who it is, I answer. "Yeah?" There's so much noise on the other end, I can barely make out that it's Blaze. "Where the fuck you at, brother? I can barely fucking hear you." I hear a curse and then shuffling noises. He must be walking outside or into another room.

"I need you to stop by the shop and pick Dani up for me. I was supposed to be done with this job Mack put me on, but it's taking longer than I thought. I don't want her driving in her condition."

I laugh into the phone. "What the fuck, man? You talk like that in front of your old lady? She's pregnant, not fucking disabled, brother." Just thinking about what Dani would do if she heard Blaze say that shit puts a rare smile on my face. Yeah, I'd pay to see that shit. Pregnant or not, she'd kick his ass.

Blaze growls into the phone, which only makes me laugh. "Can you do it or not, asshole?" I should push his buttons and make him sweat a little bit, but he knows I'd do anything for that woman, so there's no point.

"Yeah, man, I'll make sure she gets to the club safe. But I'm telling you now, when you get back, you're going to have a fight on your hands—sending someone to pick her up like she's an invalid." Blaze lets out a long sigh full of relief mixed with defeat. Yeah, he knows he's fucked.

"Yeah, man, I know. Thanks, brother." I hang up and start my bike, revving the engine. I love the growl of my bike.

***

After a grueling eight hours of training at the gym, I'm just ready for this day to be over. Knowing that I was going to see Sara today made concentrating on what I was doing extremely difficult. I got knocked on my ass more times than not while I was sparring with Connor. My rhythm was fucked up on the speed bag, and I almost broke my hand while working the heavy bag. I need to get my shit together and fast.

I take a quick shower in the locker room and head out to my bike. I've decided that I just need to talk to her. Maybe if we sit down and talk about what went on between us, I'll be able to focus better. At least then, no matter what the outcome may be, I'll know where we stand.

I make a quick stop at home to switch my bike for the truck. Speeding through all the yellow lights and taking short cuts through the alleys, I make it to Sinners Ink in record time. I park in the back, thinking this way I'll have an excuse to walk Sara to her door and head inside. "Dani girl, where are you?" I yell as soon as I walk in. Besides seeing Sara, I'm actually looking forward to seeing how Dani reacts to why I'm here.

"Be out in a bit. Just let me finish this design real quick," she yells from her workroom.

Walking into the front of the shop, I'm disappointed that Sara isn't in here—she must be here somewhere. Blaze made sure that Dani had her working every day the shop was open. When he first told me that, I was going to beat his ass for demanding she work every day with no time off, but Dani assured me she wasn't going to be here from open to close every day, and that Sara was happy to help out. From what Dani says, Sara really enjoys the work, so I didn't say anything.

Taking a seat on the couch, I pull my phone out to text Blaze, just to let him know that I'm at the shop and Dani should be at the club soon. Of course, this is assuming she won't put up too much of a fight. She doesn't make it a habit to kill the messenger, but you can bet money that as soon as Blaze gets back, there will be a fight and I hope I'm there to see it. I never tire of watching her go at a man twice her size, as long as it's not me on the receiving end of her wrath.

Five minutes later and neither Dani, nor Sara, have come into the front room. Tired of just sitting around waiting, I walk into the office to see what's taking so long.

Opening the door, Dani looks up at me as she's putting her sketch pad away. "Can I help you?" she asks in a fake, sweet voice. It's just like her to be sarcastic and bitchy to anyone who crosses her path, though it's rarely ever thrown my way. I think this pregnancy has made her lash out at everyone.

"Yeah, you can, actually. You can stop being a brat and come give me a hug."

Not one to disappoint, she seems to almost deflate completely. She walks up and wraps her arms around me. "I'm sorry, Toby. It's just been a long couple of days." I hold her a little tighter 'cause I know she's having a hard time. I know this pregnancy was a surprise and she wasn't exactly over the moon about it because she wasn't sure if she'd make a good mother. On top of that, she has Blaze acting extra protective, which doesn't help her mood, either. Since she arrived here four years ago, she's made it her mission in life to never ask for help and to never rely on someone else, so having Blaze go the extra ten miles to make sure she and the baby are safe must be hard for her. But she's gonna have to get used to it, 'cause I don't see that changing anytime soon. Fuck, if anything, it's only gonna get worse.

"You don't have to apologize to me, babe. If I had to live with Blaze, I'd be a raging bitch to everyone too," I say with a laugh, trying to lighten the mood a little. She always likes it when I bash on Blaze and Louie.

"So I'm a raging bitch now, huh? If I wasn't pregnant, I'd kick your ass and you know it, so quit being a jackass and help me close up shop, will ya?" I follow her toward the front room.

"Where's Sara? Shouldn't she be here to help you close?" I ask nonchalantly, hoping she doesn't catch the curiosity in my voice, but of course, she knows the game I'm playing and smiles her evil little smile.

"Wouldn't you like to know?"

Figuring I should leave it at that, I bring up the reason I'm here. "Well, considering Blaze said you're not to be here by yourself to close in "your condition," I'd like to know why the fuck Louie isn't here helping you out when Sara isn't. Oh, and speaking of your old man, he wanted me to take you to the club. He said he wasn't going to be back in time to pick you up."

"You have got to be fucking kidding me. My *condition*? That ass wipe is lucky he isn't here because I would shove my size seven-and-a-half boot so far up his ass that he'd be tasting leather for a month. Just fucking wait till I see him. My condition! Who the fuck does he think he's talking like that, huh?" It's a rhetorical question so I don't even bother answering. I just watch her storm around the shop, throwing magazines down on tables and kicking trash cans. I'll just let her calm down before I bring Sara back up again.

It takes her half an hour to calm down before I stop fearing for my life. Dani's sitting at the front desk, going through tomorrow's appointments, I assume, when she looks up at me, tapping my finger on the desk. "Do you mind?" she asks, but the edge isn't present in her voice anymore, so I know she isn't that annoyed.

"Why isn't Sara here helping you close?" I hope that by wording it this way, she won't figure out the real reason I'm asking, but this is Dani we're talking about, so no such luck. "I gave her the rest of the day off since we weren't busy, so she's upstairs cleaning. Why don't you head on up and ask if she's ready? I asked her before she left if she wanted to get something to eat after I close." Damn, I love this chick. She knows when to push things and when to tell me what I want to know. She's also real good at helping me out without making it obvious.

Without answering her, I head out back, past my truck, and up the stairs to the apartment Dani used to live in. It's still weird to think back on those days when Dani first came into our lives. She's a whole new person now, though she was still one tough bitch when she showed up. It was all inner strength, but now she's got the physical strength to back it up.

Knocking on the door, I listen to Sara on the other side. It sounds like she's cursing at something and trying to move furniture. When she hears my knock, she curses again as she stomps to the door. I'm not sure who she thinks it is. I don't think she'd be acting this way if she thought it were Dani, but I could be wrong. Maybe she's having a bad day.

Opening the door, she already has a scowl on her face, but when she sees me, it looks more threatening. "What do you want?" Yup, she's not happy to see me at all. I could change that in two seconds flat, but I'm not gonna push her. I want her to want me too.

"Well, hello to you too, doll," I say with a chuckle. "Dani's ready to go get something to eat and wanted to know if you were ready. She's done in the shop and told me to come up and grab ya." She looks at me with confusion before wiping all emotion off her face.

"Uh, well, I'm a little busy right now. I was moving some furniture around and if I leave now, it won't get done. By the time I get back, I'll have no ambition to do anything. Tell her I'll take a rain check." I'm so busy looking at her in her baggy sweat pants and plain white t-shirt that I almost miss her refusal.

"Oh, well, I'll just help with the furniture real

quick and then you'll be able to tell her yourself. But if you've learned anything about Dani yet, it's that she rarely takes no for an answer," I say with a smirk. It's true. No one really tells Dani no anymore unless you want your ass kicked or to be on the receiving end of her wrath for at least a week.

I can tell she's thinking about it. She's probably trying to come up with an excuse to make me go away, but she knows she could use the help. Whether she wants it or not, I'm going to help her.

"I could use the help, so thank you. And I really don't want to go out, I'm kind of tired now after doing all this." I give her a look that says she knows that ain't gonna cut it with Dani, which in turn has her smiling. "But I do know that she won't let me back out. I guess once we're finished, I'll change and we can go." I smile back at her before looking around her living room.

"So where do ya want all this?" I ask as I wave my hand at the mess in front of me. She's moved her couch to the far corner, the coffee table is pushed up against the wall beside it, and a ratty recliner is next to it.

She walks over to the recliner. "Well, I wanted to move this into a corner because I don't really use it, but as you can see, I haven't gotten that far yet." She looks embarrassed.

"Just tell me where you want everything to go and I can get it moved while you go change." As much as I want to stay in her apartment with her alone, I know Dani will be chomping at the bit to go. The woman loves to supervise and tell people what to do. God love her, but I really just want to get the girls something to eat and see if I can get Dani to talk Sara into coming to the club with us. Maybe if I can get her to cut loose, she'll open up to me a little. I want to get to know her better.

Sara looks at me like she can't believe I'm offering to help. "Okay, but you don't have to do it by yourself. I can help." I walk over to her and place my hands gently on her shoulders.

"It's no problem, doll. I'm happy to help any way I can." Giving her one of my rare, full, megawatt smiles, I look her in the eyes for a couple of seconds so she knows I mean it, then drop my hands and turn back to the mess of furniture she has spread out. "You could put the recliner over in that corner," I say as I point to the corner by the windows, "and then we could put the couch in the middle here to separate the room a little. I think the coffee table looks good against the wall right where it's sitting now." Looking around the room, I make sure there's nothing else I can see that should be changed, then look at her for confirmation to start.

She looks around to where I pointed and thinks about the suggestions I've made. "Actually, I think that would work out great. Thank you." I nod and get to work. I lift the recliner with little effort and start moving it to the other side of the room. Sara says something I can't understand, but what has me really smiling is the way she can't seem to stop checking me out. When she moves her eyes up to mine, she realizes I've caught her. She turns her head, but not before I see her blush. "I'm just gonna go get changed. Let me know if you need any help." She doesn't wait for me to respond before she rushes into her room and slams the door.

After setting the recliner in its final resting place, I turn back to move the rest of the furniture with the biggest smile I've had in…well, ever. It's good to know that she's still attracted to me, which will help my case when the time comes, though for tonight, if I can get her to come to the clubhouse, I only want us to get to know each other. If she lets it happen, then maybe she won't have such a problem with me being around more.

Once I have the living room all arranged the way I want it, I decide to move her kitchen table a little so it doesn't look so cramped with the recliner in its new spot. When I start moving some of the chairs though, I notice that the legs are a little loose, so I search her drawers for a screwdriver. Finding one, I head back over and get to work on fixing the chairs. Wouldn't want her to sit down on them and have them break.

I'm almost finished tightening the last screw when Sara walks out of her room. Her hair is down and it looks like she's curled it. She's not wearing a lot of makeup, but what she is wearing makes her the most beautiful woman I have ever seen—I shit you not.

She's wearing a red dress with thin straps on her shoulders and a black belt that wraps around her waist, which emphasizes her flat stomach and pushes up her tits. The bottom of the dress hits her mid-thigh, but it's still short enough that I'm tempted to have her go change so no one else can see her like this. Finally, my eyes land on her shoes—black, with a little red on the straps. They make her at least four inches taller and have me imagining her in nothing *but* those shoes.

Before I know it, I'm standing in front of her without even realizing I was moving. Reaching out, I wrap my hand in the back of her hair and give it a little pull so she's forced to look me in the eyes. "Are you trying to test me tonight, doll? See how long I can last before I drag you into the closest empty room and fuck you against the wall?" I don't give her any time to answer before my lips are crushing against hers.

As soon as I make the connection, she reaches her hands up to rub the back of my still shaved head. I growl because it feels so fucking good.

Wrapping her hair completely around my wrist, I give it another tug and deepen the kiss, completely dominating her mouth with my tongue, which in turn has her moaning and breathing faster. I move us backwards, hoping we hit either the table, a wall, or any fucking surface soon so I can sink inside her tight pussy.

Her back hits the wall next to the front door first, so this will have to do.

Unwrapping my hand from her hair, I move my hand down her face and neck, over her shoulder, only stopping once I reach her left breast. With my other hand, I slide it up her thigh and play with the edges of her panties. Breaking away from the kiss, my gaze roams her face until she opens her eyes and meets mine. "What do you want, Sara?" I ask, needing her to tell me that she wants this—that she needs this as much as I do.

She takes a deep breath. "I want—" but she's cut

off by a loud knock on the door right next to us.

"Yo, Sara, you ready or what?" I let out a deep sigh and release her hands from above her head, but before I let her push me away, I whisper in her ear.

"This isn't over." Then I step back and walk over to the kitchen chair I was fixing while she pats down her hair and fixes her dress before opening the door.

"Yeah. Toby's just finishing up. He's fixing my kitchen chairs for me and then we're ready." She rushes out.

Dani looks at her like she wants to question what's going on, but one look from me, she shuts her mouth. Smart woman.

Turning the screwdriver one last time, I finish with the last chair. Standing up, I wipe my hands on my jeans and head toward the girls. "All right, let's get this show on the road." I usher them out the door, check to make sure the door is locked, then follow them out to my truck. Maybe tonight will be a little more than just getting to know one another. I'm not sure I'll be able to keep my hands to myself with her in that dress and the taste of her still on my lips.

CHAPTER 6

Sara

Dinner was awkward and tense. Well, actually, that's the understatement of the year.

After Dani interrupted the most erotic kiss I have ever experienced, I've been trying to get my heart to slow back down to normal, but every time Toby looked my way with his fuck me eyes or even spoke something as simple as a food order, it was no use. His voice alone is pure sex, but when you add that to everything else that makes up Toby, any woman within a ten-mile radius is fucked, or at least they are in their fantasies.

By the time I take the last bite of my cheeseburger, I need to get away, if only for a moment. I need to get myself under control, otherwise I might just offer myself up as dessert— on a silver fucking platter.

"I'm gonna run to the bathroom and then I'll be ready to go," I say to no one in particular as I push my chair out and get up.

"All right, we'll meet you outside," Dani says as she makes a grab for the check, but Toby beats her to it. She offers up a glare that should make him flinch, but he only chuckles as he shakes his head.

"I got it, Dani girl. We'll meet you outside in a few," he says as he heads over to the counter to pay. I'd offer to pay my part of the bill, but I know when a battle is lost before it even starts, so I just continue on my way toward the back to the bathroom.

After doing my business, I stand in front of the mirror, willing myself to calm down so I can get the rest of this night over with. "You just have to last the ride home. You can do this. He's just a guy," I whisper to myself, hoping my pep talk will help calm my nerves and hormones. I don't think I'll be able to last much longer in his presence before I jump him…again. The man is too sexy for his own good; for *my* own good.

Finally feeling like I have my shit together, I walk out the door, only to run into a wall—a hot, muscled wall of man. "Shit, I'm sorry," I mumble, trying to step out of the person's hold, only to look up and see Toby before I feel him tighten his hold on me.

"I'm not. In fact, I'm not sorry at all," he says into my ear, which causes goose bumps to rise on my arms and a shiver to rack my body.

Before I can say anything or try to put some distance between us, he pushes me back into the bathroom and locks the door behind us. The next thing I know, he's spinning me around and pressing my back against the door. He leans down and growls in my ear, "I told you it was just a matter of time before I'd lose control and have to fuck you against the wall. Didn't matter if it was a bathroom or closet." Suddenly I'm being lifted up, my legs automatically wrapping around his waist, and he has both of my arms pinned above my head. His lips slam down on mine. I know deep down I should be freaking out; being pinned and held down is a trigger for me. It was proven the morning we had sex. But I don't feel even an ounce of fear. Instead, I only feel hot and needy.

I throw everything into our kiss—all the tension I've felt since the last time I was with him, all the fear about the ways he's consumed my thoughts, and how I feel when I'm around him. I put every one of those feelings into this kiss.

He groans into my mouth, then pulls away just far enough to look into my eyes. "This is gonna be quick, doll. We don't want to keep Dani waiting and I can't stand another second without being inside of you, but I promise you, later I'll take my time and worship your body the way you deserve." I'm barely able to comprehend what he just said before he's reaching between us, freeing his cock and pushing inside of me.

"Oh God!" I groan.

"Shit, you're soaking wet," Toby grunts in my ear as he thrusts in and out of my pussy furiously. He releases my hands from above me so I can hold on for the ride of my life. He grabs my hips as he thrusts hard inside of me. "Hold on tight, babe," he says before speeding up his thrusts to the point I think he'll actually fuck me stupid.

My toes start to curl inside my shoes and my

nails dig into his shoulders to the point I may draw blood underneath his shirt. I close my eyes as I feel my orgasm rising up inside me at a rapid pace; almost too rapid. I've never gotten off so soon before, and I'm fearing what will happen when I fall over the edge.

Squeezing my eyes shut, I can do nothing against the onslaught of pain and pleasure he causes me with every brutal thrust he delivers. I know that if he keeps this up, I'll come so hard I may just pass out.

Toby takes a small step back, but it's enough for him to shift me in his arms, allowing him to thrust even deeper inside of me. He's so fucking deep, I see stars and fall over into ecstasy.

I open my mouth to scream, but nothing comes out.

I barely feel him thrust a couple more times in quick succession before he stiffens inside of me with his own release. "FUCK!" he roars before he slows his thrusts, pumping into me a few more times, trying to draw out as much pleasure for both of us as he can. When he finally stills, he drops his head into the crook of my neck and presses his body against mine.

After we both calm our breathing, he slowly untangles my legs from around his waist and sets me down. When my feet hit the ground, I immediately fix my dress and run my hands through my hair. I walk over to the sink to make sure I look presentable and not like I was just fucked within an inch of my life, but on the way there, I feel wetness seep out of me and run down my inner thighs. Oh shit! We didn't use a condom.

Instead of stopping at the sink, I rush into a stall to clean myself up. I cannot believe I got so caught up that I forgot to tell him to use a condom. How could I be so stupid? I've never been so consumed with someone, even when I was young and dumb, that I've forgotten to use protection. I can't fucking believe this.

Sitting on the toilet with my head in my hands, I hear a soft knock on the stall door. "Babe, are you okay?" He sounds worried, but I can't answer him. I'm too busy freaking out. I need to get my head on straight before I can face him. I also need to find a way to ask if he's clean.

"Hello? Can you open the door so the rest of us can go to the bathroom?" a girl says loudly from outside the door, sounding irritated and bitchy. This is just what I need right now.

Standing up, I open the door and walk past Toby to get to the door. With him right behind me and the both of us walking out of a public restroom together, they're all going to know what happened.

Before I reach the door to unlock it, Toby comes up beside me and wraps his arm around my shoulders. "Follow my lead," he says before he unlocks the door.

As soon as Toby opens the door, the arm that isn't already around my shoulders gently reaches over and rubs my stomach. "It's all right, doll." What the hell is he doing? Too embarrassed to look up at whoever is standing there waiting for us to come out, I nestle my face further into Toby and keep my eyes downcast.

"Oh my goodness, is she okay?" the girl asks.

"She's fine. I'm sorry about locking the door, I just wanted to make sure she was all right." He sounds so sincere. It's incredible that he's able to make up a story so fast that no one will know what really happened in that bathroom, and for that I'm grateful.

Walking past the girl, Toby quickly ushers me outside to his truck.

"What the hell took you so long?" Dani yells as soon as she sees us walking out the door, but when she gets a good look at the way Toby still has me tucked under his arm, she rushes over and takes my hand. "Sara, what's the matter? Are you okay?" When I don't answer, she looks up and directs a seething glare at Toby. "What did you do?"

He releases his hold on me, but just long enough to open up the passenger side door, then takes my hand to help me into the front seat, leaving Dani to get into the back. "I didn't do anything to her. She's fine." Not wanting to explain to her what really happened, I just nod and turn to give her a reassuring smile.

"I'm just tired. Toby saw me coming out of the bathroom and walked me out."

Dani doesn't question what we tell her, but she does look at me longer than necessary to try and gauge my expression. I lock everything down inside of me, willing my face not to give anything away. It must work because she just shakes her head and smiles back at me.

"Okay, if you say so." As Toby starts the truck, Dani's phone rings. "Yeah?" She's quiet, listening intently to whoever is talking on the other end. "Well, I'm with Toby and Sara. We just got done eating. We were going to drop her off before coming to the club." Listening again, she waits for their reply. "Sure, we'll be right there," she says, hanging up the phone without even saying goodbye.

Leaning forward between the seats, she puts her hand on my shoulder. "I know you're tired and probably just want to go home, but Mack needs me at the club. Do you mind if we stop there real quick? I promise we won't be long." Her voice is laced with concern, probably because this would be the first time I would be going to the clubhouse. Though Dani has informed me of that way of life and how things work, I'm a little nervous about actually *seeing* some of the things she's mentioned; mainly the "club whores." Let's hope it's not too bad.

I nod, hoping she takes my lack of answer as just being tired like I said and not what it really is, which is that I'm really fucking nervous about going. But also because I can't get what happened at the diner out of my head.

Toby turns us around and heads in the direction of the club, or that's what I assume, at least. Maybe I can just wait in the truck for Dani to talk to Mack, or maybe Toby will drop her off and take me back to my apartment.

Five minutes later, Toby pulls into a lot near a row of bikes. I'm surprised when he puts the truck in park and turns off the ignition. They both get out of the truck, but not knowing what I'm supposed to do, I stay buckled in and don't move.

My door opens and Toby looks at me questioningly. I don't answer, not sure what the question is, and just stare at him. "I gotta go in to make sure everything's okay. I don't really want to leave you out here by yourself..." He leaves the sentence hanging, waiting for me to get out of the truck. When I still don't make a move to get out, he shakes his head and reaches around me to unbuckle my seatbelt. "Come on, doll, we won't be long." He physically lifts me out of the truck, only putting me back on my feet once we're right in front of the door.

"What is it with you and carrying me around all the time? I can walk, ya know," I say, but there's no heat behind my words, though I am curious.

"I'm not going to apologize. I just like the way you feel in my arms." His statement leaves me speechless. I've never had someone make me feel the way Toby does, or seem like he enjoys the way I make him feel. For him to admit he can't stop touching me because the way I feel to him is one of the most precious things someone has ever said to me. I just fear this will lead to him wanting to control me, consume me. I won't go there again, I can't. Even with Toby.

Once we are inside, I look around but I don't see Dani anywhere so I assume she's already talking with Mack.

Toby places his hand on the small of my back, ushering me further inside.

There are people everywhere—scary looking men sitting on stools at the bar, some with women between their legs, and some by themselves. There are men playing pool with a few girls standing off to the side, and men sitting on couches with women either draped over their laps or straddling them. All the girls in here are dressed in clothing that would rival a stripper.

Looking around some more, I come across a couple in the corner. Holy shit! Are they fucking? Here, in front of everyone?

Averting my eyes, I decide that it will be safer to not look around and keep my eyes down.

Toby gently urges me forward, moving toward the bar, and whispers, "I know it's a lot to take in, doll, but just stay with me. No one will hurt you here, I give you my word." I can only nod, afraid if I open my mouth he'll hear the uncertainty I feel.

When we reach the bar, Toby pulls out a stool and offers it to me. Without looking to see who I'm sitting by, I take the seat and stare at the wood that makes up the bar.

"What can I get ya?" a deep voice asks close by, but I still don't look up.

"Give me a Bud Light. What do you want, Sara?" Wanting to calm my frayed nerves a bit but not wanting to get wasted, I ask for a beer as well. Seconds later, two bottles of Bud Light are set down in front of us. Taking the bottle, I chug half its contents before putting it back down. Toby laughs softly and runs his hands up and down my back. "Relax," he says before taking a sip of his own beer.

After a few minutes, I decide to brave the room again and take another look around. I hope the couple in the back are done fucking, or at least moved their *party* into a room with a door, but just to be safe, I don't look in that general direction.

On second inspection, I notice that the men don't look as scary as I first thought. I mean, they are rough looking, covered in tattoos, wearing leather, and they're all packed with muscle, but I can tell by looking at the way they interact with each other that they don't look all that bad. I mean, I'm sure they can all be scary if the situation called for it, just like I'm sure Toby can be when he wants or needs to, but the vibe I'm getting off of these men isn't anything that would make me feel uncomfortable. Plus, knowing that Dani calls these men her family and what they've done to help her, they can't be that bad, right?

Speaking of Dani, I see her talking to an older man who must be Mack. They walk into the bar area from what looks like the hallway. He looks old enough to be her father, but he's young looking as well, if that makes sense. He's tall and broad, packed with muscle, has short, dark hair that is sprinkled with gray in areas, but his face is what catches my attention. When he speaks to Dani, he looks like a father caring for his daughter. My parents died when I was very young and then I was placed with a foster family, so I don't really remember them, but if my father was still alive I would want him to look at me that way; loving and proud, all at the same time. I can also tell that this man is most likely the scariest of them all, but probably the most gentle, as well.

From what Dani's told me, he is the saving grace she needed to get her life back together when she left her hometown four years ago. He is most certainly a man I want to know and have on my side, but I have no idea how to go about making people like me the way they like Dani.

I see her nod, then look around the room until her eyes land on me. She smiles and leads him over to where Toby and I are sitting at the bar. When they stop in front of us, Dani introduces us.

"Sara, I'd like you to meet Mack, the president of the Forsaken Sinners. Mack, this is my friend, Sara. She's helping out at the shop and staying in the upstairs apartment." Mack looks to her for confirmation on something, then turns to me and smiles while he offers me his hand.

"It's nice to meet you. Dani has told me a lot about you." Not sure what she would have told him, I just smile and shake his hand.

"Hi," I say in return, offering him a polite smile.

Mack turns his head and looks at Dani. They seem to be having a silent conversation between themselves. Just by looking at the two of them, I can tell this is something they have perfected.

When Dani looks back in our direction, she steps toward Toby. "I need to steal you for a couple of minutes. Mack, why don't you take Sara into your office where it's quieter?" Toby looks between Mack and Dani, then at me with a silent question in his eyes, asking if I'll be all right. He seems torn and guilty about leaving me. Not wanting him to worry about me when Dani needs him, I smile, assuring him that I'll be fine, and turn to Mack.

He offers me his arm and once I take it, he leads me back the way he and Dani had come from.

Once inside the small office, he leads me to a

couch that's set off to one side of the room before taking a seat next to me. "So, tell me about yourself, Sara. What brings you to our neck of the woods?" I give him a nervous chuckle. He would go right to the hardest question. I wring my hands in my lap and think about how much I should tell him.

Deciding to go with the truth, or most of it, anyway, I tell him the story that I wanted to leave home, so I left. I got in my car and just drove till I wound up here. I don't want to go into the details with him, but I have a feeling he's not going to be satisfied with my vague answer.

After I finish, he just sits there and stares at me, almost like he's waiting for me to continue, but I don't.

Standing up from the couch, he walks over to the desk and sits down behind it. He brings his right hand up and rubs his index finger along his lower lip while the other hand taps on the arm of his chair. He hasn't stopped looking at me since he sat down and I start to feel uncomfortable. I know he won't hurt me, but the way he's looking at me, I can tell he's trying to read me.

"Look. I understand that you don't know me from Adam, and you certainly don't trust me, but I just want you to know that I'm one of the good guys." He stands up and begins pacing. "I'm not sure what Dani has told you about when she first came into town, but when she came into my shop, she was running away from her old life and looking to start over. I gave her a job, a place to call home, and offered protection if she needed it. Thankfully, the only thing she was running from was herself and not some lunatic, but that's her story to tell, not mine. So, the bottom line is this. I offered her a safe haven and protection, and I'd like to do the same for you. Now you don't need to tell me everything, but I need to know enough to be able to protect you if trouble comes knocking, because I have a strange feeling that it will." He's quiet for a moment, giving time for what he's saying to sink in.

I do know a little about what happened to Dani, but not the whole story. She only told me she was once in my shoes and Mack, along with this club, helped her when she didn't have anyone. With what I know of Dani, I know that she's someone who inspires me, someone that lets me know that people can overcome their past and make their lives better. I want what she has, and if it means laying all my dirty laundry out for Mack to see, then that's what I'll do. It would be nice to have someone watch my back and be there for me for once. I don't know Mack, but I can tell he means what he says, and he'll do anything he can to help me.

Taking a deep breath, I decide that in order for him to help me, or at least let him decide if he still wants to help me, I need to tell him everything.

I motion for him to take a seat.

"What I told you was the truth, but not *everything*. I did live in New York, but with my ex-boyfriend. I'd tell you the short version, but I suppose you need to know it all?" He gives me a small smile, then nods for me to continue. "We'd been together for about five years, but during the last year and a half, things went downhill. Actually, now that I think about it, I can't say that we ever really had a 'good' relationship, but the last year or so, it was bad—the worst. He was always kind of a possessive jerk, but I just thought he was your typical alpha-male type of guy, and to be honest, I liked it in the beginning, especially because we'd been together so long, it made me feel important. As time passed, he became obsessed with being in control and was jealous over the littlest things. He would always make rude comments about me, the things I did, or what I wore. After three and a half years of going through the motions, things with him began to escalate—harsher words turning into harsher actions. His control over me became suffocating. He told me I was starting to look fat and that I dressed like a slut, so he went through all my clothes and threw half of them away before taking me shopping to buy only things he approved of. Then he demanded that I stop hanging out with my friends. He would tell me what time I needed to be home, and when I didn't always make it on time, he hid my keys, telling me that since I couldn't be back when he said, that I no longer had the right to drive. He made me dependent on him for everything." I stand up and start to pace in the same spot Mack was pacing moments before, needing to be doing something besides reliving everything Rick did to me.

"Before I knew it, he was the only one I had in my life. He had officially made sure that my friends were no longer there for me and even my co-workers stopped talking to me. He wanted me to quit so I couldn't leave the house at all, but since he liked having extra money to spend on gambling, he allowed me to continue to work. The only reason I still had my own apartment was because I'd already paid for it and I think he would take other women there. I didn't care though, as long as I didn't have to deal with him, it didn't matter. I always hoped he would get sick of me and I'd be able to go back there, but that never happened.

His jealous rants turned physical. He started with slapping, then went to punching and beating me anywhere that could be hidden with clothes. I knew I needed to get out of there, but every time I tried, he would catch me and beat me to the point that I was too scared to try again. I'd given up on the idea of ever getting away, so there I stayed." Taking a deep breath, I try to compose myself as much as possible, knowing that the worst part is coming next.

"Then one night, he came home late from work and was mad that I went to bed without him. I guess he thought I shouldn't be able to sleep unless he gave me permission to. I woke up to him grabbing my ankles and pulling me out of bed. He was yelling at me but I couldn't understand anything he was saying, he was slurring so bad. He dragged me into the hall toward the bathroom, and I instinctively started kicking out, hoping I could distract or hurt him long enough for him to release me so I could get away. I was able to catch him in the crotch, but it wasn't anywhere near hard enough. It only caused him to drop my feet and start punching me in the stomach, and a few times in my face. It hurt me enough that I stopped struggling, which allowed him to rip off my pajama pants and panties. He was going to rape me. In all the years we had been together, even when he was abusing me, he had never forced himself on me. We barely even had sex by that point, but that was because he was out screwing other women because I disgusted him. He said that I needed to lose weight before he would touch me again. I knew I wasn't overweight, but if that's how he felt, then I was good with it. It kept him from touching me."

I look Mack in the eyes. "I knew if he succeeded, I wouldn't be able to come back from that. It was one thing to deal with the hitting and verbal abuse, but I knew I wasn't strong enough to get over being raped." It probably makes me look weak in his eyes that I stayed and let it go on for as long as it did, but I need him to understand.

"My eyes landed on a small statue that must have fallen to the ground in the struggle, or maybe on his way to the bedroom, who knows, but I saw it and wiggled just enough to reach it. Rick was too busy trying to spread my legs and keep me from kneeing him in the balls to notice that I now had a weapon. Without even thinking, I hit him over the head as hard as I could, repeatedly, until he fell to the side of me, dazed from the blows, until he went completely limp. I didn't know if he was dead or alive and at that moment, I didn't give a shit. I got up, pulled on my pants, and ran out the door."

Now that the hard part was over, I felt a calmness take over my body. It actually felt pretty good telling someone the whole story. "I had found my keys that he'd hidden and I had a getaway bag still hidden in my trunk from the last time I tried to run, so I didn't grab anything from the house. I didn't go to my apartment. I just got in my car and drove until I wound up here." Wrapping my arms around myself, I look up at the ceiling and wait for him to speak.

It felt like hours, years even, before he finally spoke.

"Do you think he'll come after you?"

I almost smile, because knowing Rick and how he operates, I feel pretty confident with my answer.

"No. Even if he had looked for me, he would've given up by now."

Mack looks at me with doubt. "What if he has found you, but he's waiting to make a move?" He makes a solid argument, but he doesn't know Rick like I do.

"He would have approached me already. He isn't a patient man, so if he knew where I was, he would've made himself known already."

After thinking about that for a moment, he nods. "Okay." He stands up and walks over to me. Placing his hands on my shoulders, he gives me a reassuring squeeze. "You did good, Sara. You got yourself out of a bad situation. You did whatever it took to make sure you were safe. And I know it wasn't easy telling me that, but I needed to know. I'll keep my eyes open for any trouble, but you come to me if anything feels off or you see him around. Do you have a picture of him so I know who I'm looking for?" I nod and open my wallet. I only have one picture of him and it's from when we first got together, but he hasn't changed much.

Pulling it out, I hand it to him. "It's an older

photo, but he looks the same, just older." Mack studies the picture, then puts it in his pocket before slowly walking us out of the office and back toward the bar.

"I won't tell anyone what you told me, but I am going to pass this picture around for the guys to keep an eye out for him. They won't know it's related to you, though. I promise you that." I feel so much gratitude toward this man that I can't help but stop in my tracks and hug him tightly.

"Thank you," I whisper in his ear.

"Anytime, sweetheart. Whatever you need, you just let me know, all right?" I just nod, afraid if I say anything more I'll start to cry again and I don't want to do that in front of a crowded bar.

I start walking toward the bar, but stop short when I see Toby sitting there, but he's not alone. My sudden stop has Mack looking at me with concern, then he follows my eyes across the room.

"Is there anything going on with you and him that I need to know about?"

I should be embarrassed that he's asking about my relationship with Toby, but knowing more about Mack and the way he works, it doesn't really surprise me that he's already caught on, even if I'm only now just starting to realize my feelings. "Well, it's kind of complicated. We met at the gym, then again when he found me working at the strip club. All I know is that when I'm with him, I feel safe and wanted, but that scares me after everything I went through with Rick. I mean, I have no idea who Toby is or what he wants with me. The way he is sometimes reminds me of the way Rick would act, but I don't want to believe Toby is anything like him in *any* way. What I do know for sure is that I like the way he makes me feel most of the time, and I can't stay away from him."

Mack puts his arm around me and squeezes. "Sweetheart, Toby is an intense man, but I know for a fact that he would never hurt you or try to control you. Hell, he'd go to the ends of the earth to make sure you're safe. That's just the type of person he is; he's a fierce protector." He releases a long sigh and stands in front of me so I have no choice but to look at him. "Take a chance. Sit down and tell him about your worries. You need to be open and honest, and see where the road takes you. Who knows? Maybe he's exactly what you need." With that, he leads me toward the man in question.

"Word of advice; be confident and go after what you want. Don't let anyone stand in your way. If Toby is what you want, then stand up for him—claim him. I know you don't know a lot about our way of life, but you're no club whore. Make them give you the respect you deserve, because in our life, they're nothing. That's just the way it is." He gives me an encouraging smile, then puts his hand on my back to urge me forward. "Go get him."

With a weight lifted and realizing what I want, or rather *who* I want, and what needs to happen, I move forward with nothing but determination.

CHAPTER 7

Toby

Sitting at the bar, I have to physically restrain myself from storming into Mack's office and pulling Sara into my arms. It hasn't even been five fucking minutes and I'm already going crazy, knowing she's within these walls but I can't see her. Or maybe it's the fact that she's here, in my club, surrounded by my brothers, and knowing exactly how they react to unclaimed pussy. I'm going to have to put the word out that she's off limits and anyone who fucks with what's mine will be drinking out of a straw for the next couple of weeks, maybe even months.

I've never considered myself possessive or jealous where a woman is concerned. Sure, I can be arrogant, demanding, and I've never been one to back down from a fight or even to start one, but with Sara, I want to consume her. I want to take her away and hide her from the world. I want her all to myself, but I also want to shield her from the cruelty that's everywhere. I want to comfort her from every hurt from her past, and protect her from anyone who dares harm a hair on her head or even thinks about hurting her.

Taking one more glance toward Mack's office, I turn back toward the prospect behind the bar and order another beer. While I take a sip, I feel someone slide in close beside me. Thinking Sara is back and just getting close to me because she's uncomfortable, I turn with a smile on my face. "It's about time you came back—" When I turn to look at her, I realize that it's not Sara. Instead, it's Trixie who's sidled up beside me, looking at me like I'm her dessert for the night. Fuck, I don't need this shit right now, especially with Sara here. I didn't even consider this bullshit when I brought her to the club. I need to get rid of her before she comes back.

"What do you want, Trixie?" I ask. I don't even try to hide my annoyance. I see her flinch a little from my tone, but I don't give a shit.

After she recovers, she slips back into her seduction. "Toby, baby, I've missed you. Why you gotta be like that?" she whines. I've noticed her do it plenty of times before, and I never thought twice about her pouted out, botoxed lips, but now I can't believe it never annoyed me before. It's honestly like listening to nails on a chalkboard.

"What. Do. You. Want?" I say between my clenched teeth, not playing this game with her now or ever again. I'm done with her, so she needs to get it through her head now before I have to make an example out of her.

I turn back to face the bar and try to tamp down

my anger and irritation. I know I shouldn't really direct it at her. It's not like she knows about Sara, but she's a club whore and I'm a patched member of this club. She should know better than to come at me like this. She knows her place and knows that if I wanted anything to do with her, I would come find her. She's only good for one thing and one thing only, and I don't need that anymore, at least not from her.

Trixie places her hand on my arm to try to draw my attention back to her, but she's not getting it. "Why don't we go back to your room? Let me make you feel better, baby," she purrs in my ear, leaning in closer to me.

Turning around to move her away from me, I look over her shoulder and see Sara. Fuck! This isn't going to go down well. I know we aren't together, but there's something between us, and her seeing Trixie hanging on me isn't going to help my case. God fucking dammit!

Sara and Mack are across the room looking straight at me. I can't tell what she's thinking or what Mack thinks of the situation, but I'm nervous. This could be a turning point for us and it may not go the way I want it to.

I watch as they head toward us again after Mack says something to her. I hope it was to give me a chance, but fuck, I would completely understand if she doesn't want to give me the time of day now, seeing me with Trixie. But if she gives me the opportunity to explain, I hope I can get her to understand.

When she stops in front of me, Trixie goes rigid.

I spare a quick glance at her and see her glaring daggers at Sara. That shit's not gonna fly, but Sara speaks before I can say a word. "I'm ready to leave whenever you are, Toby." She sounds confident and not really upset, but I don't know her all that well, so I could be in for it when we leave. I also notice that she looked directly at Trixie when she spoke. Interesting.

Deciding to see how this pans out, I sit back to see what she does. I don't have to wait long.

Trixie snaps into bitch mode, not like she really leaves it often, and takes a step closer to me, placing her hand on my arm. I shrug it off, but she holds it in place. "He's a little busy right now, honey, so why don't you call someone else to take you home, where you belong." Trixie's smile is taunting. I want to put her in her place, but I want to see what Sara does more. If we have any chance at a relationship, no matter what type it is, she needs to learn to stand up for herself. Otherwise, these girls will walk all over her.

Sara just smiles at Trixie and turns back to me, not giving her anymore of her time. "Like I said, whenever you're ready. Maybe we can grab some drinks to take back to my place," she says with a smile. I'll do anything to keep it on her face.

Pulling away from Trixie, I move toward Sara, but Trixie has other ideas. This bitch is really getting on my nerves. "Listen, bitch, I don't know who the hell you think you are, coming in here and thinking you have some sort of claim with the club because you work with Princess Dani—" The way she sneers Dani's name makes my back stiffen and rage overtake my mind, but before I can do anything about her blatant disrespect, she continues, "—but you don't. You're nothing to this club, and you never will be. Toby is mine, so back the fuck off."

I keep my eyes on Sara, trying to reassure her that this is not what Trixie is making it out to be, but instead of looking hurt, I see something I've never seen before—she looks confident, slightly amused, and ready for battle with a glint in her eye. Stepping right up to Trixie, she says in a voice low enough so only the three of us can hear, "I may not be anything to this club yet, but let me tell you who you are. You are a club *whore*, which means you're only good for one thing. So, before you start preaching and laying your claim, look in the fucking mirror. You will never be anything more than a club whore, whereas I'm someone who is worth more than just a fuck to anyone who wants it." Ho-ly shit. Did she really just say that? I think I'm in love.

Sara looks above Trixie's head and locks eyes with me before finishing, "And Toby isn't yours, honey. If he's anyone's, then he's mine, so unless you want me to remove your hand from him myself, I'd suggest that you fuck off." There's fire in her eyes when she says it, and it's all for me. "Oh, and the next time you disrespect me in front of anyone in this club, I'll make sure that you find yourself fucked, and not in the way you so desperately want." Oh God, I'm hard as a rock. Listening to her lay her claim and declare that she wants me has me ready to drag her to the first available room and claim her too. She doesn't know it yet, but what she just did solidified it for me. She's mine and everyone will soon know it. There's no turning back now.

And the way she stood up for herself and demanded respect from someone she knows is beneath her, like an old lady would, lets me know that she's just as ready as I am. It also shows me that it still may take a little getting used to, but she's going to fit in just fine around here.

I step to Sara's side, ready to leave when Sara grabs Trixie by the arm in a hold so strong I can see her knuckles turning white. "And one more thing. If you ever talk like that again about Dani, I will personally make sure you find it hard to form any words for a very long time." With that said, she walks ahead of me and out the door.

I spare a quick glance over my shoulder at Trixie, and she's staring after Sara with humiliation and pure hatred. "You fucking heard my woman, but let me say it one more time in case you missed any of it. No one will take a club whore as an old lady, so you may as well just stick to the only thing you're good for—sucking and fucking. And I'd watch what you say about a brother's old lady around here, or you'll be finding yourself cold in the ground."

Leaning over the bar, I grab two six-packs of Budweiser for the road and take off after Sara. I can't wait to get her alone. I know I just fucked her an hour ago at the diner, but I need her again. After what just happened, this time will be different. She'll be mine.

***

The ride back to her place is quiet. I wanted to give her time to process what happened and what she said, because when we get inside, it's going to be game over.

Walking through her door, she lays her purse down on the table. I go into the kitchen to put one of the six-packs away, but take one over to the kitchen table. I think we'll need it so there's no sense in putting it away and having to get up numerous times for a refill.

"I'm gonna take a quick shower and change, if that's all right with you. Make yourself at home and I'll be out soon." She doesn't wait for me to respond, but I let her have this time. I can wait for a bit. If I get my way, we have all night, and hopefully every day after.

I grab two beers out of the case and make myself comfortable on the couch. Maybe I should turn the TV on so there's some background noise, or at the very least so it doesn't look like I'm just sitting here twiddling my thumbs until she comes back.

Flipping through her channels, I notice that she only has a few, so I turn the TV off and see a radio sitting on a shelf. I check out the CD player first to see if there is anything in there before looking at her collection. It seems she only has country music, which really isn't my style. Messing with the radio for a couple of minutes and not finding anything, I figure there's nothing else to do besides put something country on. I guess it really won't matter because we won't be listening to it anyway.

I've only ever really listened to country when Dani would put some on in the shop, but I never really paid much attention to it. I come across a Brantley Gilbert CD, and since he kind of looks badass, I decide to try it out. The first song comes on and it's talking about a bad boy or some shit. What the fuck am I listening to?

"Nice choice. Brantley Gilbert is one of my favorite singers." I turn around at the sound of her voice and have to take a minute to calm my dick down. She's standing by the couch in what looks like an old ratty t-shirt and boy shorts. Damn, this woman is sexy as fuck!

Clearing my throat, I answer, "Ah, yeah. I'm not really a country fan, but I didn't see anything else to choose from." I give her a sweet smile so she knows it's no big deal. I don't really care what we listen to or what's on TV, 'cause we've got more important shit to do.

I walk back over to the couch and pull out another beer, offering it to her. She takes it from me and sits on one side of the couch with her feet underneath her. "So, I guess we should talk about what happened, huh?" She's not looking at me, but she doesn't seem hesitant to talk, which is good. I think she's more nervous than anything else. I can work with that.

"I think that would be a good idea," I say as I sit down opposite from her, not wanting to crowd her.

After she takes a sip of her beer, she leans over and sets it on the floor in front of her. "I'll start." She takes a deep breath, then releases it slowly before looking up at me. "I like you, more than I

probably should at this point in my life right now."
She stops, but doesn't look away. I take a drink of
my beer and wait for her to continue, not wanting to
interrupt or say anything until I know where she's
going with this. "I was in a bad relationship when I
was in New York. I don't want to get into the
specifics, but it wasn't good. Winding up here, I
figured I would start fresh with my life; get a job
that I liked, find a place, maybe make some friends.
Which, by the way, you've been the one to help me
single-handedly with all those things, but I sure as
hell wasn't looking for a relationship. I didn't want
a man in my life unless it was friendship, and
honestly, I thought if I were friends with a guy, he
would either be really old or gay." That statement
makes her laugh and has me smiling.

"But then I met you within the first few days of
getting to town and you turned everything upside
down. There was something about you that drew me
in, but it scared me. It still does, actually, but I had
to find a job and a place to live so I put you out of
my head. Then you showed up and saved me at the
strip club that night. It was like you were my dark
knight, hell-bent on charging into my life, but
saving me from others and myself at the same time.
That night at your house was a turning point for me,
but I guess I just didn't know it until today."

Picking up her beer again, she takes a drink and
goes on. "I knew there was something about you,
and then we had sex, which was amazing, but as
much as I enjoyed it and enjoyed being with you,
there are things about you that scare the shit out of
me. You're so strong and intimidating. Don't get

me wrong, those aren't bad qualities, but in my experience, it can lead to bad things. Regardless, there's something about you I can't resist. I came here to start over and live my life the way I wanted to, and if I protect myself from every little thing that scares me, that's not living, it's hiding. I don't want to hide anymore. I'm just unsure how to get past some of my hang-ups and fears without pushing you away. I want you to know I want to try; I want to try this with you, if you want to try it with me." I know she means what she says.

Reaching over, I take her beer out of her hands and place both bottles on the floor on the side of the couch, then I take her by the hand and pull her over onto my lap. I can't stay away from her anymore, I just need to touch her. "I understand being scared and I know you have a past that isn't pleasant. Shit, my past isn't sunshine and roses, either. I don't know what happened or how your ex treated you, but you need to understand that I'm not him. I know it probably doesn't come easy to you, but please just trust me. I would never hurt you." I pull her chin up so she's looking at me as I say the rest. "But I want to see what this is between us too. There's something here, we both feel it, and I want to see where it takes us."

I lean in to give her a quick kiss on the right side of her mouth. "I'll be patient with you. I'm going to need you to be patient with me too because I've never been in a relationship before." Then I kiss the left side of her mouth. "So if you promise to trust me, I promise that I will never hurt you and I will always protect you." Then I kiss her fully on the lips.

When she pulls back, she has the most beautiful smile on her face that I have ever seen. "I trust you, Toby." She leans back in to kiss me, but we need to talk about what happened at the club first, so I pull back just an inch, but it's enough.

Smiling, I give her one more peck on the lips, then turn her on my lap so she's straddling my hips. When she settles on top of me, I realize my mistake. I can feel her hot pussy through the thin layer of shorts she's wearing. Fuck! Maybe this was a bad idea, but we need to get this all out of the way before anything else happens and I don't have the strength to move her away from me. "About what happened tonight at the club..." I let the sentence trail off, knowing she'll understand what I mean. She laughs nervously.

"Yeah, about that...look, I'm not going to apologize for the things I said, but I do apologize if it upset you. That wasn't my intent, but after hearing about the club from Dani and then my talk with Mack, I felt confident in how I judged the situation and what I said. As far as what she said about being yours..." She looks me straight in the eyes as she says this, but before saying any more, she leans in close and brushes her lips across mine so softly I can barely feel them. "I don't care if you've been with her before. The only thing I care about is you being with me, and only me, from now on."

"First of all, whatever happened between her and I meant nothing, and it's been a while since we've been together, but since I've met you, I haven't even *looked* at another chick. So, me being with you and *only* you is no fucking problem, doll, but you're mine now too. I hope you realize that." I wink so it doesn't scare her, but I want her to know that I'm serious.

She smiles, so I know she gets it and I haven't scared her off. Good, now we can get to the second part. "And about what you said to her, you have nothing to be worried about. To be honest, if you hadn't said anything, what I would've said would've been so much worse, but I'm glad it came from you. It shows that you demand respect and won't take her shit or anyone else's. I know you don't know the ways of the club yet, but I'll get you there, babe. You're already off to a great start. What you did tonight wasn't bad. If anything, it was great." When she nods, I decide it's time to get to the important stuff. "Now, where were we?" I ask, but I don't wait for her to respond. I just dive right in and take her lips in a hard kiss.

She doesn't disappoint. She meets my desperation and adds her own by biting my lower lip. Growling into her mouth, I grab her ass and stand, not breaking our connection.

Walking over to her bedroom door, I kick it open and drop down on her bed. Lifting up onto my elbows so I don't crush her, I break the kiss, but keep my lips on her body. I kiss her jaw, down her neck, and over her breasts. I take one of my hands and push the bottom of her shirt up, baring her naked nipple to my hungry mouth and suck hard while flicking my tongue on the hard peak.

"Oh God, Toby, that feels so good," she moans

as she runs her hands over my shaved head. I move over to her other nipple and suck it deep into my mouth before biting down.

My hands move south as I continue torturing her tits. When I reach her shorts, I can feel that she's so wet she's soaked through the material.

"These need to go," I say before I rip her shorts off, along with her panties. Looking down, I see her bare before me. "Fuck. You have the prettiest pussy I've ever seen." Spreading her legs, I run my finger through her excitement. "You wet for me, doll? How bad do you want my cock inside your pretty pussy?" Even though she got off both times we had sex, it felt rushed. I want to take my time with her tonight—build her up so high that she never wants to come back down.

"Yes, I want you inside of me."

Stroking her with my finger, I position myself on the bed so my face is level with her pussy. I can't fucking wait to taste her. Starting at the bottom, I give her a long, hard lick, then replace my finger with my tongue by swirling it around her clit. "Ah, yes, please!" Knowing she's close, I let up, not ready for it to end yet.

I can see surprise and frustration on her face, but it all goes away when I pull myself up so I'm kneeling between her legs. I grab my belt and slowly unbuckle it, pulling it through the loops. "Do you trust me, Sara?" I raise my belt up so she can see it and grab one of her hands, so she understands what I about to do. I can see uncertainty and fear reflecting back at me, but she shakes it off and nods her head once. "I need you to say it, doll. Do you trust me?" She doesn't hesitate this time.

"Yes. I trust you." I reward her with a kiss as I take both of her hands and pull them above her head. When I lift my head, I make sure she's looking at me.

"I won't hurt you. If it becomes too much, just tell me, and I'll stop. I promise." Again, she doesn't hesitate.

"Okay."

I lift the belt and wrap it around her wrists, making it loose enough that it doesn't hurt her, but tight enough that she can't get out. Then I wrap the other end through her metal headboard. Once she's restrained, I run my hands down her arms, over her breasts, and back down to her pussy. "If you want me to stop, you'll tell me, right? Let me hear you say it before I go any further." She's still wet, so I know she's still with me, but I need to be sure she understands the rules.

"Yes," she says on another moan.

"That's my girl."

Done talking, I drive my tongue back into her pussy—I'm done messing around. I want to hear her scream my name and come all over my mouth.

Flicking her clit with my tongue, I take two fingers and push them inside of her. She squeezes me so tight that I can't move. Knowing I won't be able to hold off much longer before my need to feel her around my cock is too much, I start moving my fingers in a fast pace and take her clit into my mouth and suck, hard.

"*Oh fuck!* Yes, Toby, *yes!*" I hear her scream seconds before I feel her convulse on my fingers and her taste explodes in my mouth.

"That's it, doll," I say as I continue to lick and suck until I feel her relax into the bed.

Pulling my fingers out, I kiss my way up her body until I'm level with her face.

It takes her a couple of seconds to come back down to earth and focus her eyes on me. "You ready for more?" I ask, hoping she's not done yet. I want to feel her squeeze my cock and feel her juices run down my thighs.

She pulls at her restraints and lifts her lips to mine for a hungry kiss. "Yes, I want your cock inside me." She doesn't need to tell me twice.

I hurry to pull my shirt over my head and rip my jeans and boxers off. Within seconds, I'm balls deep inside her pussy and she's squeezing me so fucking tight. "Shit, you feel so fucking good." I pull out slowly so only the tip of my cock is inside her before I slam back home.

I continue at a slow, but hard pace, never getting enough of the way I feel as I reach the end of her. I'm so deep that I don't know how I'm not hurting her, but I can tell I'm not.

She starts pulling at the belt that holds her hands. "Please, I want to feel you." Reaching up, I release the belt and rub her arms before she wraps them around my neck, pulling my lips down to hers.

Her pussy starts to slowly contract around me, telling me she's close again, and I'm not far behind. Pulling my mouth away from hers, I look into her eyes and say, "Come with me, Sara. Show me how good my cock feels inside your pussy." As soon as the words are out of my mouth, she clamps down hard on my cock, screaming my name. Thrusting once more, I follow her into oblivion. "Fuck, doll. Fuck!" Spilling myself inside her, I feel lighter and happier than I have my whole life. This woman was made for me.

Pulling out, I roll over onto my back and pull her on top of me. Running my hand from the top of her head to the top of her ass, I just breathe her in while my heart rate slows.

Minutes pass, or maybe it's hours, but she finally raises her head to look at me. "We never used a condom," she says quietly. Trying to gauge where her mind is at, I look for any sign that she's freaking out, but I don't see anything.

Reaching up, I push a stray piece of hair behind her ear. "I'm sorry. I just lose my mind when I'm around you, but I've never *not* used a condom before you. I get checked every six months, and I'm clean."

She smiles at me before leaning down to kiss me softly. "It's okay. You do the same to me. But so you know, I'm clean too." With that out of the way, she lays her head back down on my chest and quickly falls asleep.

Closing my eyes, the last thing that runs through my head is that I'm one lucky fucker that she's agreed to take a chance on me—on us.

CHAPTER 8

Sara

It's been two weeks since that night at the club, and things have been going great with Toby. We see each other every day, either downstairs in the shop, at his house, or in my apartment. We've even spent some time at the clubhouse, though I'm still a little uncomfortable there. It has more to do with some of the things I see than it does with the people there. I actually like most of the guys. I've even talked to a few of the girls, but most of the club whores—I don't really like. It's not because of who they are or that they sleep with the men there. It's more because of how they treat me like I'm beneath them. Not that I think they are beneath *me*, but I know where they stand in the club, and I know where I'm hoping to stand in the club: beside Toby.

Toby and I have talked quite a bit about things I've done since I've been here, people I've met here, and Toby talks about the club and his fighting career. He also told me a little about his past, but mainly just that his mother was a junkie and never cared for him. He said he's been fighting since before he can remember.

I've told him about some of my dreams for the future and some happy memories I had as a kid; like getting a puppy for my sixth birthday and having him till I was fifteen. I miss that dog to this day, but I'm hoping that once I get more settled, I can get another dog.

I plan to tell him more about my past in time, and I hope he tells me more of his too, but for now, we're happy with the way things are and just living in the present, only thinking about the future. I don't think I've ever been this happy before in my life, but there's a part of me that keeps waiting for him to change. I keep thinking that my past will repeat itself, and that scares the shit out of me.

I've caught myself a few times being scared of not doing something right and how he'll react, but I try to put a stop to it right away. I don't want to punish him, or myself for that matter, for someone else's actions. What Rick did to me really messed me up, but Toby isn't Rick and I need to remember that. I think I'm getting better, but I hope soon those fears will go away completely. Then I can be truly happy, and I think Toby might be someone who can help me with that.

Hearing my phone buzz, I look at the clock and realize I was supposed to be downstairs ten minutes ago for work.

Thinking it's Dani asking me where I am, I unlock my phone as I push out the door.

Toby: Got any plans tonight?

I stop walking and give myself a moment to bask in my happiness. Really, we rarely go even a few hours without talking or seeing each other.

Me: I'm working late tonight, but do you want to hang out after?

I start walking again, wanting to get in the shop before Dani gets upset. I don't think she'd really get upset with me, but she's been so amazing, and with everything she's doing to help me out I don't want to push my luck.

By the time I make it to my desk, I hear my phone buzz again, but before I can look to see if he's going to come over, Dani appears from her station with a customer right behind her. "Sara will ring you up and make sure you're all squared away with your aftercare. Let me know if you have any problems," she tells him, then looks over at me. "Meet me in the back when you're finished up here, okay?" I just nod and watch her walk away without saying anything else.

After the customer leaves, I quickly make my way to the back of the shop, not wanting Dani to wait any longer than necessary. Shit, I hope she isn't pissed. This is the first time that I've been late, but I don't want her to think that since we've gotten closer, or that Toby and I are together, that I would start taking advantage of her.

When I enter the back room, she's sitting on the counter in the break room. I still can't decipher what she's thinking or what her mood is like. Her face is, for the most part, expressionless. "I'm sorry I was late. I just got caught up cleaning, but I promise, it won't happen again, I swear," I rush to assure her, but she doesn't say anything. She just stares at me like she's expecting more from me, and I get nervous.

I start to fidget with my shirt and stumble on my words. "I, ah, I-I can stay later tonight and clean up, or I'll come in early tomorrow to make up the time." Still, I get no reaction from her. She's still just sitting there, staring at me. I can't take it anymore, so I drop my eyes and head over to the coffee maker to start the brew. I think today is going to be one of those days that I'll consume mass amounts of caffeine because of my nerves, which will only make my jitters worse, but I'll do it anyway.

While I'm pouring water into the machine, I hear her clear her throat, which frightens me so much that I jump. I finish with the coffee and turn around to face her again, hoping she ends my suffering.

When my eyes meet hers, her lips twitch, which could either be a smile or a sneer, I'm not really sure at the moment. "Will you...will you just say what you're thinking already? You're freaking me out." At least if she were yelling at me, or shit, even firing me, I'd know where I stand and try to figure out what I need to do to fix it.

Jumping down from the counter, she slowly stalks toward me. I didn't notice out front before, but now that I'm really paying attention to her, I see that she's wearing a cute pair of cut-off jean shorts, a white tank top, and her leather jacket. Since the tank top is tighter than I've seen her wear lately, I can tell that she's starting to show her pregnancy. I want to squeal, jump up and down, or hug her because it's so exciting, but I'm not doing shit till I know what's up. It's so fucking frustrating!

When she's right in front of me, in my personal space, she crosses her arms and stares at me, hard. "Well, what do you have to say for yourself?" she says in a *don't fuck with me* tone. Thinking she's talking about my tardiness, I rush to explain myself again.

"I'm so sorry I was late. I just lost track of time. I swear to you, it will never happen again. And I'll—" I'm cut off when she holds up her hand to stop me, not letting me finish.

"I don't want to hear any of that bullshit," she says in a low voice, which scares me more than if she would have yelled in my face.

Feeling completely defeated, I drop my head. "Are you going to fire me?" I whisper, not being able to stand the thought of not only losing my job and most likely the apartment too, but I find myself more upset with the fact I've disappointed her and let her down. Dani has been so good to me and I don't want to lose her as a boss, but what's more, I don't want to lose her as a friend.

I snap my head up in surprise when she bends over and laughs so hard, her whole body shakes. I'm confused, and maybe a little irritated, that she finds me getting fired amusing, but I figure it would be best to just let her get it out than to interrupt her. No sense in making matters worse, right?

When she finally calms down, she wipes a few tears that have fallen in her fit of laughter, and straightens back up to look at me in amusement. "You really think I'm upset with you about being late, or that I'd actually fire you over it? Come on, Sara, I'm not that big of a bitch." She laughs again, then settles down before saying, "I'm talking about you and Toby, girl. When are you going to give me details? I've been patiently waiting for you to come to me and tell me what's been going on, but I get nothing. So now I'll get it out of you, even if I have to use mass amounts of alcohol." She ends with a laugh.

I let out the breath. "Oh my God, you scared the shit out of me. I seriously thought you were pissed at me. Why didn't you just say you wanted to know that? I would've told you if you'd asked." I've never really had girlfriends before, or at least the type that I've confided in. I mean, let's face it, I haven't had anything in the relationship department in a while that I'd want to brag or gossip about with another girl. Yet it would be nice to sit down and talk to her about him, especially since they're good friends. Maybe I can get some more insight into who he is and what to expect out of him. He's told me a little bit about his life, but it's mostly from his time being in the club. I don't really know about his past, about what made him who he is today, but I haven't given him details on some things about my past either, so I can't really blame him. We'll get there eventually, or I hope we do.

Maybe now would be a good time to mention some of my fears and see if she can give me some advice on how best to mention them to Toby without him freaking out and thinking he's doing something wrong. That's the last thing I want him to feel. Walking over to the small couch in the break room, I let out a little laugh. "I don't even know where to start." I try to figure out what I should say, but Dani interrupts.

"Just tell me what's going on with you two." She sits across from me on one of the chairs and waits.

"Okay," I say, then tell her from start to finish about the chain of events that led up to today. I tell her about attending the self-defense class and how Toby was the instructor. I tell her about getting a job at the strip club, and how I hated it but needed the money. She told me that Lyle is a part of the MC, but he doesn't hang out at the clubhouse often. When I told her about the guy that attacked me at the club the night Toby was there, she yelled and cursed, but was just glad nothing major happened. I tell her how Toby took me home with him and we had sex for the first time. I don't go into specifics, but I tell her how being with him made me feel both elated and scared. I talk to her about my fears, but that I don't want to feel like this anymore.

When I look up at her, she has a look of pity, but it's quickly replaced with understanding. "Look, Sara, I get where you're coming from and why you were scared, I really do. When I first got here, I was hesitant to open up about what happened to me, but if you ever want to get over what happened and move on you need to talk about it. You need to tell the people who care about you, the people you care about, what happened. We can help you. Not just help protect you, but we can be there for you too. We're a family, and whether you think so or not, you're a part of that family. You have been since you got here, you just didn't know it." Her words make me so happy, but sad too. I wasted so much time being scared and not opening up to everyone.

"I know that now, and you all mean so much to me. I'm just sorry I didn't realize all that until talking with Mack that night at the club. He was so nice and understanding, even offering to help me if needed. I knew you were all good people and I had nothing to be afraid of, but that was easier said than done. For some reason, talking with Mack that night put everything into perspective. Like you said, we're a family." I have a family now. For so long, I've felt so alone, and now I'm not.

She smiles sweetly at me with a look of admiration on her face. "Mack really is great. He's like a father to me. I'm glad that you feel comfortable around him. He really is an amazing man and will do anything it takes to make sure his family is safe." I nod because I agree with her. Mack really is great and I'm glad that he's in my life.

"Things have been good, great even, since we talked about what we both wanted. We haven't discussed anything more about us as a couple, or even officially made it known to each other that we are a couple, we just are. I'm really happy though, Dani. He's truly amazing—you all are. I'm so grateful I met all of you and now have you in my life." I tear up at the end, but they're happy tears. I finally feel like the past is behind me and I can finally move on with my life.

I notice that Dani has tears in her eyes as well, but she tries to make light of it. "These damn pregnancy hormones, I tell ya. I can't go one fucking day without crying. Even those animal shelter commercials make me cry. I hate it!" I hope that she knows she can be herself around me and not put up her tough-girl front if she doesn't have to.

Pulling her over to me, we hug and wipe our eyes. "All right, bitch, back to work. I'll be out once I fix my face." With that, she gets up and walks over to the bathroom across the hall.

Heading out front, I sit at my desk and look through the appointment book. Today is actually a slow day, which I'm grateful for.

I hear my phone buzz in my purse, remembering Toby's text message from earlier. Shit, I forgot to text him back. Grabbing my phone, I hear the bell on the front door jingle, but instead of looking up to greet whoever it is, I unlock my phone and say, "I'll be right with you."

Whoever walks in doesn't respond, and that's fine by me. I really need to let Toby know I wasn't ignoring him. Just as I'm pulling up my messages, the person speaks, and the voice has me paralyzed with fear. "Hello, Sara. Miss me?"

Looking up, I see Rick leaning against the desk with a cruel smile on his face. The way he's looking at me, I can tell he's trying to act as normal as possible since we're in a place of business, but I see the danger lurking in his eyes.

I sit back straight in my chair and try to push

myself further away from the desk to get further away without him noticing. I need to distract him. Maybe if I wait long enough, someone will come in and he'll have no choice but to leave. "W-what are you doing here, Rick?" I stumble over my words, my fear making it hard to talk.

As soon as the words are out of my mouth, he drops the smile. "Why, I'm here to bring you home." The smile is back, but it's even crueler now, letting me know what waits for me. I can't let this happen. I'm not leaving with him. I'm finally getting my life back and have people who care about me. No, I'm not leaving with him; not now, not ever.

Getting my first boost of courage since the moment I realized he was here, I sit taller and look at him defiantly. "I am home. I'm not going anywhere with you, so you need to leave." I get up and make my way around my desk to head for the back of the shop, but I forgot what type of man he is. He wouldn't show up here and leave without me; he would take me with him, kicking and screaming if he had to.

I barely make it three steps away from him before he rushes me and pulls me back by my hair, which causes me to cry out. "Did you forget who the fuck you were talking to, bitch? I said we were leaving, even if I have to drag you out of here by your hair." He turns us around and starts pushing me toward the door, but he doesn't release my hair.

"J-just leave me alone, Rick," I cry. This cannot be happening! Things were going so well. I can't let him do this. He can't get me out of the building because if he does, I'll never get away from him alive.

He doesn't answer, he just yanks on my hair even harder. "Shut the fuck up!" He pushes me again, when suddenly I hear a gun cocking from behind. Thinking he now has a gun and it's pointed at me, I stop and close my eyes, praying this isn't the end.

"Let her go," Dani says in a low, menacing voice. Oh my God, Dani, no! What if Rick lashes out and hurts her?

I try turning around to plead with Dani to back away. I don't know what I would do if something happened to her because of me. I only make it halfway around with Rick still holding my hair in his fist, but it's enough for me to see that Dani has her gun trained on his head and she's not paying any attention to me. Her sole focus is on Rick.

Rick pauses for only a moment, stunned, before he relaxes, not thinking Dani will shoot. "Why don't you put that gun away, little girl, before you hurt yourself?" Rick says evenly, then starts to back up slowly, still holding onto my hair. Fuck, my scalp hurts, but there's nothing I can do. I feel so helpless. I wish now I would've kept going to those self-defense classes. Maybe then I would know how to get myself out of this mess.

"I wouldn't take another step if I were you." She sounds so commanding and badass right now. If it were any other situation, if we both weren't in danger and I wasn't so scared, I would hoot and holler that she's amazing.

Her words make Rick laugh, but it's quickly cut

off when he takes another step back and Dani fires a round at his feet. I look down and see that the bullet landed right in front of his big toe. "Last chance, motherfucker. Let her go or the next shot won't be a warning, it will be your death shot." Rick pauses. He lets go of my hair, but still has a hard grip on my arm.

Peeking at him through the corner of my eye, he looks like he's weighing his options, and maybe even a little scared.

Finally, he releases my arm and pushes me forward. "Fuck this," he says as he gives one last glance toward Dani, probably to make sure she won't shoot, before walking backwards again. When he gets the door open and is almost outside, he looks at me and what I see makes me shiver in fear; I see a promise in his eyes—a promise of pain.

CHAPTER 9

Toby

I've been sitting around for the last hour waiting to hear back from Sara about tonight. It's not like that's strange since I know she's working, though. Sometimes she just gets busy and can't return my text immediately, but I have a bad feeling. I feel it deep in my gut that something isn't right, yet I don't know if it has to do with her not answering me or if it's something to do with the club. But my gut has never steered me wrong before, so I've learned to never dismiss it.

Knowing I won't be able to calm myself down until I hear from her, I decide to call her. She's never not answered when I call her phone, even when she's with a customer. It helps that when we first got together, I told her that even though the MC businesses are mainly legit now and we rarely have problems, it's still very important for her to answer her phone if I ever call, just in case there's an emergency she needs to be aware of. She's still new to everything, but I think she's coping and managing everything pretty well.

Picking up my phone, I dial her number and listen to it ring. It goes to voicemail, so I hang up and dial again, but it goes to voicemail again. The feeling I have in my stomach just got worse. Something is wrong.

Grabbing my keys, I head for my truck, not sure what type of situation I'll encounter when I arrive at Sinners Ink.

Pulling into my parking spot out back, I open the door, but before I even get one foot out of the truck, I hear a gunshot ring out. I take my phone out of my pocket as I reach into my glove box to grab my gun. "Yeah?" Mack answers after two rings.

"Gunshot at Sinners Ink and the girls are there. Not sure if Louie is inside or not. Get the boys and haul ass, I'm going in." I don't wait for him to respond before I hang up and run to the back door.

Opening it as quietly as possible, I step inside and pause, listening for anything that will give me an idea of who's inside, how many, and where they're located, but it's quiet. Not a good sign, but it doesn't mean it's bad either.

I move into the break room to clear it when I hear a man's voice from the front. It sounds like he's saying "fuck it," or maybe "fuck you," I can't be sure. Stepping into the hallway again, I quietly move toward the front. I wish I knew how many were inside. If I knew what I was dealing with, I wouldn't have to be so cautious.

I'm almost there when I hear a thump, and then someone crying. Fuck being careful, I'll just shoot any fucker who isn't Sara, Dani, or Louie. Fuck the consequences. My girl needs me.

Running into the front room, I see Dani on the floor in front of the door with Sara in her arms. I do a quick sweep of the room to make sure no one else is inside and rush over to them. "Are you girls okay? Are you hurt?" I ask, afraid to move them since I have no idea what's happened.

I spot Dani's gun lying close beside her, so at least the girls had some sort of protection, but I need answers. I need to know who I'm dealing with, how many, and what they're after. I feel so helpless right now and I fucking hate it.

Kneeling in front of the girls, I reach out my hand to touch Sara's head but as soon as she feels me, she flinches back and burrows into Dani more. What the fuck?

"Dani. I need some fucking answers right now," I say a little harsher than I intended, but I'm so far inside my rage my head is spinning.

Dani looks at me and I see a mixture of pain and anger on her face. "Help me move her to the break room, then we'll talk." I nod, afraid to say anything else and scare Sara any more than she already is.

I move closer to them so I can grab a hold of Sara to move her. "Sara, honey. Toby's here and he's going to pick you up and take you into the break room. You're safe. Nobody will take you away from us, okay? Everything will be all right, I promise." Dani speaks firmly, but quietly to Sara. When she looks back up at me and nods, I reach out and take Sara into my arms. She comes to me easily now that she knows it's me, but I feel her shaking in

119

my arms, crying out in fear or pain, I'm not sure which.

When I stand up and move toward the back, I stop and say to Dani, "The boys are on their way. Should be here any second. Do not go outside. Wait in here with the door locked, then flag them down to let them know the coast is clear when they get here and meet us in the back." She nods and turns toward the front door, keeping a lookout for the guys while I move toward the break room.

Laying Sara down on the couch, I kiss her head, her eyes, her nose, and then her mouth. She doesn't kiss me back, but I wasn't expecting her to. "Are you injured, doll?" I ask, praying she's just shaken up. It takes her a couple of seconds to register my question, then another moment to do a mental inventory before she shakes her head no. Thank fuck for small favors.

"That's good. That's real good. Can you tell me what happened?" The bell above the front door jingles, which tells me the boys are here. I feel Sara stiffen in my arms and see her shaking her head back and forth. "Hey, it's okay. It's just Mack and the others. You're safe. I won't let anyone hurt you. I'll kill anyone who tries."

"She all right?" Mack asks. I nod, hoping it's the right answer.

In the small amount of time she's been here, she's become like another daughter to Mack. I know he would do anything for her, as would I, and I know since she means so much to both of us and Dani, the rest of the brothers would go to the ends of the earth for her too. It's an amazing feeling knowing I have my brothers behind me and my woman.

I try to step back so Mack can come closer and see for himself that she's scared, but not hurt. Before I'm out of reaching distance, she grabs for me and pulls me back. We've come so far these last couple of weeks, and it feels good that she's not pushing me away.

I look behind Mack and see that Skinner, Louie, Tom Tom, Blaze, and Dani are all standing back, waiting for Sara to recover enough to talk about what happened. Blaze is holding Dani from behind and rubbing his hands across her stomach. Shit, he must be fucking livid knowing something could've happened to Dani and the baby. He's been even more anal about her safety now that she's pregnant. Fuck, I wouldn't be surprised if he locks her away in a safe house after this.

Speaking of Blaze, he's not patient enough to wait for Sara to speak, so he turns Dani in his arms to look at her. "What happened, Baby Girl?" Wanting to know just as much as him, but not willing to put Sara through more hell than she has to go through right now, I eagerly wait for Dani to speak.

"Sara and I were back here talking. I'm not sure for how long, but when we were done I told her to go up front and that I'd be up in a bit 'cause I had to use the restroom. It was only a couple of minutes later I heard Sara and she sounded scared, then I heard her yell, so I grabbed my gun out of my purse and went to the front of the shop. Some guy was pulling Sara toward the door by her hair. She was trying to get away, but he had a tight grip on her. I snuck up behind him, held the gun to his head and told him to let her go. He turned around and saw me, but didn't see me as a threat until I shot at his foot. He finally let her go and took off. That's when Toby came in."

"Do you know who he was?" I ask Dani, thinking it's someone from a rival club or a new player. She shakes her head and looks at Sara.

Knowing I need her to talk and tell us what she knows, I brush my finger down her face. "Baby, I know you're scared right now, but I really need you to tell us what you know. Do you know him? What he wanted?"

She looks away from me and tries to sit up. Not wanting to let her go, I try to hold on to her, but she's not having it. When she's sitting by herself on the couch, she moves as far away from me as possible. "I know who he is and what he wanted," she says quietly, looking down at her hands. I try to be patient and wait for her, but I'm all out of patience.

"Sara, tell me."

Before she speaks, she looks at Dani, then Mack, then back to me.

"It was Rick, my ex-boyfriend. The one I left back in New York."

I look at Mack, who seems to have already figured it out. I get the feeling he knows more about what's going on than I do. He comes closer and kneels in front of her. Placing his hand over hers, he asks, "Was he here for you?" What the fuck! Why do I not know anything about this ex, besides the fact she left him and they didn't have a good relationship? God dammit! I knew something happened, but I didn't get the full story and didn't want to push her to talk about it. I have no idea what he did to her and had no clue to even watch out for him. Why wouldn't she tell me this?

"Yes. He said he was here to take me home. I didn't know what to do or how to get away. I didn't want to yell out for help because I didn't want him to know Dani was here and hurt her or the baby, but she saved me." She pauses and looks at Dani. "You saved me. I can't thank you enough. I don't know what would've happened if he took me." Sara starts to shake again, so Dani moves closer to comfort her, but Blaze holds her back. That's when I notice him glaring at Sara. He blames her for putting Dani in danger.

I get up to tell him to stand the fuck down, but what Mack says next stops me cold. "I've had an eye out for him, but no one saw him come into town. I have no idea how long he's been here, but I promise you, sweetheart, he will not get close enough to try and take you again." And that's the moment the whole room explodes.

"You fucking knew about this? You knew about him but didn't think it fucking necessary to tell me?" I yell at Mack. President or not, he fucked up. This is my woman. If there was someone out there looking for her, someone that meant to cause her harm, he should have fucking told me. Fuck, she should have told me.

Mack stands to his full height, now in full president mode. "Calm the fuck down, Toby. It wasn't your call, it was mine. Sara told me about him, but we weren't sure if he would come after her or not. I was keeping an eye out for trouble, and if I saw something happening, I would have brought it to the table." I step closer, wanting to get in his face, but having enough sense to not go that far.

"You were keeping an eye out, were you? Well, guess what? The fucker got past you. He was able to sneak in, right under our fucking noses and get to her. He almost fucking succeeded!" Knowing I'm getting close to crossing the line, I back up and try to calm myself. It would not be good to knock out my president, but I sure fucking want to.

Next, Blaze steps forward and looks even more pissed than I feel. "You son-of-a-bitch." He moves like he's going to punch Mack, but before he can get close enough, Louie grabs him and holds him back. Fighting Louie, he continues to scream, "You fucking knew about this and let her," he points an angry finger at Sara, looking like he wants to choke her, "work next to Dani? You put her and my fucking baby in danger!"

"You better calm yourself, brother, before you say or do something you'll fucking regret," I growl at him. Mack should have told us what he knew, but I'll be fucking damned if I let him take his anger out on Sara.

Dani storms past us all and stands beside Sara. "You all need to shut the fuck up. Sara told Mack what happened and Mack made the call to keep it quiet. You all need to quit acting like whiny fucking bitches and man the fuck up." She's raging fucking mad. Dani pissed is a scary sight to see on any given day, but when you fuck with someone she cares about, like she does Sara, she's going to rip anyone apart that tries to hurt her—even if it's one of us.

Blaze must realize this at the same time, because he stops fighting Louie and takes a deep breath. "Baby Girl, you need to understand that this isn't just about her anymore. Her being near you puts you in danger and I can't fucking have that. I'm sorry, but until this is resolved, either she won't work here anymore or you won't. Either way, she's not to be around you." He went there. He should know better than anyone that nobody tells Dani what to do.

Dani literally growls at him, then moves to sit beside Sara. "First of all, fuck you, Blaze. Second, let me tell you what is going to happen. You, Mack, and Toby, are going to go back to the clubhouse and figure out what your next move is going to be. I'll be staying with Sara upstairs while Louie and one of the prospects stand guard. She and I will both continue to work downstairs during the day. You'll just have to post more men outside and Louie will just have to deal with his shit and start coming back to fucking work. *That* is what's going to happen." She takes a breath and levels him with a stare that would have even me cowering. "And lastly, if you ever talk to someone I care about like that again, or try and tell me what to do and how to run my business, you will be at the wrong end of my gun, regardless of who you are to me." With that, she stands up and pulls Sara up beside her. They walk right past us and head upstairs.

When we hear the door close to Sara's apartment, Blaze grabs a nearby chair and throws it across the room. "Fuck!" Yeah, I don't think that went the way either of us wanted, but at least we now know what happened and who we need to find. Now I have a fucking target.

***

When we get back to the clubhouse, Mack calls us to Church. When everyone is seated, he tells us what we need to know and shows us all a picture of this Rick fucker.

When the picture is finally passed to me, I notice it's the same guy he asked us a couple of weeks ago to be on the lookout for, but he never told us why. I look up at him when I toss the picture down. "You should have fucking told us." I try to keep my voice even, but I can tell by his glare that I didn't succeed.

"Listen, all of you. I did what I thought was best for everyone. I got all the information I needed from Sara and we didn't think he was a threat. We now obviously know different, but the point is, I did what I did because it was the right thing to do. I gave you all a heads up and told you to be on the lookout for him. It shouldn't have fucking mattered if you didn't know the details or not. If I tell you to watch for someone, you better fucking do your best and watch for him, no matter what the reason behind it may be. Getting your panties in a bunch now won't change anything. That son-of-a-bitch came into our town and fucked with one of ours. The only thing left for us to do is to find the fucker and put him to ground." No one says anything, but I can tell that even though Blaze, Louie, and I are still pissed, we all know he's right.

When no one answers him, he growls, "Do you fucking understand?" We all nod and say yes, then we start planning.

***

It's past two in the morning before we're done going over everything we know about Sara's ex and figuring out what we're going to do.

Tom Tom and Skinner are going to work on getting us some background information on him so we know who we're dealing with. Slayer and Louie are in charge of setting up recon on him; where he lives, where he works, where he likes to hang out, the people he associates with. Once we have eyes on him, Slayer will be keeping tabs on his whereabouts. Blaze and I are in charge of setting up around the clock security for the girls. Knowing they will most likely stick together for a while, especially after what went down in the break room, we need extra muscle to handle them both together. And once we have the fucker, I'll be the one to rip him apart after I torture him for fucking with what's mine.

Knowing I won't be able to sleep without at least checking on Sara, I head to her place.

I spot the prospect positioned outside the back door that leads up to her apartment. "Anything?" I ask, hoping there's been no activity while I've been at the clubhouse, but also secretly hoping there has been so I can take all my anger and frustration with Mack and Sara out on someone deserving of it.

"Nah, it's been quiet," he responds.

I nod my head. "Louie around the front?" He better not be fucking slacking off or I'll put a bullet in his leg.

"No, he's upstairs with the girls." That information makes me feel equal parts relief and even more pissed off. On one hand, I'm glad that he's taking this seriously and is close to them in case something happens, but on the other I'm pissed because he should be outside, making sure nothing gets anywhere close to them. Plus, leaving the prospect out here by himself doesn't sound like a good idea to me. Sure, he should know how to handle himself, but he's still a fucking prospect. I trust Louie more than I trust him. It's shitty, but that's just the way it is.

I don't say anything else and walk up the stairs. I take out my key that I still had from when Dani was staying here. Opening the door, I don't see any of them anywhere. Deciding I'll find Louie later and get on his ass about not being out front, I go in search of my girl.

I find her sleeping, curled up in bed with Dani lying beside her. They both look so peaceful. If shit wasn't so heated right now, I would probably enjoy seeing the two women in my life cuddled up together in bed, but I'm too on edge for that.

Seeing movement out of my eye, I notice Louie sitting in a chair in the corner of the room. I motion for him to follow me to the living room. He does and sits down on the couch, rubbing his hands across his face in exhaustion. "So, we got a plan yet?" he asks me in a quiet voice. Sitting down, I relay everything that happened during Church and what we're going to be doing.

He nods his head in agreement, but doesn't comment. I'm surprised that he hasn't said much, so I ask him, "What's going on with you, brother?"

I can tell he doesn't want to talk about it, but then to my surprise, he whispers, "Nothing, man. It's just been a long couple of months. First, shit with Dani, then Harlow leaving without an explanation, and now this thing with Sara. Shit's been hitting the fan non-stop and I'm just exhausted." I understand how he feels, but now is not the time to be off our game.

"Look, we're all tired and pissed about what's been going on, but I need you on your toes. If you're going to be guarding Dani and my woman, I need to know your head's in the game." I hate putting him on the spot, but things are different—this situation is different. We aren't talking about some random person being targeted or someone fucking with our business. This is my girl we're talking about, so I need him to understand.

Rubbing his face one last time, he stands up and looks me in the eye. "I've got this, brother. No one will come near either one of them, and that's a fucking promise." With that said, he stands up and starts to move back toward the bedroom, but I stop him.

"Get some sleep. I'm staying here tonight." With a nod, he walks out the front door, but I'm betting he'll be outside tonight instead of going back to the clubhouse to get some sleep. The shit that happened today got to more than just Blaze and I; Louie's feeling the heat too.

After locking the door and checking all the windows, I head back into the bedroom. I just need to see her face again to reassure myself that she's okay.

First, I walk over to the side of the bed Dani's lying on. She's rolled over onto her side so she's facing away from Sara. Brushing her hair to the side, I drop a kiss on top of her head, then walk around to Sara's side.

She looks so peaceful sleeping. Looking at her now, you would never know the hell she went through today. I crouch down in front on her, just so I can stare at her beautiful face; memorizing every feminine curve. Lightly running my hand from the top of her head down to her lips, I whisper, "I don't know what I would do without you, doll. You've come to mean so much to me." I'm quiet for a minute, watching her, hoping I don't wake her. When she doesn't even twitch, I lean over and kiss her softly on the lips. "I think I'm falling for you, and if that's what this feeling is, I don't want it to stop." Kissing her one last time, I stand up and head out to the living room to sleep on the couch. I'd give anything to curl up beside her and hold her all night, but it's not an option tonight.

CHAPTER 10

Sara

It's still dark out when I wake from a dream. Rick came back for me, but when I roll over and see Dani lying beside me, I realize it wasn't just a dream, but my mind replaying the events of the previous day.

I can't believe he found me, but what puzzles me even more is the fact that he came all this way to get me. I honestly thought that even if he did look for me, he wouldn't look for long, and if he found me, I didn't think he would actually come here to drag me back to New York. I believed that once he realized I was truly gone, he would cut his losses, but I was obviously being naïve. At least he didn't succeed. I shudder to think of what would've happened had he gotten me into his car. I don't think I would have made it even to the state line intact.

Getting out of bed as quietly as I can as to not wake Dani, I head into the bathroom to splash some water on my face, trying to wash away the fear and hopelessness I feel. Rick found me and tried to take me away from this new life I've made for myself, and away from the people I've grown to think of as family, but what scares me even more is that I put Dani and her baby in danger just by being in the same building as her. I don't want her to get caught in the crossfire of my past. I don't even want to think of how much it would hurt to have to leave my new home, but that might just be what I have to do to keep those I care about safe.

Drying off my face, I walk into the living room, wanting to get something to drink, but come to a stop when I see Toby sleeping on my couch, shirtless. If that isn't a sight for sore eyes, I don't know what is. He is stunning—not too muscular like some of those steroid eating gym guys. He's tan all over, and his face is relaxed, yet it still has a hard look. He's the perfect man, both inside and out.

Now that I see him, I remember him coming into my room last night. I thought I had dreamt it because I thought Louie was here to watch over us, but seeing Toby on my couch, maybe it wasn't a dream after all. If I didn't dream about him coming into my room to make sure I was okay, maybe I didn't dream the words I thought I heard him say. *I don't know what I would do without you, doll. You've come to mean so much to me. I think I'm falling for you.*

Hearing those words in my head again, I smile. He really cares about me. I was pretty sure he was feeling the same thing I was starting to feel, but I've been wrong about people before. So, if I'm right, and he did say those things to me while he thought I was sleeping, then we feel the same way.

Knowing he's here with me, wanting to be close and protect me from my past, I don't think I could go back to my bed and sleep without him if I even tried. I just need to hold him and have him hold me too.

Forgetting about getting a drink, I quietly walk over to the couch, trying to figure out how I can crawl in beside him without waking him. I have no idea what time he got done doing what he was doing at the clubhouse, but he wasn't here when I finally fell asleep after one in the morning.

Realizing there is no way that I'll be able to sneak in beside him, I decide to just lay down beside him as much as I can and pray I don't wake him up.

I'm surprised when I get situated that he didn't wake up. Instead, as soon as I lay down beside him, he wraps his arms around me, almost instinctually knowing that it's me and that I need him right now.

Sighing, I close my eyes and run my hands lazily up and down his chest. "Thank you for being here for me. I know we have a lot to talk about, but having you here makes me feel safe and cherished. I've never felt that way before," I whisper, not wanting to wake him, but needing to say it anyway.

I kiss his chest. "I've already fallen for you, Toby, but when I fell, instead of just letting me crash and burn, you caught me. So if you fall, I'll catch you too and hold you close to my heart." I kiss him one more time over his heart and fall asleep, feeling complete.

***

I wake up alone on the couch and hear raised voices coming from what sounds like my bedroom.

Taking a quick look around, I spot a black sweatshirt on the floor. Tiptoeing over to it, I pull it over my head and smile when it smells like Toby. It covers up my shorts and goes almost down to my knees, so it looks like I'm not wearing anything underneath. Since there are people in my room, there's no way for me to grab a pair of sweats, so it looks like this will have to do for now.

Walking as quietly as I can to my closed bedroom door, I stop and listen, trying to figure out who is on the other side and what they're arguing about. I don't feel right eavesdropping on what is probably supposed to be private, but they are in my apartment, and I have a feeling I know what it's about.

"I don't give a fuck that she's your friend and employee. What I give a shit about is that she's a walking fucking target, and you being near her makes you a target. It puts you in danger, and that I will not fucking allow." This comes from Blaze.

"You won't allow it? Who the fuck do you think you are? You are not my fucking father, Zane!" Dani whisper yells.

"I'm your old man, the fucking father to your unborn child, the man who loves you and would do anything to make sure you're safe. It's not just you anymore, Dani. You need to think about our child! You can't be careless and walk around half-cocked all the damn time!" Blaze fires back at her. "And no, I'm not your fucking father because if I was, I wouldn't be here now, would I? But I am here because I fucking love you. I'm trying to do what's best for you and our baby, so quit being fucking difficult and listen to me."

I briefly wonder where Toby is during all this, but then I hear him. "Look, Blaze, I understand that you're pissed off. Hell, I'm pissed too, but you need to calm the fuck down before you do or say something you'll regret. Yelling and demanding isn't the way to get Dani to do what you want. You fucking know this, brother," Toby says sternly. "And Dani. We aren't trying to tell you not to be around Sara, or at least I'm not, but you need to be more careful. Like Blaze said, it's not just you anymore. You need to be more careful."

"Back the fuck off, Toby. Why don't you just fucking worry about keeping Sara away from Dani and let me handle my own woman?" Before anyone can answer, I hear a crash and someone say, "Son-of-a-bitch," before I hear what sounds like a scuffle.

Not wanting to hear anymore, and definitely not wanting Toby to fight with his brother over my situation, I open the door, but am stunned by what I see.

I thought for sure Toby and Blaze would be going at it, blow for blow, but it's not Toby and Blaze, not just the two of them, anyway. Dani was the one who threw a punch at Blaze, connecting with his cheek. Toby jumps in trying to contain Dani, but that only seems to enrage both her and Blaze even more.

"Let me go, asshole," Dani yells.

"Get your fucking hands off of her!" Blaze hollers at the same time. Toby is trying to contain Dani, Dani is still trying to get at Blaze, and Blaze is trying to get Toby off of Dani. If this situation wasn't so serious and if they weren't fighting because of me, I would laugh, but it is because of me, so instead I walk further into the room and do my best to get in the middle of them all. "You guys—stop it—right fucking now!"

As soon as Toby realizes I'm in the room and trying to break everything up, he drops his hold on Dani, and instead reaches for me, pulling me behind him. Dani, no longer held by Toby, pushes Blaze away when he tries to do the same with her, and walks over to me.

We all just stare at each other, the three of them trying to catch their breaths.

"You all need to stop. Please don't fight over me. I'm not worth it," I whisper the last part, not really meaning for them to hear, but knowing it's true all the same.

Toby pulls me further into his arms and holds me. "Don't say that, doll. You're worth it to me."

Dani comes up and places her hand on my shoulder. "And you're worth it to me too. Sara, you're family, and we protect our own. This," she waves her hand around the room, indicating what I just broke up, "is nothing. Families fight. That's all this is. But don't worry, you're going to be fine and so will the rest of us. Nothing that a little time in the ring won't solve," she says, directing her glare at Blaze. She turns her eyes back to me. "Please don't worry about this or about what happened yesterday.

The guys are on it and I'm not leaving your side till this is resolved. Nothing is going to happen to you, I promise. And me? I can take care of myself, so no worries." She gives me a little smile, which I try, and probably fail, to return.

"Dani—" Blaze starts, but he's cut off.

"I'm heading down to the shop to clean up and get ready to open. Why don't you take a shower, get some coffee, and come down when you're ready." She says to me, completely ignoring Blaze. She gives me a hug then turns around, sends one last glare toward Blaze, then leaves the room. A couple seconds later, I hear the front door close, then it's quiet in the apartment.

I look at Blaze and see that he's still staring at the door.

Toby breaks the silence. "I'll go make some coffee while you take a shower, then we can talk, okay?" I nod, walk over to my closet to pull out some clothes, then walk toward the bathroom. Before I'm out the door, I see Blaze pinning me with a look that is both threatening and concerned at the same time. Is that even possible?

Closing the bathroom door quietly behind me, I turn around and lean against it, letting out a long sigh. This is all one big clusterfuck. Why did Rick have to come here? He's fucking with more than just me now; he's messing with everyone around me, breaking them all apart in the process.

I hear two sets of footsteps walking past the bathroom door, so I lean my ear against the wood and try to see if I can hear anything. The only thing I can make out are murmurs, no words. Well, guess

I'm not going to get anything else, so I may as well get in the shower. The faster I can get dressed, the faster I can talk to Toby and figure out what I should do now.

Once out of the shower and dressed, I walk into the kitchen and see that Blaze is no longer here, but Toby is. I walk up behind him and place my hand on his shoulder. "I'm sorry about what happened yesterday, and that it's causing everyone to worry and fight," I whisper. I hate knowing I'm causing people who are normally so close to fight.

Toby turns around and wraps his arms around me. "You have nothing to be sorry for, doll. I'm just glad that you're okay. I don't know what I'd do if you were taken or hurt." My heart beats faster at his confession, which reminds me of last night and the whispered words that were said between us, though I'm not sure if I imagined his words and if he even heard mine.

He kisses the top of my head before pulling away. Grabbing my hand, he pulls me over to the table where I notice two coffee cups. Once we both take a seat, we just stare at one another, both trying to wrap our heads around the events of the last twenty-four hours.

Figuring it's time I tell him about my past, I start by telling him how I met Rick, then about how he went from perfect to a nightmare. By the time I'm finished with my story, Toby is gripping his coffee cup so hard, I'm surprised it doesn't shatter in his hands.

He doesn't speak. He just stares at the table, trying to gain some type of control. When he finally looks up at me, I see so many emotions within the depths of his eyes: anger, pain, concern, and love? I can't be sure, but I think that's what I see, or maybe it's just what I want to see. Regardless, he lets out a deep breath and grabs my hand. "I'm so sorry you went through that. I wish I would've met you years ago to prevent all the pain you experienced." He looks so lost and helpless that for a moment, I imagine him as a child. He's only told me a little about his past. I know that he grew up without a father, and his mother wasn't a very good person. I also know that he fought a lot, but I don't really know the reason why.

I squeeze his hand and give him a reassuring smile. "It's not your fault that happened to me, Toby. If anything, I should have known better. I should have gotten out of that relationship at the first sign of trouble, but I was weak and too afraid to be alone. I had nothing and no one. I only had him." I hate that he now knows exactly how weak I was, but he deserves to know the truth and what he's getting himself into so he can choose for himself if he thinks I'm worth it.

"Doll, you are anything but weak. If you were weak, you wouldn't have left. You would still be in New York, suffering through everything he did to you. But you did leave, and that makes you strong. That's what makes you a fighter—a survivor. I promise you that from now on, you don't have to fight this alone. I'm here, and I will kill anyone who tries to take you away from me." The look in his eyes tells me he's serious, and even though I don't want him to kill anyone, it makes me happy that he's willing to fight for me. That he thinks I'm worth it.

Standing up, I go over to him and sit on his lap. I snuggle up against him, my head under his chin, and breathe him in. "I don't know what I would do if I never met you. You make me want to be stronger, better. Thank you for being here for me," I say, squeezing him tighter, wishing I could become one with him so we never had to be apart.

Laying his cheek on top of my head, he whispers, "Always, doll. I'm not going anywhere."

We sit there for a while, neither of us talking, just holding each other. I don't want to move, but I know I should go downstairs and get to work. I also need to be down there with Dani, just in case Rick comes back. This isn't her fight, and I don't want anything to happen to her, or cause any more problems between her and Blaze.

"What's wrong?"

Needing to hear what he thinks I should do, I say, "I'm worried about Dani. Blaze was so mad about her being near me, putting her and their baby in danger. I just don't know what to do. I want to protect her and stay away, but I also don't want to go into hiding or make her hide out because of me. I don't want to lose her as a friend." I curse Rick for probably the hundredth time today.

Toby looks at the wall on the other side of the room, probably trying to decide how to respond. "One thing to know about Dani and Blaze; they are always fighting about something. That's just what they do, how their relationship works. No matter how fucked up that sounds, it's just them. He's worried about her and the baby, but he shouldn't have put that on your shoulders. It's not your fault your ex came here. I also agree that Dani shouldn't put herself in unnecessary danger, but I am glad she was with you and was able to stop him from taking you. We're just going to have to be more careful, and that's for all of us. If you don't want to stop working or hanging around Dani, then don't. Blaze will get over it. We all know Dani can take care of herself, at least long enough for us to get here, and I feel safer if you aren't by yourself at any time. So, this is what we're going to do. I'll be staying here with you, or you'll be with me at my house, or the clubhouse. When you're at work, we'll post extra guys outside to make sure you both are safe. If you have to go anywhere, you'll have an escort to make sure nothing happens." I look at him a little dumbfounded. I feel like they're going way overboard with having people watch me every second of every day.

"I know it seems like a lot, but it's all necessary. Until we know he's not a threat anymore, you will always have someone with you. I also need you to keep your eyes open and tell us if you see anything suspicious, or if he tries to contact you in any way. Can you handle all that?" I still think it's a little too much, but I nod anyway. "I need to hear you say it, doll. Will you be able to handle not going off on your own and telling me if you see anything we should know about?"

"Yes, of course, Toby. I can handle it. Now you promise me that if something happens, you'll tell me too. I don't want to be in the dark about this. I'll tell you if I see him or hear from him, but I expect the same from you. Please," I say. I know there's a good possibility that they'll be out searching for him, and if that's the case and they find him before he can come to me again, I want to know about it.

Toby smiles and places his hands on both sides of my face. "That I can do," he whispers, then he kisses me tenderly on the lips.

When I'm finally able to pull myself away, I walk with him down the stairs and into the shop. Dani is already with a customer it seems, so Toby and I go into the break room. "Remember what we talked about. Don't leave here without letting someone know, and most certainly not without taking a brother with you. I've already programmed the phone numbers of all the brothers into your phone, so if you need anything, don't hesitate to call someone. I'd prefer that you call me or Mack, then we can figure out if we need anyone else. I'm gonna head over to the clubhouse and talk with Mack and the guys and I'll be back in a couple of hours." He gives me a quick kiss, then walks out the back door.

Taking a deep breath, I walk out to the front room and sit at my desk. Staring at the front door, I can't help but remember what happened here yesterday. I can't stop thinking about the look in his eyes when he left. He'll be back, and when he does, he'll do whatever it takes to get to me and make me pay for leaving him. I just pray that Toby and the club can stop him before he gets close enough to carry out his punishment, because if not I know I'll pay with my life.

CHAPTER 11

Toby

It's after one in the morning by the time I head back to Sara's apartment. I hope she's not sleeping yet. I feel like I haven't touched her in years, when really it was the night before her ex turned up.

After our talk this morning when she finally told me what happened with her ex, she had to get downstairs to work and I had to get to the clubhouse so we could discuss our plan of action. I'm pissed that we have nothing on that motherfucker who tried to take my girl away from me, and even worse, we have no fucking idea where he's at now. The only thing we do fucking know is this: he's not back in New York, he hasn't used his credit cards or his phone, and even though we're pretty certain that he's still in the area, we can't fucking find him. It's frustrating as hell, and I can't even go to the gym to work out my anger unless I take Sara with me, but of course I'd rather work out with her in a different way. Hence, I hope she's not sleeping.

Parking in the back of the building, I get off my bike and notice that the prospect isn't outside. Where the fuck is he? He should be right here, keeping watch and making sure that Rick doesn't get anywhere near Sara. If anything happens to her on his watch, I'm personally going to kill him.

I walk quietly up the stairs, prepared for anything. I almost hope that fucker is here so I can kill him, but that would mean he would be near Sara, so that isn't going to happen. Once I figure out where the prospect is, he's going to be in a world of hurt.

When I reach for the doorknob, I hear laughter—male laughter. What the fuck? Swinging open the door, I stand in the doorway, confused, and pissed off by what I'm seeing.

The prospect is sitting at the kitchen table laughing at something and Dani is sitting beside him, smiling. Sara walks in a couple of seconds later, holding what looks like a platter of chicken wings in one hand and two beer bottles in the other.

They all turn to look at me, but when I make no move to walk further into the room or say anything, all of their smiles falter.

"H-hey, Toby. I didn't know you were coming over tonight," Sara says as she places the wings and beer on the table, then walks slowly over to me. I cross my arms and give her a soft look, then harden my stare as I look at the prospect.

I don't say anything, just glare. Either people wither under my quiet glares, or they take it. I wonder which one the prospect will be. I can usually tell a person's character by how they react.

The prospect actually surprises me; he doesn't look away, but matches my stare, though his isn't as tough. That would be disrespectful. It's good to know he's aware of that and willing to take what I give him like a man, whether it's a beating or mutual respect.

Dani's the one who breaks the tension in the room. "If you're here to bitch and moan, then you can just turn your ass right back around and leave. We already had one Debbie Downer come by already. So if you're here to rant, I'll kick your ass out just like I did his. You guys just never learn. Just because I'm pregnant doesn't mean I can't kick some ass." She gets up and heads over to the couch, murmuring what sounds like "Stupid jackasses think I'm fucking disabled? Please. I'll make *them* fucking disabled."

I try to hide my smile, knowing if she sees it, it'll only make her even madder, but Sara doesn't miss it. She puts her arms around me and whispers, "Please don't be mad. We didn't like that he was down there all by himself, so we invited him up here. I know he's supposed to watch over me, but he can do that from here too, can't he?" I squeeze her back and kiss the top of her head before I grab her hand and lead her back into the kitchen.

The prospect stands when we reach him, so I offer him my hand. "Thanks for watching over my girl." He shows his surprise at my gesture and words for just a moment before he hides it and shakes my offered hand.

"Not a problem, man. I know I should have stayed downstairs, but the girls said they would bring everything outside and sit with me there if I didn't come up. I figured it was best to just give in than have them out in the open." This time, I don't try to hide my smile.

"Yeah, that sounds like them," I say, then chuckle.

"When you're done kissing ass, bring over those wings, would ya? I'm starving over here," Dani interrupts without even looking our way.

Sara releases my hand and grabs the food, along with Dani's water, before joining her on the couch.

The prospect laughs then walks to the door. "If you all don't need anything else, I'm gonna head out." I walk over and clasp him on the shoulder.

"Check around the building, then head on back to the clubhouse. Someone should be here soon to stay outside tonight. When you get to the clubhouse, Mack will let you know what's going on."

He nods, then looks once more toward the girls before heading out.

I make my way over to the couch, pick Sara up, and place her on my lap after I take her spot. "Are we watching a movie?" I ask. The girls don't say anything for a minute, so I move my eyes away from the TV and look at Sara first, then Dani. They're both looking at me like they're waiting...for what, I have no idea. "Or are we just gonna sit here and girl talk? Hey, maybe I can get one of you to paint my nails and I could braid your hair," I say in an overly excited voice, rubbing my hands together in front of Sara. That has them both looking at me like I'm high, which was not the response I was looking for.

Dani, again, is the one to speak first. "Cut the shit and tell us what happened at the club. I assume you all had a little powwow about what our next move is?" Dani has never been one to stay out of club business.

She'll never let it go if I don't say something, so I decide to give her just the basics. "We just went over the information we gathered about Rick; when was the last time he was home, if he's used his credit cards and/or phone recently, things like that. We've got our ears to the ground and have called some of our allies around the area to keep their eyes open." I hope they don't ask if Rick has made any movements. I really don't want to have to see the worry and fear on Sara's face if she knows we can't get a lock on Rick.

I can see that Dani wants to ask more questions, but her phone rings, interrupting her before she can get anything else out. "What do you want?" she growls into the phone. I never knew a woman who growled before or who is as intimidating as Dani. She's something else, that's for sure.

She gets up and starts pacing around the room, looking madder and madder as the seconds tick by.

"I already told you I'm staying here till this shit is resolved, and I'll continue to stay here after until you get your head out of your ass and quit being an egotistical jackass! I'm about done with your caveman act, so if you think you can just club me over the head and make me compliant like some weak-ass bitch, you are dead wrong," she yells into the phone before hanging up.

Sara looks at me with concern, then at Dani

when she finally comes to sit back down with us. "Dani, I appreciate all that you're doing, but I don't want you to fight with Blaze over me. Maybe's he's right, maybe you should stay away for a while. I don't know what I'd do if you got hurt because of me," she says with tears in her eyes. I wrap my arms around her even tighter, trying to let her know without words that I have her.

When Dani looks over at us, I notice tears in her eyes as well. Dani isn't one to cry—ever. I don't know if it's the pregnancy or if this is really getting to her. "I'm not going anywhere, Sara. I'm right where I need to be, and if he doesn't understand that then he doesn't really understand me."

We're all quiet for a while after that. As much as I want to agree with Blaze so Dani is safe, I know this is who she is. She'd never back down from a fight or leave a friend in need. I know he's probably going insane with worry and is rightfully pissed off at the whole situation, but she's right. He needs to trust her judgment and stand behind her. Maybe he'll soon realize that it's better to fight with her than against her.

It's not long after that Sara goes to lay down with Dani and I check all the windows and the door before I remove my shirt and lay down on the couch. I want to be in bed with Sara so much I physically ache for it, but I know Dani needs her right now and Sara needs her too.

About ten minutes later, I feel Sara slip under the throw blanket I have lying over my bottom half and cuddle up beside me. I instantly take her in my arms and situate her so she's lying on top of me.

"Goodnight, doll," I whisper into her hair. She lets out a sigh of contentment and falls asleep almost instantly. I can no longer fight it; I'm in love with this girl.

***

I wake to the sound of someone turning the doorknob. Gently moving Sara off me, I rise and quietly walk to the door, hiding, so I can see who's coming in. This gives me the advantage of taking care of any threat.

The door slowly swings open and I see a man dressed in black walk inside. After he closes the door gently behind him, he slowly crosses toward the living room, looking around the room as he goes.

Not wanting him to get any closer to Sara, I creep up behind him and point my gun to his head. "Not another step," I hiss at him, not wanting Sara to wake and freak out, but the threat in my voice is real.

The man raises his hands a little to show that he's not armed. "It's me, brother. Stand the fuck down," Blaze orders.

I push the end of my gun into his head harder to show that it's no joking matter. "You know better than to sneak in here when shit's going down, brother," I say before lowering my gun. Motherfucker just about lost his head.

He laughs softly, but when he turns, I can see the sneer on his face. "I wouldn't have to sneak in to see my woman if it weren't for the shit your woman brought to our fucking doorstep." I've about had it with his shit. If he doesn't watch it, he's not only gonna lose his girl, he's gonna lose a couple teeth too.

I walk into the kitchen and turn on the light above the stove. Blaze follows behind, but he looks toward the bedroom where Dani's sleeping.

Grabbing a couple of beers out of the fridge, I hand him one before we both sit down at the table.

After he takes a long swallow, he lets out a long sigh, running his hands through his hair. "I don't know how much longer I'm gonna be able to handle this shit, Toby. If she doesn't come home soon, I'm gonna carry her there, kicking and screaming, and handcuff her to the bed." Looking up, I can see how tired and wary he is.

"Just give her some space, man. You should know by now that making demands and telling her what to do is only gonna piss her off even more and push her further away. I know this situation sucks and you just want her safe. I do too. Fuck, she's my best fucking friend and having a baby, but she's smart and stronger than you give her credit for. She wouldn't do anything to put herself, the baby, or anyone else she cares about in danger." He needs to understand this. He may have known her when she was growing up, but he also knows that she's not that scared little girl anymore. She's a fierce woman that knows how to protect herself and those she loves. We, the club, made sure of that.

"I fucking know how strong she is, and that she's smart, but she's my fucking woman, pregnant with my fucking baby." He abruptly stands, almost knocking his chair over in the process. Leaning down so he's at eye level with me, he says with venom, "But I'll tell you something *you* don't fucking know. If something happens to my girl because of that bitch in there," he points to where Sara is sleeping peacefully, unaware of what's transpiring a few feet away from her, "I will make her pay; whether you're fucking her or not."

I don't give him time to fully stand up straight, I just shoot out of my chair and hit him hard and fast with a right cross. He doesn't even have time to recover before I deliver an uppercut that I know will knock him on his ass. It's not enough to knock him unconscious, but that's not what I was going for, at least not yet.

Once he's on the ground, I drop down and place my knee to his throat; not enough to choke him completely, but enough to make him uncomfortable and unable to move. "Make a threat against the woman I love again and I swear on my fucking life that it will be your last," I spit at him.

I hear a sharp intake of breath and turn my head to see Sara standing close behind me with her hand to her mouth. The ruckus must have woken Dani too because she comes storming out of the room, gun in hand. "What the fuck?" she says more to herself than to the rest of us, looking between a shocked and scared Sara, and Blaze on the floor with me holding him down. "Somebody gonna tell me what the hell is going on?" Dani's more confused than pissed, though she's still got that glint in her eyes that shows she's close to being pissed too.

I put a little extra pressure on Blaze's throat before I let him go. "Nothing. Blaze was just leaving. Right, *brother*?" I don't look at him till I'm beside Sara, wrapping her in my arms, but when I do lock eyes with him, I can see that this may be over tonight, but we'll be having words again soon.

"I just came by to check on ya, Baby Girl. I haven't seen you since the other day and I missed you," he says a little hoarsely. Dani softens a little at his words, but knowing her, she's still gonna make him work for it.

"I miss you too, Zane, but I think you should go. We can talk about whatever happened tonight tomorrow." Blaze doesn't look my way again, which is fine by me.

I lead Sara back over to the couch to sit while Dani walks Blaze to the door. I can hear them whispering, but can't make out what they're saying.

"Are you okay? What happened?" Sara asks, concern lacing every word. I hug her close to me and tuck her head under my chin.

"Everything's fine. It's nothing for you to worry about."

The door closes and Dani comes to stand in front of us. "I don't know what the fuck happened out here, but right now, I just don't care. I'm fucking tired as hell and just want to sleep." She looks at Sara and says a little more calmly, "I'm gonna message Louie tonight and tell him to be in the shop tomorrow with you. He'll be able to take my appointments or we can reschedule them for another day. I'm gonna take the day off to get some rest and try to straighten Zane out. If you need anything

152

though, you call me—anything at all. Got it, babe?"

"Yeah, of course. Get some sleep and don't worry about me. Louie and I will be fine tomorrow."

Dani looks at her a little skeptically before finally heading back into the bedroom.

I let out a long sigh as I lean back and pull Sara with me. "Let's get some sleep. It's been one hell of a night." I scoot us down and situate us on the couch again, just like we were before Blaze showed up.

When we finally settle, I close my eyes and think about all that happened tonight. I've never fought with one of my brothers before, at least not in a non-joking sense or in the cage. Sure, we've had disagreements. We may yell at each other, but I've never taken a swing at a brother, meaning to inflict real damage. And I wanted to *kill* Blaze. The shit he said tonight, threatening Sara like that, was a mistake. I find it hard to believe he would make a threat like that, no matter how pissed he is. I mean, he knows Sara isn't just anyone to me—she's no club whore—and she's Dani's friend. She's a part of this club, this family, whether it's official or not.

When Dani was in trouble a couple of months ago, we all banded together and would have done anything to make sure she was safe. What happened to her had nothing to do with the club or any of its women, but we still stood behind him to help find her and then took care of the clean-up after shit went down. Of course she's been a part of the club longer than Sara, but still. If our roles were reversed, Dani in Sara's position and vice versa, I would never threaten to take care of Dani the way Blaze threatened Sara.

Tomorrow, I'm gonna sit down with Mack and Blaze, and we're going to hash this shit out once and for all. I know with Mack there he'll be able to put everything into perspective, for both of us. Plus, I know he'll give his own beat down if necessary. Dani is like a daughter to him, has been since the day she walked into the ink shop looking for a place to live and work, but Sara is also like a daughter, only maybe in a different sense. Like how some parents will call the friends of their children their child as well. Like their adopted children, that's what Sara is to Mack, I think.

I'm also going to officially claim Sara as mine. Maybe that will help if any of the other brothers have a problem doing whatever it takes to make sure she's safe. Most of them love Sara already, but I want to make it official for more than the fact that it will make her property of the club, of me. I want my claim on her so she knows she's mine and I'm hers. I'll do whatever it takes to protect her and show her she has a family in me, and in the club.

Putting all of that out of my mind, I try to relax so I can sleep. I'm gonna need it to be in the same room with Blaze again tomorrow. "Did you mean what you said earlier?" Sara whispers, interrupting my thoughts. I thought she was asleep, but she must have too much going on in her head, just like me.

"Did I mean what?" I don't know what she's asking, so I want to be sure before I answer.

"When you said you loved me?" I didn't even realize I'd said that out loud, but now I remember.

When I threatened Blaze; if he threatened the girl I love, he'd regret it.

"I didn't mean for it to come out this way. I wanted to wait a little while and tell you myself when it was just you and I, but yeah, I meant what I said," I tell her as I turn her head so she's looking at me. "I knew there was something about you when I first laid eyes on you. Then, after spending time together, I knew you were someone special. You've come to mean so much to me. I'm not even sure where I end and you begin anymore, but I wouldn't change it for anything. You're the girl I'd fight the world for, Sara. So yes, I love you." I kiss her gently on the mouth, then lay her head back down on my chest.

I wasn't expecting her to say anything back—it's not the reason I said it to begin with. Shit, I didn't even think she heard me, but she kisses my chest and sighs happily. "I'm glad you love me, Toby, because I'm in love with you too," she whispers. I squeeze her tight and close my eyes again, basking in the feeling. Neither of us say anything else in that moment because there's nothing left to say. It's already perfect.

No matter what life throws at us, I know we'll be okay. She knows that I love her and will fight whatever stands in our way. She loves me. For the first time, someone loves me for *me*. She makes me feel so at peace, like I don't need anything else in the world but her. And that's a great feeling, one I've never known before.

CHAPTER 12

Sara

When my alarm goes off at ten in the morning, I realize that Toby is no longer on the couch with me. Opening my eyes, I listen and let my eyes wander around the room. It's quiet and I don't see anyone here, or at least in the kitchen. Dani may still be sleeping and Toby could be in the bathroom.

Getting up slowly, my back cracks and hurts a little. I'm sure it's from sleeping on this crappy couch for the past couple of nights. How the hell does Toby do it? He's so much bigger than me, it has to be even worse for him. I hope he isn't feeling it too bad, but maybe I can give him a nice massage. That would give me a good reason to touch him. It's not like I need a reason, but it will give me an excuse to take my time and really explore his body.

I walk into the kitchen first to start the coffee. I won't be able to get through the day without at least a cup before I go to work. I head toward the bathroom.

Seeing that the door is open and the light is off, I know no one is in there. Dani could still be sleeping and if Toby isn't here, I'm sure he just had to get back to the club. I know everyone is on high alert now that Rick is here. Gah, I still can't believe he found me. Why can't he just forget about me and let me live my life in peace? Oh yeah, that's right. Because he likes to torture me and inflict as much pain as he possibly can, both physically and mentally.

Once I'm done in the bathroom, I tiptoe into my bedroom. The light is off and the curtains are closed, so it's still a little dark in the room, but not dark enough to hide that the bed is messed up and empty. I guess both Toby and Dani snuck out this morning. I'm a little hurt that they didn't even bother to wake me to let me know they were leaving, but I understand too. Just sucks.

Flipping on my light, I walk over to my closet to grab clothes for work, but on my way over, I spot what looks like a note lying on my pillow. Opening it up, I can tell right away it's from Toby.

Doll—

Was gonna wait till you woke up, but got a call from Mack that I was needed at the club. You looked so peaceful that I didn't want to wake you.

I'll call you later. Have a good day at work. Don't let Louie fuck with you. If he does, I'll kick his ass.

Can't wait to see you tonight.

<3 Toby

His note puts a huge smile on my face. I love that he was thinking about me. He even put a heart at the end. Though he said he loved me last night, I thought maybe he'd hope I forgot, or just wouldn't say anything more about it. I know he didn't write 'I love you' specifically, but the heart is enough for me.

After I pick out my clothes, I head out to the living room to search for my phone, wanting to send him a quick text before I have to be at work. I know he probably won't get it for a while since he's busy at the club, but whenever he looks at his phone next, it will be there.

Me: Just found your note. Thank you! Will talk to you later tonight. <3 P.S. I'm sure Louie will be fine.

I jump in the shower, wash my hair and body quickly, then get dressed. Not really wanting to do anything special with my hair, I put it in a messy ponytail, throw on some mascara along with some lipgloss, and I'm ready to go.

When I walk out into the living room, I notice my phone blinking. Unlocking it, I see that I have two messages from Toby.

Toby: Not sure what time I'll be there. Got a lot

158

to do here.

Toby: And Louie better not cause any problems, but if he does, call me and I'll straighten his ass out.

I'm not sure why he thinks I'll have problems with Louie. He hasn't been around much since I've been working in the shop with Dani, but the couple of times he has been there he's been really quiet.

I'm a little disappointed that I might not get to spend time with Toby tonight, though. He's been late the last couple of nights, working out the details of what they're going to do about Rick. I feel really bad that they're all working so hard to make sure I'm safe, but it does make me feel better knowing they have my back and are helping me. I don't know what I would do if I had to deal with him all by myself. I'd probably end up dead or lying somewhere in a ditch, broken and bleeding. If not that, I'd probably end up hiding away somewhere, too afraid to go outside for fear of him finding me again and taking me away. I'd rather be dead than have to endure any more time with him, whether he's inflicting pain on me or not.

Me: I'll try to wait up for you. Want to spend some time with you, seems like I haven't really seen you in forever. I miss you...

After I hit send, I put my phone in my purse and walk out my door to head downstairs, but run right into a solid wall of muscle. "Umph!" I try to catch myself, but end up falling on my ass. Looking up, I'm met with a hard stare from Louie. "I'm sorry, I didn't know you were out here," I say as I pick myself up off the floor. He doesn't even try to help me or ask if I'm all right, just stands there with his arms crossed.

Once I'm standing again, he says, "Just makin' sure you get down to the shop without breakin' a nail or getting yourself kidnapped." Wow. Someone is in a shitty mood today.

"Oh. Well, thanks, I guess," I mumble, then walk around him and down the stairs. He follows me down, but doesn't say anything else. Looks like it's going to be a long day.

***

Things have been slow today at the shop, but surprisingly, the day has gone by fast, thank goodness. We only have a few more hours until closing.

I only had to call two of Dani's customers to let them know she wasn't going to be in today and reschedule. They weren't pissed, which I was thankful for. Louie took the one appointment that I wasn't able to reschedule and we had a few walk-ins, which weren't anything too crazy.

I've stayed up front most of the time, only venturing into the back for something to drink or to use the bathroom. I've only talked to Louie when I needed to, letting him know when someone was here for their tattoo, or asking if he wanted something to eat when I was calling to order something. Louie, on the other hand, either shook his head yes or no to answer me, or used as few words as possible.

When it was slow and we didn't have anyone here, Louie stayed at his station, either drawing something or messing around on his phone. I worked on cleaning the front room, straightening and organizing my desk, and waiting to see if Toby would text me. So far he hasn't, so he must be really busy at the club.

Louie seems to be bothered by something, but since I'm not really close to him I don't feel comfortable asking him what's going on. I feel like his behavior today is something completely out of the norm for him though. Maybe it's because it's the first time we've had to work together without Dani here as a buffer, or maybe he's pissed about the extra work he now has to do with the club because of me. I don't know, but I want to ask him what his problem is. I don't want to tell Toby that he's being a jerk and have him come in here to fight my battles for me. I figure it will be best to wait till it's almost closing time to ask him about it. Then, if he says something that I don't like or things get even worse, I won't have to deal with it for long before I can just leave.

We have another walk-in, a girl that only wants a small rose on her ankle, then it's quiet for the rest of the night. With nothing else to do, I decide to read a book that I downloaded onto my phone last week. I don't know what Louie is doing, but he stays at his station and remains quiet. I don't even hear him messing around with his equipment.

I get caught up in my story and before I know it, there's only about a half an hour before we close, unless of course someone walks in wanting something, but I'm fairly confident no one will since we haven't had anyone come in for at least an hour and a half. I figure now is the time to confront Louie and see what's up with him. If anything, maybe I can help since I'm not really in the know with people around here and I can give him an unbiased opinion.

Getting up, I put my phone in my back pocket and walk toward his station. "Hey," I start, figuring I'll start with small talk. Maybe I can warm him up to me.

He's sitting in the reclining chair that the customers sit in to get their tattoo, doing something on his phone. He doesn't even look up when he hears me, he just asks, "What?" Okay then, this is going to be harder than I thought. I'm really glad I waited till it was almost time to leave to talk with him now.

"I, ah...I wanted to ask if you were a-all right?" I hate sounding nervous. I stumble over my words, but I've always been that way.

This time when he hears me, he looks up from his phone. "Why wouldn't I be?" There's a definite edge to his voice. Yeah, there's something there, something bothering him.

"Well, I know I don't know you very well and we haven't been around each other that much, but you just seem so closed off today—pissed even. I just wanted to make sure you were all right. If you wanted to talk, I'm a really good listener." There. I put it out there that I was just worried about him, noticed that something was off with him.

Louie laughs almost evilly before standing up and walking over to me so that we're almost toe to toe. "You want me to talk to you? Tell you what's wrong?" I don't like the tone of his voice, but I can't back out now, though I wish I could. Louie is a scary guy to begin with, but he's downright frightening when he's like this.

Shakily, I nod.

"All right. You want to talk, let's talk." He turns back around and walks to the other side of the room and leans against the wall. "Well, let's see. First there was Blaze coming in, stealing the girl I wanted. In the process, I feel like I lost my best friend, even though she's still around and I work with her. Then there's the girl that turns my world upside down and pisses me off at the same time. I don't know what to do with myself half the time. Then she up and leaves, not saying how long she's gonna be gone or where she's going. On top of everything else that's going on, there's you. You come here with all your baggage and shit, put Dani in danger and cause shit between her and her old man, putting rifts between brothers. And let me tell you something, we never go against our brothers. You may not have intended for any of that to happen, and I'm not saying it's completely your fault, but you had a hand in it. If something would have happened to Dani, your hands may not have been completely stained, but they would have been very dirty. So yeah, I'm a little closed off, but I'm more *pissed* off. And no, we are definitely not friends," he growls the last part.

The whole time he was talking, he never looked away from me, not afraid to show me his anger or the way he feels about me.

My eyes are burning with unshed tears, but I try my best not to let them fall. I don't want to give him the satisfaction of knowing how much he just hurt me. I stay quiet, not knowing what to say, trying to keep the tears at bay.

He pushes himself away from the wall and comes toward me. When he's side by side with me, each of us not looking at each other but at the opposite wall, he says, "Thanks for the talk. I feel so much better now." With that, he walks out of the room and goes outside.

As soon as I hear the front door close, I fall to my knees and let the tears fall. If I thought I felt horrible before, knowing that I brought my shit to their doorstep and inadvertently put Dani in danger, and then seeing how Toby and Blaze fought last night, it's nothing to how I feel now after listening to Louie put it all out there. He's absolutely right. If something happened to Dani, it would be my fault, and Toby fighting with his brother—that's all my fault too.

Needing to just get out of here, away from everything, I get up and go to my desk. I turn off my computer, grab my purse, and walk out through the back.

I don't see anyone out here, so whoever is supposed to be watching the outside of the shop is probably out front with Louie or walking around to make sure everything is as it should be.

Not wanting to go up to my apartment, but also not wanting Rick to be able to find me if he's looking, I decide to walk down a couple of blocks and get a taxi. I'm not sure where I'm going to go, I just know I need someplace quiet so I can think and get away for a while. Everyone will just think I'm upstairs and Toby won't be back for at least a couple of hours anyway, so no one will know I went out by myself.

I hail a taxi and ask him to just drive for a while. When the meter hits twenty-five dollars, I ask him if he could take me to a place that's quiet, maybe a place people go to stare at the stars. Probably not the best thing to ask a taxi driver—take me someplace quiet—in case they are rapists or murders, but I take the chance, not finding it in myself to be concerned. Ten minutes later, we pull up to what appears like a lookout point. I thank the driver, pay the toll, and get out of the car. There's a small parking lot with only a few cars parked and a trail that leads up a hill. There's a sign at the bottom that says there are five different cliffs with a lookout, so I go to the top one. If I'm lucky, no one else will be up there and I can be alone to clear my head and think.

It takes me about half an hour to make it to the top, but once I'm there and look out over the town and up at the stars, it's worth it. Why haven't I been out here before now? It's breathtaking—quiet and peaceful, beautiful and majestic. I think I've found my new favorite place.

Since I don't have a blanket, I just find a nice grassy area to lay down. The ground is a little cold, but feels nice on my overheated skin.

I spend a little bit of time looking for the few constellations I know, then try to see if I can pick any of my own out. I find a little comfort in doing something that I used to do so much of as a child; make shapes or animals out of the clouds or stars.

When I close my eyes, my mind replays the events of the past few weeks; that first night at the club with Toby, spending as much time with him as possible, getting to know him, and then falling for him. Then I replay the day in the shop where Dani and I really talked about what was going on with Toby and I, feeling like we were real friends and not just employer and employee, being grateful to have met her and to be able to call her my friend.

Then it shoots to images of Rick pulling me by my hair, listening to him put me down and call me a bitch, and me trying and failing to fight him off. When Dani came to my rescue and Rick gave me that look before he left. I remember the fighting, everyone yelling and pissed off that Mack knew and didn't tell anyone. Toby and Blaze wanting to kill each other, then Dani fighting with Blaze. The last image I see before I fall asleep, laying there under the stars, is of Toby and I lying on the couch, and him telling me he loves me.

***

In my dreams, I replay everything again, but the ending's a little different.

Everything stays the same until I get to the part

166

where Rick appears. He came into the shop, told me he was taking me back home with him and started dragging me out of the building. Dani came into the room and held the gun at him, but instead of it scaring him away, it made him angrier. He swung out, his fist connecting with Dani's face, which made her drop the gun.

Rick leans down to pick the gun up and points it at Dani. I yell and try to get his attention off of her, but it's too late. He pulls the trigger. There's so much blood surrounding her. She's so still, like she's sleeping, but I know better.

Suddenly, Rick disappears, and in his place is Toby and Blaze. The way they're looking at me, blaming me, and they're so angry I put her in danger. It's my fault she's dead. I try to tell them how sorry I am, that I didn't mean for it to happen, but they don't hear me.

Then Toby is holding a gun and it's directed at me. I yell and plead, tell him I love him and I thought he loved me too, but he just shakes his head and snarls at me that he could never love someone like me. When he pulls the trigger, instead of the pain, I'm teleported back to New York, and back to Rick. "You're mine now, bitch!" he yells before leaping forward and wrapping his hands around my throat and squeezing.

Jolting awake, I reach up to my neck, gasping for air. It felt so real, all of it. The pain I felt in my dream about Dani dying, Toby not loving me, and knowing I'm never going to get away from Rick, it's all there. I can still feel it all.

Dropping my head to my hands, I start to cry again. I cry for putting Dani in danger, I cry for not being worthy of Toby's love, and I cry for myself. I just want to disappear and take all of my troubles with me. If it would guarantee safety for those I've come to love and care about, then I would gladly disappear, but it doesn't work that way, unfortunately.

I hear a twig snap, and fear pulses rapidly through my body. My nervous system is really taking a ride tonight—I'm all over the place.

Staying very still, I try to look around without drawing attention to myself. I have no idea how long I've been here, but I suddenly realize it was a big mistake to come here by myself. It could be Rick. He could have followed me here and found me. No one knows I'm even gone or where I am.

My heart is beating loud and fast. I'm afraid whoever made that noise will be able to hear it and it will bring them right to me, but then I hear a voice that has my heart beating fast for a whole other reason. "Sara?" It's Toby. I have no idea how he knew I was here, but I'm so thankful it's him and not someone else.

I stand up and see him about ten feet away from me. He sees me instantly, but instead of waiting for him to reach me, I start running and don't stop until I'm in his arms. "How did you find me?" I ask after a couple of minutes, not wanting him to let me go, but knowing we should probably get out of here. I don't want to be here anymore anyway. I still can't get that dream out of my head.

"I tracked your phone. What the fuck were you

thinking, Sara? You just fucking left without telling Louie you were even leaving work. Everyone thought you just went home, but when I got there after you wouldn't answer your phone, you weren't even there. Everyone's been worried and out looking for you. So tell me, what the fuck where you thinking coming out here by yourself?" He sounds equal parts relieved and pissed. I know I shouldn't have left, or at least not without telling anyone where I was going, but he doesn't need to yell at me. Doesn't he understand what I'm going through, or have a clue what I'm feeling?

Stepping out of his arms, I glare at him. "I just wanted to get away and be alone. I'm sorry I didn't fucking tell Louie I was leaving, not like he'd fucking care anyway," I say, just as pissed. I can't deal with all of this. "Just take me home." I don't wait for him to respond, I just start making my way back down the hill toward the road.

He doesn't try to talk to me on the way down the hill, nor does he say anything as I climb behind him on his bike.

As soon as we make it to my apartment, I jump off and go upstairs.

When I open my door, I don't expect anyone to be there, but sitting on my couch and around my kitchen table is Dani, Blaze, Louie, Mack, the prospect who was up here the other night, and a few guys whose names I can't remember.

Dani stands up and rushes toward me as soon as I walk in the door. "Oh my God, are you okay? I was so worried something happened to you!" I feel bad that I worried her, but I just don't think I can deal with anything else tonight.

"I'm sorry I worried you. I'm fine though, really. I just want to go to bed." I step out of her embrace and head to my bedroom.

"Yeah, sure, of course. Let me go to the bathroom and I'll come with you." I hear Blaze growl just as Toby walks into the room.

I look at him, then at Dani. "No, I'm fine. I think you should go home tonight, Dani. I just want to be alone." I say the last part while looking at Toby, trying to get my point across that I don't want him here either. It's not that I don't want Dani here, it's more that I don't want to cause any more problems for her or put her in anymore danger. At least for the night, she can be home with the man she loves and be safe.

I don't wait for her to respond, but as I close my door, I hear her say, "If you're sure." I hope she understands and doesn't think I'm ungrateful for all she's done for me. I'm just at my end for tonight and I don't even know what time it is.

As I climb into bed, I can hear the murmurs of people talking but I can't make out the words. Realizing I don't even have the energy to care, I just close my eyes and fall asleep. I hope tomorrow is a better day.

CHAPTER 13

Toby

After Sara closes her bedroom door, I stand and stare after her. I have no idea what the fuck happened today, but whatever it was, it's not a good thing. I could tell right away when I found her tonight that something was wrong. At first she was relieved and happy to see me, though maybe a little hesitant and curious, but then she turned distant and pissed off.

Looking over toward where Louie is leaning against a wall by the kitchen, I point at him and growl, "You. Outside, now." I don't wait for him to answer or to make sure someone is staying inside to make sure Sara is safe. I just know that one of my brothers will be here.

Once I'm outside, I start pacing, trying to figure out what could have happened to make Sara go off by herself tonight. Whatever happened though, I have a feeling it has something to do with Louie, and if it wasn't him specifically, he'll at least be able to give me a rundown of what could have happened. When I left this morning, things were fine, so something happened between the time she woke up and the time I found her tonight.

I hear rather than see Louie come outside behind me. Before I can even question him about Sara's behavior, he starts talking. "Look, I don't know what happened today. One minute we're both working quietly together, not really talking unless we needed to, then the next, shit just got outta control." Having no clue what he's talking about, I give him a look that tells him he better start explaining before I lose my shit.

He runs his hand through his hair in frustration. "It's just things have been so fucked up lately. I mean, first with Dani and Blaze getting together, then her getting kidnapped. I feel so fucking guilty about it that I just want to kick my own ass. I let my hurt feelings get in the way of our friendship, and I wasn't there for her when she needed me. If I wasn't so selfish and ass hurt over her wanting to be with Blaze and not me, she wouldn't have been taken in the first place." He's the one pacing now while I'm standing still in shock at what he's saying. I knew he took Dani and Blaze getting together hard, but I had no idea he was still feeling guilty. The fucker keeps everything locked inside until it just explodes.

"Then things with Harlow got fucked up and before I could apologize or make things right, she just up and fucking leaves without saying why, where she's going, or how long she'd be gone. Shit, she didn't even say if she was coming back!" He's still pacing, but now he's starting to get angry. He's kicking rocks or anything else that comes into his path. "And now there's this shit with Sara. I know she didn't mean for this shit to follow her, or for Dani to get involved, but she did. She fucking did because it's Dani we're talking about, and of course, she has to be the fucking badass, the fucking hero, and save the fucking day. She could have been hurt, man. Her and the baby! And again, I should have fucking been there. If I was there the day that fucker Rick tried to take Sara, he would already be in the ground. Dani wouldn't have put herself in danger and this shit wouldn't be hanging over Sara's head. You and Blaze wouldn't be fighting and everything would be fine. I just can't fucking deal with all of this shit. I feel like it all comes down to me being a dipshit and not being there. It all comes back to me." He stops in front of the building and is breathing heavily. Then he lifts his fist and punches the side of the building. "Fuck!"

I know he needs to vent and let out all his frustrations, but punching a brick wall isn't the best way to do that. Plus, he still needs to tell me what any of that has to do with Sara going off on her own tonight and the way she's acting now.

When he pulls back to punch the wall again, I'm instantly behind him, holding his arm back. He looks over his shoulder at me, at first with an angry glint in his eye, then it disappears and is replaced with a look I've never seen on Louie before—regret.

He drops his head and I feel his arm go slack, so I release him. "So what does any of this have to do with my woman taking off tonight and putting herself in danger?" I have a feeling I know, and I'm so fucking close to taking a page out of Louie's book and punch shit too, but I need to know for sure; I need to know exactly what happened so I can fix this shit.

He steps away from me, probably knowing that it's a good idea to put distance between us. "Like I said, we were both working quietly together, only talking when we had to, but then at the end of the day, she came into my station and asked what was wrong; said that I was acting closed off or some shit, and that she was willing to listen. I just snapped. It was like a switch was flipped and everything that's been going on, all that shit just came out. I told her about Dani and Blaze and feeling like I've lost my best friend. I told her about Harlow leaving and how it drives me fucking crazy not knowing where she went, what happened, and when or if she'll even be back. Then about the shit that followed her here, and how it could've hurt Dani. I was pissed, but I didn't mean to make her feel guilty, I really didn't. I walked out front to calm down and then I went back in to make sure she was okay and apologize, but she wasn't there. I assumed she just went home. I stayed out back, watching, until you showed up."

I've never been so at odds with any of my brothers, and now I feel like I'm at war with not one, but two of them. I want to deck Louie and bash his face in until he's unrecognizable. Then I want to go at Blaze and do the same thing, but I know I can't. I just don't understand how they can act so heartless when it comes to Sara. I mean, yeah, she brought her past with her, but it was unknowingly. She would never have put Dani or anyone else in danger on purpose. I just wish they would see that, or think before they said shit that made things worse on me and her.

I have no idea where her head is now, but I do know that the shit from Rick fucked with her big time. Then add to that the way Blaze has been acting, and now Louie, it's no wonder she's being distant. I probably didn't help matters when I got pissed at her for leaving without protection. She probably wanted some alone time, time to process what has been happening, and then I go and fuck that up by yelling at her. Fuck, this is all just a big pile of fucked up shit.

"I'm sorry, man. I didn't mean for any of this to happen, for her to take off on her own. If something would have happened, I wouldn't have been able to ever forgive myself. I'm sorry," he breathes out as he turns so his back is to the building, then slides down so he's sitting. I follow his actions and sit beside him.

"I know, man, I know. I fucked up too. I never should have yelled at her when I found her tonight. I think I fucked up even worse than you and Blaze. I fucking love that girl, and instead of just taking her in my arms and making sure she was all right and just being happy I found her, I got pissed that she left and made her feel even worse than she probably already does." How in the hell am I going to make this shit right with her?

We are both quiet for a couple of minutes, each

probably trying to get a handle on what's going on, though I bet Louie is probably going through a lot more than that in his head.

Not really wanting to dig into his head right now, but thinking this might be the best time to do so, I ask, "What happened with you and Harlow?" We don't look at each other, but I can see out of the corner of my eye that he stiffens at the mention of her name, and then he laughs softly.

"What the fuck didn't happen with her might be the right question." I don't say anything. I let him gather his thoughts and wait for him to elaborate. "When she started working at the shop, at first, I just liked to push her buttons. She always seemed so proper and innocent, but was always sassy. It was confusing as fuck and a complete contradiction, but I liked it. I would always mess with her by slapping her ass or making smart ass comments, and she would give it back to me times ten. I've never met someone besides Dani to give as good as she got. It was like a breath of fresh air. You know how it is, having girls paw at you, do whatever it takes to jump on your dick, but not her. We became friends. I could talk to her about anything and not have to worry about putting on this tough guy act or worry about her getting clingy. She couldn't care less about my cut and what it could give her. The day before she ran, we slept together. It just kind of happened, but I had no idea how innocent she was, man. The way she'd act when I was messing with her, I never even thought there was a possibility she was a virgin. Afterwards, I tried to talk to her about it, but she completely shut down on me. I thought it was probably best if I left it alone and let her talk to me about it when she was ready, but when I came into work the next day, all she left was that note." That's bad fucking luck. I had no clue he and Harlow were getting close, not even as friends. Shows how much I've been out of the fucking loop.

I clasp him on his shoulder, offering what little support I can. "I'm sorry. I had no clue." When Dani and I spoke at the club a couple of weeks ago, the night Sara met with Mack, she told me how she and Mack were concerned about Louie, but I didn't really see it. Now, it's painfully obvious they were right. "It doesn't excuse the shit you pulled tonight, but I understand it a little better now. But let me say this—if you ever do something that upsets my woman again, or do anything that puts her in danger for any reason, even from herself, I will make you regret it." I don't need to say anything else. He knows exactly what I'm talking about. I just hope that now I can make things better with Sara.

An hour later, everyone has left the apartment except for Dani and Blaze. Sara has been in her room the whole time, and when Dani went to check on her she said she was dead asleep.

"How are you holding up, Toby?" Dani asks as she sits beside me on the couch. My head is in my hands as I lean forward with my elbows on my thighs.

"What am I gonna do, Dani? I have no idea how to even begin to fix this shit. Her ex is still under our radar, shit's falling apart between the brothers, and now I feel like I'm losing her. I am completely in the dark with what I need to do." I sigh, then finally lift my head to look at her, hoping she has some advice for what I should do.

Dani's quiet for a long time, making me uncomfortable. I mean, she's a chick. She should know how to fix this, but she doesn't say anything. She just looks at me with pity. I fucking hate it when people pity me.

I move to stand, but she places her hand on my arm. "Oh, sit the fuck down. I don't pity you, you dipshit." She knows me so well. Sometimes it amazes me how much. I never really had friends before the club, but with her, it's so simple and comes so naturally. It feels like she's more than just my friend, she's like the sister I never had.

"Well, what the fuck was that look for then?" I ask as I sit back down.

"That look was because I feel helpless. I can't tell you what you need to do or how you should fix this. There's more going on here than I even know. Only you can make this right; with Sara and your brothers." She's fucking right and I hate it. I hate that she can't help me with this.

Dropping my head into my hands again, I say, "Yeah, I know."

Blaze walks back into the room and looks over at us on the couch. "You ready to go home, Baby Girl?" Since the moment I called Dani and Blaze to tell them Sara was missing, I haven't seen them butt heads or argue even once. It's a nice break. These two always seem to fight, but I was getting worried for a little bit there.

Dani looks at Blaze for a while, probably deciding if she wants to be a bitch, but finally deciding against it. "Yeah, just let me go check on Sara one more time, then we can go." Without waiting for an answer, she heads into the bedroom, closing the door behind her.

I stand up and approach Blaze. "I see you two have called a ceasefire," I say with a soft chuckle. Those two really are something else, and most times I enjoy watching him sweat a bit over Dani, but I'm full out exhausted.

Blaze laughs a little too. "Yeah, so it seems, though who knows how long it will last." I nod, agreeing with him. With Dani pregnant now, you can bet her crazy bitchiness will come out again sooner rather than later.

"Look," Blaze starts, "I know the way I acted and treated your girl was wrong. It just makes me insane to think of Dani and the baby being in any sort of danger. I lost my head there for a bit, but I know if it were Dani, you would have my back no matter what, so I'll try harder to remember that. Now I can't promise if shit starts getting hot again and Dani is close by that I won't flip the fuck out, but I will do my best to remember that it's not her fault and direct my anger and frustrations elsewhere." Knowing that's as close to an apology as I'm going to get, I nod.

"I'd appreciate that, and you know I'd always have your back and do anything to make sure Dani is safe, along with the baby. I also hope you understand that I need to make sure *my* girl is protected as well, and that goes for anyone who tries to hurt her, even you."

At that moment, Dani quietly walks out of Sara's

room and takes Blaze's hand. "Let's go home. I feel like I could sleep for a year, but first, I could eat a cow." That makes us all laugh, but then Dani gets a serious look on her face and it's directed at me. "Fix this." That's all she says before they leave.

Knowing there's a prospect outside, I forego doing a search around the building, but check the windows and door before I tiptoe into the bedroom.

Sara's lying on her side, as close to the right side of the bed as she can get without falling off. I hate the thought of her doing that because she didn't want to be close to me.

Removing my shoes, socks, and shirt, I crawl into bed and pull her closer to the middle of the bed, then tuck her in close to my chest. I will fix this. I'll make her see that I love her and would do anything for her. I'll apologize for the way I acted, but she can't fucking do something like that again. I was so scared that her ex got to her, I was two seconds away from going on a rampage and killing everyone in my path to find her. I'm just glad I found her and have the chance to make it up to her.

* * *

I wake up to Sara trying to sneak out of bed. Keeping my eyes closed, I pull her back and hold her tighter. "Don't go yet," I croak. After watching her sleep for a while, then just holding her close to me, I finally fell asleep. I feel like I've only been out for seconds, I'm still tired as shit.

She tries to wiggle away again, but I squeeze my arms. "I have to get up and get downstairs. I'm gonna be late." Her voice sounds sleepy, but there's still defiance and distance there that I don't like.

I pull her back and move her so she's lying underneath me. I look down at her, but she tries not to make eye contact, and that kills me. "I'm sorry, doll. I shouldn't have yelled at you last night. I was just so worried and scared that something had happened to you. Then when I found you, I was just pissed that you left and didn't tell anyone. When it comes to you, I just need to know you're safe, especially with your ex gunning for you. It doesn't make up for how I reacted, but I am sorry. I can't promise it won't happen again, but I can promise that I will always do whatever it takes to make up for it."

She doesn't say anything, but she finally looks at me. I try to gauge what she's thinking, but there's a wall up and that feels even worse. I'm starting to think it's not going to be as easy as I thought for her to forgive me.

When she tries to get up again, I let her. "Look, I know you were worried and I'm sorry I put you in that position. I wasn't thinking when I left, but I just had to get away for a while. There's just so much going on right now that I'm losing sight of what's up and what's down, but the way you reacted, like you didn't even care about my feelings or what I'm going through, that hurt, Toby. It hurt a lot." She grabs clothes out of her closet, then when she's at the bedroom door, she pauses before turning around to face me. "I won't leave without letting someone know again because I know it's the right thing to do—the safe thing to do. I can forgive you for what happened last night, but I can't forget the way it made me feel. I need some time to think about everything that's happened and figure out what needs to happen now. Just…please, give me some time, okay?" She sounds so defeated, but if that's what she needs to come to grips with everything before we can move past this, then that's what she'll get. Doesn't mean I like it, though.

Getting out of bed, I walk over to her. I don't touch her, but I make sure to hold her eyes. "I can give you time, doll, but I'm not going anywhere. I'm still gonna be here every night to make sure you're safe and I'm still gonna be around because I don't think I can't not be close to you. I will let you be and give you the time you need to figure your stuff out." Leaning down, I place a soft kiss on her forehead, then to her lips, before I get dressed and head into the kitchen.

I make a pot of coffee because I know she needs as much as she can get before going to work, then I sit and wait quietly for her to finish getting ready. Once she's done getting dressed, I hand her a to go cup and walk her out.

When we reach the back door to the shop, I pull her into a hug. "I love you, Sara…always." Then I kiss the top of her head and get on my bike, ready to head to the club. I'm going to find that fucker Rick and take care of him so I can get my woman back.

***

It's hours later, and we still don't have shit on Sara's ex. How can this piece of shit just disappear like that and not leave a trace?

Needing a break, I head out to the bar for a beer. No one is manning the bar, but it's no matter, I'll just get it myself.

I end up grabbing a couple long necks and a bottle of bourbon. I think I'm going to need it today with everything going on. Can't find the fucker I'm looking for, shit with Louie and Blaze, then Sara being distant. I've sent her a couple of text messages, just to see how her day's going, and I'm only getting one word replies. I know she said she needed some time, but I didn't think that she'd cut me out like this. The sooner we can get past this shit, the better.

On my way back to the chapel, Trixie sidles up next to me. "Hey, stranger," she says while grabbing onto my arm to stop me. I'm really not in the mood for this shit today and frankly, I'm about done with her games.

"I'm not in the mood to deal with your shit today, Trixie." I move to leave, but she yanks on my arm to pull me to stop.

"What the fuck is your problem, Toby? We used to be real good together until that bitch of yours came into the picture," she practically spits at me.

Slamming my beers and bottle of bourbon on a nearby table, I grab hold of her arm hard enough that I know it will leave a bruise, swing her around, and push her against the wall. "If you value your life, bitch, you will do best to never speak about Sara like that again. In fact, don't even think about her again, or the last thought you'll have is why you had to be a stupid fucking cunt and go against me. I will fucking kill you without remorse or even a second thought. Stay away from me and stay the fuck away from my girl. You got me?" I growl at her in a low, deadly voice. I've only ever used that tone with men that have crossed me, but there's always a first time for everything.

Trixie looks at me with fear and she's trembling so much that if I wasn't holding her arm so tightly, she'd probably drop to the ground.

When she doesn't answer me, I bring my face closer to hers. "Do. You. Fucking. Understand. Me?" I say through clenched teeth.

"Y-yeah. Yes, I-I understand," she stutters. Good, the bitch is scared. Maybe now she'll know I'm not fucking around.

"Good. You seem to have forgotten your place around here. It's on your back for anyone who wants a fuck, so you better watch your mouth from now on. I will not warn you again. I push off the wall and give her one last hard glare before picking up my drinks and making my way back to the room where we have all our computers and shit set up to find Rick.

"Took you long enough, asshole," Tom Tom says once I walk into the room.

"Shut the fuck up and get back to work. I want to have sights on this asshole by the end of tomorrow, if not sooner." I bring my beer to my lips, taking a healthy swig before going over my game plan for when we find the man we're looking for. I think I'm gonna have to make him suffer extra for all the shit he's making everyone go through, and especially what he's put Sara through, then and now. Yeah, his death isn't gonna be fast, that's for sure.

CHAPTER 14

Sara

Today has been nothing but shit. Waking up wrapped around Toby, I wanted so bad to just forget everything that happened yesterday, but I can't. After everything I've been through, I will not be a doormat anymore, not for anyone.

I know how worried he must have been, and I really do feel bad about just leaving like that, but the way he handled it was all wrong. The way he jumped right into anger frightens me and pisses me off at the same time. I don't care how concerned or afraid he was, or pissed off that I put myself in danger. He should never have yelled like that. He said he loved me. Well, in my eyes, you should never direct any type of anger at that person, no matter what the circumstances may be.

Then there's what happened with Louie. I understand where he's coming from, and I had no idea he was dealing with more than just the shit that's going on with my ex being here, but I had nothing to do with that stuff. Why did he have to take it out on me? All I wanted to do was offer up my ear to listen and maybe help him if I could, but for him to direct all that on me was wrong on so many levels. It was even worse how he made me feel so guilty about Dani, like I don't already feel horrible about the situation as it is—he had to rub it in my face that my past could have gotten Dani hurt, or worse.

Oh, we can't leave Blaze out. He, more than anyone else, has a right to be angry about what went down and how Dani was involved, but again, that wasn't my fault. I didn't ask Rick to show up and cause trouble. I didn't ask for it to happen at Dani's shop, and I definitely didn't ask for Dani to stand up for me and risk herself and her baby. Not that I'm not grateful, because I am. I don't think I could ever repay her for what she did for me, but I didn't ask her to do it, and if I could change what happened, I would tell her to just hide and whatever happened to me would just have to happen. At least it wouldn't be on my conscience that she got hurt trying to save me.

The guy that was getting his tattoo interrupts my thoughts. "Do I pay you, or wait for Louie to come out here?" he asks.

"I can take care of it. Did he give you the instructions for your aftercare?" I already know what he was getting and what Louie quoted him, so I don't need to go back and ask him what he's charging, thank God.

"Yeah, I got it right here," he says as he reaches into his back pocket and shows me the piece of paper. "But there is one thing he didn't give me."

Not sure what he's missing, I stare at him in confusion. Usually the only thing you get after a tattoo is the aftercare instructions. Sometimes you get a business card, but those are sitting right in front of him, hard for him to miss.

"What are you missing?" I ask.

"Your phone number." he says almost innocently, but there's a cockiness in his eyes that pisses me off.

"I'm sorry?" Maybe I heard him wrong. Maybe he asked for the number to the shop or for Louie in case he has questions about his tattoo or scheduling another.

"Your number, babe. I'm taking you out Friday."

I'm speechless. Having a random person hit on me is uncommon enough, but the way he just assumes I'll accept…I can't believe my ears.

Before I can answer, I feel Louie walk up behind me. "You got a pen, I'll give you her number." Louie says, which as me turning around, shocked that he would give him my number. What the fuck is he doing?

The guy in front of us rushes to grab a pen, then holds it over the back of his aftercare instructions, eager to write down what Louie gives him.

"Louie—" I start, but he ignores me.

"Okay, you ready?" The guy nods, a sick smile plastered on his face. Not wanting anymore to do with either of them I stomp away, but Louie's next words stop me.

"Her number is: She's the property of the Forsaken Sinners. If you so much as even *look* her way again, I will beat you so bad that your mama won't be even able to ID your body." His voice is even but the edge I hear makes me want to piss myself, and it wasn't directed at me. "You got that, boy?"

I turn around just as the guy stumbles over his words, his face white as a ghost. "Y-yes. Yes, s-sir." Then he takes off toward the door like the devil himself is after him.

"Oh, and one more thing." Louie says. "Don't ever come back here. You're done at this establishment."

After the door closes, I thought Louie would immediately head back to his station, his good deed done, but he doesn't. He just stands there by my desk, looking anywhere but at me.

"What the hell was that?" I ask, trying to keep the fear and anger out of my tone. I never knew I could feel both at the same time, but I do in this moment. Fear after what I just witnessed and anger at what he did to me yesterday.

"That was me protecting what's ours," he says without looking my way.

When he looks at me after a few awkward moments, I see no remains of the aggression he just showed minutes ago. I only see remorse in his eyes. It's so unexpected that I'm speechless. From everything I heard about him before I met him, how he acted last night to me, and how he just threatened that guy, I didn't think he was capable of feeling remorse.

"I, uh...I want to talk to you about last night—apologize, really," he says slowly. I forget

189

about my previous question and his cryptic answer, all the fear I felt moments ago is gone, and now all I feel is anger.

"What? Did Toby put you up to this?" I ask calmly. It makes me mad that Toby thinks he needs to baby me or make people be nice to me. I want everyone who is part of the club to like me and be nice to me, but I want them to *want* to like me, and *want* to be nice to me, not because Toby is threatening them, or whatever it is he does to get his way.

"Toby didn't ask me to do anything. I feel bad about what I said last night and was planning to apologize before I even realized you had taken off on your own. Which, by the way, was really fucking stupid." I open my mouth to yell at him for calling me stupid, but he beats me to it. "And before you get all bent outta shape, I wasn't *calling* you stupid, I said what you *did* was stupid. There is a difference. I know I didn't act like it last night, but I care about you and don't want anything bad to happen to you." Now I'm stunned speechless again. He cares about me? But why? I'm nothing to him. Last night proved that much.

When I find my voice, I ask, "Why would it matter to you what happens to me, Louie? You don't even know me. Like you said last night, we aren't friends. We're barely even co-workers, and after last night, I'm sorry, but I just don't believe that you care about me or about what happens to me." He looks at me like it's simple, easy to understand.

"I know I don't know you, but Toby and Dani

know you, and that's good enough for me. And like I said, I'm sorry about what I did last night." Does he really think that because I'm friends with Dani and seeing Toby that that means he needs to be my friend or like me?

"Look, Louie, I appreciate your apology, but you don't need to be nice to me just because of Dani and Toby. Let's just go back to the way things were before last night, working quietly together. I'll stay out of your way and you won't talk to me. It's just easier this way."

I turn back to my computer to finish what I was doing, but Louie isn't done yet. "I'm not being nice to you because of them. I'm just saying that they trust you, so that means I want to trust you as well. It's not going to be an automatic friendship by any means. I know we have to work on it, the *both* of us, and I'm gonna fuck things up, it's what I do best. Just ask Toby." He laughs a little before getting serious again. "I don't do anything I don't want to do, none of us do, so when I say I care about you, I mean that. You can continue with the way things were, but eventually, you're going to have to let me in. You offered a shoulder yesterday, now I'm offering mine. Just think about it, okay?" I don't look up from the computer, but he doesn't linger, either.

This is all just a little too strange for my liking. I mean, why want to be my friend after being so mean and cold last night? Whatever. He can do what he wants, but it doesn't mean I'm gonna jump on the friendship train with him. Friendship takes a lot of work from both people, so I think we'll just see where this goes and then I can decide if he's genuine or not.

***

The next couple of hours go by without problems. Louie stays in his room unless he's walking a customer out and I stay at my desk, unless I'm taking a customer back to him or getting a drink from the break room.

It's weird, but I can feel the difference with Louie and me. Even before what happened last night, there was always this wall or something between us. I felt weird around him, like I needed to watch my step, but now it's like we're both working in harmony with each other. It's kind of nice, actually. I'm not worrying about what he thinks or if he's gonna snap at me again, I'm just doing what I need to do and not thinking about anything else. Even Louie seems more at peace with me, or maybe he's just good at putting on a front. Regardless, my day has been getting better, so I'm not gonna complain.

About an hour before closing, I pull my phone out of my purse to call Dani. I noticed that we're short on some supplies and was gonna put an order in, but don't want to do it without her approving it first.

I've had my phone on silent, so I wasn't aware of anyone trying to contact me. I have several missed calls; one from an unknown number, one from Dani, and a couple from Toby. I only have two voicemails though.

Deciding to check my messages before calling Dani back, I hit the button for my voicemail. The first message is from Dani. "Hey, girl. Just wanted to check in, see how you're feeling today. Give me a call later, maybe we can get dinner. Later, babe!"

The next message is from Toby. "Doll, I really wish you'd answer your phone, or at least text me to let me know you're okay. I know you're still upset about last night. I called Louie to make sure you were safe, but would really like it if you would call me 'cause I'd really like to hear your voice. I'm still at the club, so if I'm not there by the time you get off work, Louie or the prospect will be staying with you till I can get there. I love you, always." Just hearing his voice brings back all the turmoil I felt last night. I have a lot to think about, but don't want to get into it right now. That personal conversation with myself is for a night I'm alone, preferably with a bottle of wine.

Next, I notice the text messages from Toby.

Toby: Hey, doll. Just wanted to see how your day was going.

Toby: Still at the club. Miss you.

Toby: Wish you'd answer me back, but at least I know you're safe. I'm sorry about last night. I really hope you can forgive me. Please text me back. I love you, always.

Figuring I should let him know I got his messages and quell his worry, I text him back.

Me: I'm fine, Toby. I just need time. <3

I want so badly to tell him I love him too, but for now the heart will have to do.

It's not that I don't love him anymore. I'm not sure there is anything he could do to make me not love him. But I need to figure out what is best for me, and to do that, I need to keep a level head and as much distance as this shitty situation will allow.

Dialing Dani's number, I wait for her to answer. "Hey, babe. I was just thinking about you," Dani says as soon as she answers. I laugh.

"Well, you know what they say about great minds. Anyway, I was going through some of the inventory and noticed that we're running low on some things. Did you want me to put in an order for you?"

"Yeah, I think that's a good idea. Do you need me to come down and help you with it, or do you have it covered?" I pull up the order document that I'd already done before calling her.

"I actually already have the order filled out. I was just waiting for your approval. I can go ahead and send it now and CC you on it too so you'll have it," I say proudly. I've been trying to learn as much as possible about all the things Dani does here so hopefully I can help her out a lot more, especially once the baby comes.

"Oh my God, you are amazing. Yes, go ahead and send it out, though you don't need to CC me. They usually send me a copy once they ship anyway." I hit the send button as she continues to talk. "Oh, while I've got you on the phone, I called earlier but you must have been busy. I was thinking maybe you could come over and hang out for a bit tonight. Zane said he could pick you up, or maybe Louie can bring you by after close?"

I don't really want to go over there, especially if Blaze is going to be there, but how do I say that without hurting Dani's feelings? "Actually, I'm not sure. I'm pretty tired and was just going to head upstairs and go to bed. Maybe another night?" It's not completely a lie because I am tired. The last couple of days are starting to drag me down, so even though I wasn't planning on it initially, it sounds like a good plan now.

"Oh, uh, okay. Sure. Another day then," Dani says sadly.

I've never really heard her sound sad before. I've heard her angry, I've heard her upset, and of course I've heard her happy, but I don't recall a time that she's ever really been sad. Knowing I'm the cause of it doesn't sit well with me, not one bit.

"I guess I could stop by for a little bit, but I don't want to be out long," I concede. Maybe she'll be okay with that compromise, though I hope I don't have to see Blaze. That would be weird.

Dani instantly becomes happy again. "Great! I wanted to show you some things I picked up for the baby. I'll order some pizza, then maybe after we're done eating Toby will be done at the club and he could take you home." Not sure I want Toby to take me home but knowing it's probably for the best, I agree. Toby would be better than Louie or Blaze any day. The least amount of time I have to spend with either of them, the better. I know I can't get out of seeing Louie since I work with him, and Toby, of course, will be with me every night at some point. But Blaze? Now he's someone I don't care to see.

"I'll message Toby to let him know what I'm doing and to pick me up when he's done. I should be done here in about an hour. Do you think you could call one of the prospects to pick me up?" I ask, but before Dani can answer me, I hear Louie behind me.

"No need. I'll take you." I turn around to tell him it's no problem, but he cuts me off. "I'm taking you, end of discussion." Knowing there will be no getting out of it, I just nod and watch him walk into the back.

"Okay then. I'll see you when you get here." With that, she hangs up and I get back to work, almost wishing I could work longer.

When we're ready to close up, Louie walks up to my desk. "You ready to go?" he asks nicely.

"Yeah, I'm just powering everything down. I can meet you out back," I say without looking up from my computer. Maybe if I give him the cold shoulder or act like a bitch long enough, he'll revert back to his old self around me, but realistically, is that what I really want? No, not really.

He doesn't say anything, but after a couple of seconds, he finally heads toward the back. Thank goodness. I hate it when people just stand there and watch me as they wait for me. Grabbing my purse, I make sure the front door is locked, turn off all the lights, and head out back to meet up with Louie.

When I walk outside, I don't see him right away

'cause he's not by his bike. Then I hear a door slam a little further down the lot and notice someone getting out of a truck. Wait, that's Toby's truck. What's he doing here? He didn't reply back to my message about me going to Dani's and him possibly picking me up, but I didn't think that was because he'd be picking me up here.

Just as I'm about to question him, I notice that it's not Toby, but Louie.

"Why do you have Toby's truck? Something wrong with your bike?" It's not like I haven't ridden on a bike before, so I'm not sure why he would feel the need to get the truck instead of just taking his bike.

"No, there's nothing wrong with my bike." He closes the door behind me once I'm inside the truck. When he gets in on his side, I look at him, waiting for him to elaborate, but I get nothing.

For some reason, I'm bothered by this and want to know, so I ask again. "So, if there isn't anything wrong with your bike, why are we using Toby's truck?" He's quiet as he pulls out of the parking spot.

Once we're on the highway, he finally answers. "Because it would be disrespectful to Toby to have you ride behind me on my bike. I don't know how much Toby has told you about club laws, but that's one of them. Once a brother has laid claim to a woman, she shouldn't be on the back of anyone's bike but her old man's." That's interesting. Toby hasn't told me much about the "laws," but we've spoken a little about their way of life. I guess he hinted about different rules, but we haven't gone over them in detail.

"But wait a minute. You said she *shouldn't* be on the back of anyone's bike, except for the man who's claimed her. As in, it's not really a law?" I'm actually curious about this, not trying to be a smart ass. I find it kind of fascinating the way the club lives and thinks.

Louie glances at me for a few seconds. He must see the curiosity in my eyes because he laughs a little before answering me. "No, it's not a *law*. More like a rule of thumb, or a code between brothers. Like I said, it would be disrespectful, so I told him I was borrowing his truck." I nod and think about what he's said. I guess I can see how it would be considered disrespectful to a brother if he saw the woman he was seeing on the back of another brother's bike. I've never even seen Dani on any of the guys' bikes, but I guess I just assumed that was because she was pregnant, but maybe it's because of the same reason I'm not riding behind Louie right now.

We make it to Dani's house in what seems like no time at all. As soon as we pull up, instead of keeping the engine running, Louie surprises me by turning the engine off and getting out of the truck. Before I can even gather my stuff and open my door, he's already there.

Hopping down from the truck, I walk beside Louie. Without even knocking, he just walks right in. "Yo, where's my beer, bitch?" Even though the words sound cruel, I can tell by the smile on his face and the tone of his voice that he's messing around. Dani confirms my suspicions when she walks into the room smiling.

"Go get your own beer, bitch!" she yells back before coming up to him and giving him a hug.

After she lets him go, he goes off to get a beer and find Blaze, I would guess, and Dani walks up to me. "You look nice," she says before pulling me in for a hug as well.

When she releases me, I look down and laugh. I'm wearing an old pair of jeans and an old t-shirt. "If I look nice, then you look like the Queen of fucking France." That has us both cracking up.

Heading into the kitchen, she asks if I want a beer. I nod and wait while she grabs a bottle for me and a bottle of water for herself, then we head out back where they have a porch swing set up. It looks cozy and relaxing.

We're both quiet for a couple of minutes, just swinging and enjoying our drinks. "So, do you want to talk about what happened yesterday?" Dani asks, finally breaking the silence.

Not really in the mood to talk about it, I shake my head. "Not right now, if that's okay?" I don't look at her, just down at my lap while I pick at the label on my beer bottle. She reaches over and places her hand over mine, stopping me.

"Of course it's okay, but I'm here when you're ready to talk about it. You can tell me anything and I won't judge, I promise."

Finally looking up at her, I smile and squeeze her hand. "Thanks. Why don't you show me the baby stuff you were talking about?" She's instantly giddy, which is another thing I've never seen Dani be, and grabs my hand before leading me inside the house and up the stairs.

CHAPTER 15

Toby

I'm still staring at the computer screen, waiting for something to pop out at me, something I missed to show me where this fucker is hiding. I've never had so much trouble finding someone before, and this dickhead is supposed to be an amateur, at least that's what we're assuming, anyway.

It's quiet in here, just the way I like it, but the quiet suddenly vanishes when Tom Tom comes barreling into the room. "We've got a lead. He was spotted a couple of towns over, heading into a strip club." I stand up as soon as he says he's got a lead. It's about fucking time.

As I grab my jacket, I say, "I want someone on him. Make sure he doesn't leave." Tom Tom nods and puts his phone to his ear.

Going down the hall, I open the door to Mack's office to let him know we're rolling out, but he's not alone. Our "house mom," KitKat, is currently on her knees in front of Mack, bobbing her head to a fast rhythm up and down his dick. "Sorry, Pres, but we got a lock on him. Tom Tom and I are heading out. Blaze and Louie are with the girls now, but I'm gonna send them an update to let them know to keep them there until we have the fucker." It wasn't my intention to interrupt and cut off his happy time, but he pushes Kat aside, not nearly as rough as he would have if it were any other club whore, and stands.

"I'll notify Blaze and Louie, but I want to roll heavy. Get every other available brother ready to ride in five," Mack says as he rights himself, buckling up his pants.

I leave his office and let Tom Tom know the plan, then head into the main room to see who's here.

Five minutes later, we're rolling out of the clubhouse. There's seven of us total; Mack, Skinner, Tom Tom, Slayer, Lyle, Ryan the prospect, and myself. We should have no problem getting our hands on him and neutralizing any problems that may arise.

The only thing that makes us nervous is that this is the first time we've gotten a lock on him. We have no idea if he's playing alone or if he brought someone else in. We know he has money, so he could easily pay some muscle to help carry out whatever plan he has, and we know he has a plan. Otherwise, he wouldn't be here anymore—he'd be home.

Regardless, with the seven of us, I know we'll be able to handle whatever comes at us. It'll be a piece of cake—even if this is a fucking trap, which it very well could be.

***

It took us only about thirty minutes to reach the town where Rick was last seen, a couple of minutes to find the strip club he was supposed to be at, and less than a minute to figure out he was no longer there.

"You have got to be shitting me! Which dipshit was supposed to keep his eye on him and make sure he didn't get away?" I yell at Tom Tom. I can't fucking believe we were this fucking close to having him, and now he's gone—again. Who knows when he'll turn up next.

Tom Tom looks pissed off as well, but tries to hide it, probably because he can tell I'm hanging on by a thread. "I called in a favor to a guy I used to hack for. He said he was close and would keep me posted," he says.

"Yeah? And where the fuck is this guy now, huh? Some fucking favor." I am beyond reason and not watching my tongue anymore. We should've fucking had him and we don't.

"All right, just calm the fuck down, Toby. Tom Tom, call your guy and find out what happened. Skinner, take Slayer with you and talk to everyone inside, show them the picture and see if they remember anything useful. Lyle, head back. I want you at the door for the next couple of days in case he stops by our strip club. I don't know why he came here, but it can't be as simple as him needing a little peep show. Take Ryan with you to help out,"

Mack orders.

After everyone leaves and does his bidding, it's just me and him. "Call and check on the girls and let the boys know what's going on. I'm gonna put some calls out to surrounding clubs to have them keep an eye out. I think it's time to bring more allies in."

As much as I don't like the idea of relying on anyone other than my brothers, I know that it's a good decision. The more eyes we have out for Sara's ex, the easier it should be to track him down. Maybe we should even call in reinforcements from a few of our other chapters. We could use the extra men to find him faster.

Walking over to my bike, I take out my phone and dial Blaze.

He picks up after the first ring, probably waiting for an update. "You got him?" he asks as soon as he answers.

"No," I growl into the phone. "Tom Tom's man is nowhere to be found and neither is that fucker, Rick." I hear Blaze shuffling around or moving, hopefully somewhere away from the girls so they don't hear. We didn't want to worry or upset them so we didn't even tell them we had a lock on him.

"Son-of-a-bitch. What's the plan now?" he asks.

I give him the rundown of what's going on here and what we're gonna do now. "How are the girls?" I ask, hoping they're still none the wiser.

"They're upstairs looking at baby shit," he tells me.

I laugh a little, even though I feel anything but happy.

"Of course they are. Anyway, you think you can keep Sara there till I get back? Not sure how long it's gonna be yet."

He's quiet for a little bit, which has me worried. Blaze is rarely quiet. Finally he says, "I'm not sure. I'll do my best, brother, but unless we tell her what's going on, it may look suspicious if I ask her to stay." He's got a point.

"Okay, well could you get Dani to keep her there?" I don't want her at home, even if Louie stays there with her. At least at Dani and Blaze's house, I know Louie and Blaze can protect them both better.

"Well, I could ask her, but you know Dani. She's gonna ask more questions than your girl would." Ugh, why does this have to be so fucking difficult?

"All right, just make sure Louie stays sharp. Everyone else is busy doing shit so it's just gonna be him." I know if it comes down to it, Louie will protect Sara with his life. I just hope it doesn't come down to that.

"She'll be fine. Just do what you gotta do and get back to her. I'll let you know when they leave and Louie will keep you updated on his end. Be safe," he says before he hangs up.

Making my way back toward Mack, I relay my conversation with Blaze. "The girls are safe, so let's get to work on our end," he says, then I follow him into the club to help question people.

***

Two and a half hours later, we have no

205

information. No one even noticed Rick coming inside here, and none of the cameras were live so we can't even look to see what he was doing here. Shit, maybe it wasn't even him in the first place, or it could have been a ploy to get us away from Sara. Blaze messaged me about a half hour ago, saying that Sara was still at his house, which surprises me, but makes me feel a lot better. I know she'll be safe there.

Lyle checked in about an hour ago, telling us that the club is clear and he'll stand guard at the door for the rest of the night. He has the prospect sweeping the inside to make sure nothing is missed. If that fucker tries to enter our club, we'll have him.

Tom Tom hasn't been able to reach his guy that was supposed to be here, so we've decided to put word out that we're looking for him too. As soon as we find him, we'll question his loyalty and know why the fuck he wasn't where he said he would be. It's because of him that we may have lost our opportunity to grab Rick, *if* he was here.

With nothing else to do here, we decide to head back home.

Sitting on my bike, I pull out my phone to send a group message to Blaze and Louie before we hit the road.

Me: On my way. Should be there in 30.

Once on the road, I take the time to think about what I should say to Sara if she asks if we have anything on her ex yet. I want to keep her informed as much as I can so she knows the danger is real and to watch her back, even though we have someone with her at all times. I don't want to give her too much to frighten her, but I can't *not* tell her anything because I promised her if we had anything, I'd tell her. Then I think, technically, we don't have anything, so maybe it would be all right to not say anything?

I also think about what I should do to get her to forgive me for how I acted. I knew it wasn't going to be as simple as just telling her I was sorry, but I didn't think she'd still be this distant, or say that she needs more time to think about everything. I just don't get it. She knows I love her and that I was just worried that something had happened to her. Why is she still mad at me?

When I'm about five minutes from town, it finally dawns on me. Everything that she lived through with her ex has shaped her into the woman I love today, but it has also shown her what she doesn't want in her life.

I came across as angry, and even though she knows I would never hurt her, I've made her doubt me. How could I be so fucking stupid and blind? I was so quick with my anger, and though I wasn't meaning to direct it at her, but at what she *did*, that's not how she saw it.

If that's what's going on in her head, I have a lot to make up for. I don't care if it takes me years to prove I'm the right man for her, I'll do whatever I need to make her see I would never hurt her.

Pulling up outside of Blaze and Dani's house, I cut the engine on my bike and hurry up the walk. I need Sara in my arms, if only to reassure myself that she's here and that she's all right.

As soon as I get up the stairs, Blaze and Louie are already there with the door open, waiting for me. "So?" Louie asks.

"Nothing new. Mack is calling in some favors, asking people to keep an eye out. I don't particularly like it, but we need more ears to the ground and people watching out for him. He's also going to tell some of our sister chapters about what's going on, see if any of them can spare some men to come help us out. Hopefully with the extra eyes and man power we can find him again so we can make the grab," I say the last part through clenched teeth. I just want the fucker found and taken care of so Sara doesn't have to worry about him anymore.

"We also have eyes out for the guy Tom Tom called in. Since he wasn't there and obviously didn't hold Rick for us, we want to know what the fuck happened. Not sure if he was compromised, or if he was taken out, but we want to bring him in to figure it out. If he's a problem, we'll have to deal with him too. Tom Tom isn't too happy right now." That's actually an understatement, but they know him as well as I do. You don't bail when someone cashes in a favor.

They both nod. "So what's the plan? What do you need from us?" This comes from Louie.

"Well, I'm not sure if you're scheduled every day, but I need you to be there, regardless if you're working or not. I want you in the shop and close to Sara at all times. If Dani is there, you'll stick close to both of them. I don't see Rick targeting Dani alone, so until we decide differently, your main goal is Sara. I also want you close after hours if that's at all possible. I'll be staying inside the apartment with her, but it may not be a bad idea for you to be inside as well, or at least in the shop or outside. We'll rotate people to help you, but I want you close to her at all times until we finish this." He nods his approval, so I move to look at Blaze.

"Like I said, I don't think Dani is a target, but I want to be safe, so keep her close and make sure she's carrying. When she's with Sara, I want at least four men on them at all times. When they're not together, Blaze, I think just you being with Dani is enough for now. Our main concern is Sara. We need to make sure she's covered." Blaze doesn't look too happy, but he agrees.

"I also want to get Sara trained to use a gun. Maybe we can bring it up around Dani and they can go together. Dani can give her a rundown. Other than that, let's just keep our eyes open and be ready. If you see the fucker around but he's not making a move, let's get a tail on him until we come up with the best plan of action to remove the threat. But if he makes a move, do whatever it takes to take him out before he gets close to either of the girls. You got me?" I look them both in the eye and see a mutual understanding. I know they won't let me down.

With all of that out of the way, I ask, "What are the girls doing now?" This question has Blaze smirking and Louie fidgeting.

Blaze is the one who answers. "They're still upstairs looking at all the baby shit Dani made me buy and talking about planning a baby shower, or some shit. I don't fucking get it, man. She's barely a few months along and we don't even know if it's a boy or girl, yet she has me buying everything under the fucking sun for the kid. If she keeps this up, I'm gonna have to take up another job to pay for all this shit." He's still smiling, so I know he's not really pissed off, just a bit irritated.

I laugh with him and smack him on the back as we head inside. "When's the big day to find out what you're having?" I ask, knowing he's excited to prove it's a boy. We all think it's a girl, mainly because we think it would be funny as fuck to see him carrying around pink shit. I can't even imagine how protective he'll be if it's a girl though. Heaven help her, that's all I can say. One overprotective caveman for a father and big, scary bikers for uncles.

"We can find out in about a month, I think. Dani's been playing with me, saying she doesn't want to find out the sex until she delivers, but fuck that shit. I need time to prepare." Walking into the house, I can hear the girls laughing upstairs and it's music to my ears.

My girl. She deserves the sun and moon on a fucking platter. I would do anything, buy her anything her heart desired, if it meant she'd be happy and I could hear her laugh like this all the fucking time.

We walk quietly up the stairs, hoping to catch the girls in a rare moment, when they're carefree and not worried about anything.

At the top of the stairs, I hear Dani say to Sara,

"Do you want kids?" I'm shocked by the question, but I find myself eagerly awaiting her answer. I've never really thought about having kids, but with Sara, I would have a hundred if that's what she wanted. I don't know if I'll be a good father, but for her and our babies, I'd die trying.

"Oh God, I have no idea. I used to think so, but now I'm not really sure."

"Well, I think you would make a great mother, and Toby would be an amazing father," Dani says quietly, but with certainty.

Sara laughs. "And who says if I have children that it would be with Toby?" My whole body goes stiff and I can feel my temper flare. I'm not angry at her, I'm angry at the idea of her being with anyone besides me and that she doubts me so much that she would even consider that we won't be together to have kids when the time comes. Never fucking happening.

I take a step to interrupt them, but Dani speaks again before I make it to the door. "Oh, come on. I've seen you two together. You may be fighting or whatever now, but you and Toby…you two look to me like that forever kind of love." As much as I want to hear how Sara will reply, I'm also scared to know, so I knock on the door to make my presence known.

"Hey, doll. You ready to head home?" Sara looks up at me and blushes, but I'm not sure if it's from embarrassment or lust.

They're both sitting on the floor in front of a bare crib. Sara stands, then helps Dani up after her. "Yeah, I didn't realize it was so late," she says as she looks at her watch.

When she walks by me to head out the door, I grab hold of her hand and lace my fingers with hers before leaning down and kissing her head. "I missed you today," I whisper so only she can hear me. She doesn't say anything, but I could hear her quick intake of breath. I hope it's because she likes to hear that I miss her, and because she missed me too.

At the bottom of the stairs, we say our goodbyes to Dani and Blaze, then head over to my bike. Louie is right behind us, but goes directly over to my truck. I'm happy to know that he didn't put my girl on the back of his bike.

Once Sara is behind me, I squeeze her leg before starting my bike. Revving the engine, I look behind me and smirk. "Hang on, doll," then I peel out onto the road and head toward the highway. Once there, I really open her up. Sara once told me that she loves the feeling of being on the back of my bike and going fast. It scares her, but it also makes her feel free, and I'll always give my girl what she wants.

***

Five days later and we still haven't gotten shit on Rick. After that one lead, he's gone dark again. On top of that, Sara is still acting funny around me and the guys. Dani's even noticed a change in the way she acts around *her*.

I'm grasping at straws here, but last night, a conversation I had with her at the beginning of our relationship came to mind. We were talking about our childhoods, well, she was, and she mentioned a dog she had growing up. She said that when she got older, she wanted to get a dog, but she just never got the chance to do it.

I talked with Dani this morning and she's fine with Sara having a dog in the apartment, even said she could bring the thing to work with her if she wanted.

After calling around to shelters and pet stores all morning, I finally found a dog that I think will be perfect for her. He's a Chihuahua mixed with some Dachshund. He was rescued from an abusive owner a couple months ago; severely malnourished and afraid of his own shadow, but after being nursed back to health and cared for by a foster family, he's finally ready to be adopted.

I'm heading to the shelter today to pick him up, but first, I need to stop and pick up supplies we'll need for him at the apartment.

When I arrive at the shelter, I notice that they have him out and ready to go.

I approach him slowly, holding my hand out so he can smell me. I've done some quick research and know that when dealing with a dog that was abused, you need to take things slow, get them to trust you. Sometimes it can take months, years even, but sometimes they can sense a good soul. I think that's what happened today. He was hesitant for only a couple of minutes, then wouldn't leave me alone.

I sign all the paperwork and load him up in my truck. Before heading back home, I look at him sitting in the passenger seat. "What are we gonna name ya, buddy?" The people at the shelter and the foster family he was staying with was calling him

Rex, but he's not attached to it they said, so we could change it if we wanted to. I was going to let Sara name him, but I think it will be better if he already has a name when I give him to her.

"What about Butch?" He just stares at me. "Okay, not that one. Hmmm…Spike?" He yawns, so I take that as a no. "How about Oliver? I used to have a friend named Oliver when I was growing up. We called him Ollie, but he moved away and I heard years later he was killed overseas." I don't know why I'm explaining this to a dog, but I am.

He must like the name because he starts barking like crazy and I laugh. "Okay, okay, settle down. Oliver it is." He actually looks smug.

When I pull up outside of Sara's apartment, I grab Ollie and head into the shop. She should still be working and Dani's here today, and I know she was excited to meet the dog when I told her about it. I think she just wants to see the reaction Sara gives when she sees me with a dog.

Since I came in the back, I have a clear view of the front room where Sara is before she even realizes I'm there. Dani saw me walk through, so she drops what she's doing to come out front.

Before I have a chance to say anything or grab Sara's attention, Ollie decides to start barking, which makes Sara jump about ten feet before turning around to see where the noise is coming from. When she sees me, I think she's stunned at first. I let Ollie down on the floor and he takes off, heading directly to where Sara is sitting at her desk.

The dog wags his tail the whole way, so hard he almost tips himself over. It makes me laugh, which has Sara lifting her confused gaze from the dog to me. "W-who's dog is this?" she asks in a quiet voice.

Walking up to her, I pick Ollie up and rub his ears. "This little guy is Oliver, Ollie for short. I adopted him today from a local shelter. He was rescued a couple months ago from an abusive owner. I know you said that you wanted a dog, so I got Ollie for you." She has tears in her eyes, but still doesn't say anything so I continue, "I wanted to give you something that you didn't have, but wanted. I wanted it to be something that would give you roots here, something that would make you happy and show you how much I love you. I'm sorry for making you doubt me."

Now her tears are falling in full force, so I pull her into my arms. "Shh, don't cry, doll." This only makes her cry harder, but then Ollie starts licking her face, which has her tears turning into laughs. I knew getting him would be a good thing.

She takes the dog from my arms and sits back down with him. "Hello, Ollie. I'm Sara. You and I, we got a lot in common, you know. We both came from a shitty place, but we were both rescued by Toby over there." She looks over at me at that last part and smiles. "He's an amazing guy, isn't he?" Ollie barks in answer, which has Sara looking back at him. "You and me, we're gonna be all right. We're both finally where we belong."

CHAPTER 16

Sara

It's been almost a month since Toby brought Ollie home, and even though I fell in love with him instantly, I love him more each day. He's like my baby and best friend mixed into one. I take him everywhere with me. Thankfully, Dani's okay with me bringing him to work because I just can't find it in my heart to leave him alone.

I actually can't believe how amazing Ollie is. Toby told me about how he was rescued from an abusive owner, but looking at him now, you would never know. I'd like to think that if someone didn't know the hell I went through, that they would think the same thing about me.

Having Ollie makes me think things will finally be better for me; that we'll be able to fix the problem with Rick and not have to worry about him anymore, and that things with Toby will get back to the way they were before things took a shit. I also hope that I'll become more at home within the club.

I want to feel like I belong here, and I think I'm finally starting to.

Things with Toby have been getting better since then as well. After we went home that night, we sat down and had a long talk. I told him I understood that he was worried and angry I left, but the way he acted reminded me of the way things were with Rick. He wasn't happy about me comparing him to my ex, but I think he understood on some level too, and maybe even agreed with me.

He promised that no matter how worried or upset he was about something, whether it had to do with me or not, he would do better to not take it out on me or be so quick to anger. I, in turn, promised that I wouldn't take off again on my own, and if I felt the need to have some alone time, I would at least take a guard to have someone close by if needed. He wasn't happy with that at first, telling me that I shouldn't be alone for any reason, but I was firm that sometimes it's necessary. He finally caved.

As far as I know, we haven't gotten any word on Rick's whereabouts, but it's not for lack of trying. Toby told me they have recruited some outside help to keep eyes out for him. I can tell he isn't happy about that, but if it means keeping me safe and finding him faster, then he would get over it.

Since everyone has been working non-stop— Dani and I at the shop with Louie always nearby, and everyone else in the club working hard to find Rick—we decided that since today was a Sunday, we all deserved a day to relax and just enjoy each other's company, so we're having a BBQ at the clubhouse.

I've been there with Toby a few times in the past month, but only for an hour at the most. I'm a little nervous about being there all day, unsure of who will be there, but I feel more comfortable in my relationship with Toby, and the whole club, for that matter. At least the couple of times I've been there Trixie wasn't around, so maybe she won't be there today.

After Louie's apology, he's been on my ass about getting over that night at the shop and what was said between us. At first, I was determined to keep my distance, but he's gradually wearing me down. It probably helps that he's been like my shadow, always with me. He's become my personal guard when Toby isn't around. Shit, even when Toby's with me, Louie's still nearby. He's actually a big goofball, and I can see why Dani considers him one of her best friends.

I still don't like to be around Blaze, but at least he doesn't seem as hostile toward me anymore. He hasn't necessarily apologized, but his actions have shown that he understands this wasn't my fault. He still doesn't like the fact that Dani and I hang out or when I'm working at the shop and she's there, but he doesn't say anything anymore about me putting her in danger. Maybe he's just lulled by the fact that there are always at least two brothers with us, guarding us, at all times.

Things with Dani and Blaze seem to be better as well. I think since he hasn't outright demanded her to stop being around me or isn't telling her what to do as much, is helping with that though. One thing about Dani, she doesn't take demands from anyone.

Toby interrupts my thoughts when he comes into the kitchen. "You about ready?" he asks. I've been baking up a storm this morning and making some cold salads to bring to the BBQ. To me, if you don't have brownies and at least a couple macaroni salads it's not really a BBQ. Some people say the meat makes the gathering, but I think it's all the extras on the side. You can grill anything at any time, but unless you have goodies and side dishes, it's not really a party, at least in my opinion.

"Yeah, just let me put the brownies on a platter and put the salads in bowls with lids and I'll be ready," I say as I start cutting the brownies into squares so I can place them nicely on a party platter I picked up at the store last night.

He walks into the kitchen and wraps his arms around me. "You look sexy in that dress," he says huskily. I laugh shyly and push him away a little so I can run my hands down my dress, smoothing out any wrinkles.

When he looks over my shoulder and sees the brownies, he says in a gravelly voice close to my ear, "I think we should just leave those here. I'm pretty sure no one at the club likes brownies, so I wouldn't want them to go to waste." His warm breath in my ear makes me shiver, but I do my best to shake it off, knowing he's trying to distract me.

"Nice try, Bubba, but not gonna happen," I say with a laugh.

I hear him groan before turning me around to face him. "Ah, come on, doll. Those assholes don't deserve your treats," he pouts. A true fucking pout.

"You just want to keep them all for yourself."

219

Feeling him move one of his hands, I turn my head to make sure he doesn't grab any of the brownies, but he stops me with a steamy kiss. Forgetting about the brownies, I wrap my arms around his neck and pull him in closer to me. His lips are soft and hard at the same time. I could live off his taste alone.

Before things get too out of hand and we never make it to the BBQ, I reluctantly pull away. "As much as I want to stay here and kiss you all day, we need to get going. You deserve a day to relax and have some fun, and Dani wants to show me some new baby stuff she bought yesterday. So, if I'm not there, I'll never hear the end of it."

I move away from him just as he steps to the side. "I forgot that uh, Dani said she left a sweatshirt here. I'm gonna check in the bedroom for it." He doesn't turn around to look at me when he speaks, just keeps walking toward the bedroom. It's a little suspicious, but I decide to let it go.

A couple minutes later, I'm finished putting the brownies on the platter and have the cold salads in containers.

As I'm walking into the living room with everything in hand, Toby comes out of the bedroom empty handed. "Didn't find the sweatshirt?" I ask, still a little suspicious.

"What? Oh, uh, no, I didn't. She must not have left it here after all," he says slyly.

When he notices all the food in my hands, he comes over to help by reaching for the platter of brownies. "Here, let me help." As he reaches out, I notice something on the corner of his mouth.

"What the hell," I say, more to myself than him. With him holding the brownies, I stack one of the salad bowls on top of the other and reach out to remove whatever is on his face. Pulling my hand away from him, I see what looks like brownie crumbs.

"How did that get there?" he asks, but I can see the guilt on his face. I almost laugh, but try to keep a stern face as I grab the brownies out of his hands and replace them with the salads.

"I think you better let me carry those. Wouldn't want any more to accidently end up on your face," I tell him. He looks at me sheepishly, but doesn't argue. Good man. "Come on, Ollie. Time to go," I call out and watch as he races toward the door.

Once we're downstairs with Ollie at our heels, we load everything up into his truck. With us bringing food and of course, my new puppy, it's just easier to take the truck instead of the bike, but I know he wishes we were on his bike. I almost offer to drive for him while he takes the bike, but then I remember that his bike isn't even here. Plus, I don't really want to pull up to the clubhouse by myself. I'm not ready for that yet, even though Toby would be right behind me.

With both of us sitting in our seats and Ollie secured beside me, Toby starts the truck. "Ready?" I nod, then we head to the clubhouse. When we get halfway there, Toby's phone rings. "Yeah?" he answers. I find it funny that he answers his phone like that, but I've learned that pretty much everyone around here does that, even Dani.

"Jesus, are you *trying* to be in the doghouse?" he

says into the phone.

He's quiet for a moment, then says, "Okay, man. We'll turn around and be there shortly. Hopefully having Sara with me will save me from hearing her bitch about you the whole way there." Toby laughs. "Good luck with that, brother." Once he hangs up the phone, he looks over to me. "Minor change of plans," he says as he turns the truck around, "Gotta go pick up Dani."

We pull up to their house and see Dani and Blaze outside arguing.

Stepping out of the truck, I wait for Toby at the front before heading up the walk. I notice Ollie standing on the center console, looking out the windshield. I smile at him and motion for him to sit and laugh when he doesn't obey. Yeah, we have a lot to work on with him, but I have no problem taking my time.

When we're closer, I can hear Dani yelling, "When the fuck are you going to stop treating me like I'm sick or disabled, huh? I'm fucking pregnant, you jackass!" Are they still fighting about this? I swear, it's the same damn thing with them. Most of the time, I agree with Dani. There's being protective and wanting to do what's best for your girlfriend and your unborn child, but the way Blaze goes about doing things, you'd think he likes making her mad. Either that, or he's just plain stupid and has a death wish.

Blaze stands his ground, looking just as mad. "And when the fuck are you going to realize that you're fucking pregnant and understand that you can't do everything you used to fucking do, huh?"

See? He has a point, but he's going about the wrong way.

"I know that I can't ride the fucking bike until after the baby is born, you dipshit. I don't need you to fucking remind me of this every fucking day. But what I don't get is why we don't just drive the truck to the clubhouse *together*? Toby drives his truck when it's needed, why can't you? You feel you have to ride the bike to make you look manlier? Well, newsflash, fucker. It makes you look like a chump having some other guy taking care of your girl." Uh oh.

I'm surprised though when Blaze just takes a deep breath, calming himself before he takes the last step that separates the two of them and takes her gently by the shoulders. "Baby Girl, why do you always have to get mad at me for wanting to make sure you and our baby are safe? I'm not doing any of this to make you mad, or because I don't want to take care of my girl. I'm doing it because I would fucking die if something happened to you or our child. So please, just please, listen to me when I say I love you and only want to keep you safe." Wow. That was completely unexpected. I've only ever known Blaze to be hot-headed, and frankly, kind of scary, but this…this is a side of Blaze I'm not sure anyone has ever seen before, besides Dani maybe.

Dani starts to cry. "It's okay, Baby Girl, I got you. I'm right here and not going anywhere," he says into her hair while rubbing her back.

When she calms down enough, she looks at him. "I'm sorry, Zane. I don't know what gets into me sometimes. I just want to be close to you, not have you pawn me off on someone else all the time." Blaze looks heartbroken at what she's just admitted.

"Dani, I'm not trying to pawn you off on someone else. I just need to make sure I have my bike at the clubhouse in case something goes down and I need it. Toby's is already there, that's why he's taking his truck. Please understand. I fucking love you and would never do anything on purpose that would make you feel like I'm trying to get away from you and our baby." Oh my God, Blaze is such a sweetheart. Who the fuck knew?

I don't even realize I'm crying until Toby pulls me closer to him and whispers, "You okay?" I just nod my head and wipe the tears off my face.

Toby and I turn around to give them a little privacy, but it's not long before they walk up to us. I smile softly at Dani to let her know I'm here for her, while Blaze looks sharply at Toby. "If you breathe a fucking word of what you just saw to anyone, I will fucking kill you. You got me?" Dani and I laugh quietly and wait for Toby's reply.

Toby is dead serious when he answers, "I got you, brother. I'm fucking pussy whipped by my girl too." Blaze looks at him for a second with a promise of pain, but then he laughs.

"That you fucking are, brother."

We all load up into the truck and head to the clubhouse with Blaze following us on his bike and Ollie hanging his head out my window with his tongue hanging out. Life is good.

***

Trixie

I'm sitting at the bar, waiting for all my carefully constructed chips to fall. I used to think this club was my home, my family, but now I know better. This club isn't anything but pussies and bitches. I look forward to the day that every person who is a part of this club, or has any connections to this club, rot in fucking hell.

When I first started sleeping with Toby, it was just a good time. Then, even I can admit, it was a ploy to move up within the club. I really liked Toby and the way that man can fuck. Yeah, I definitely wasn't hurting in the orgasm department with him.

But he was always so closed off; only came to me when he needed to let off steam or when he was drunker than usual. I thought I could wear him down, and for a little while, I thought I was well on my way to becoming his old lady, but then that bitch had to come to town and steal him away from me.

Things were bad enough when Dani got here and I wasn't even fucking the guy she was pretty much with, though I'm not gonna lie, I did try a couple of times to get Blaze to fuck me with no luck.

I had been with the club for a couple of years when she showed up. Mack had taken an instant liking to her and adopted her right away. Then she became close with Louie and Toby, which at the time wasn't a big deal to me. I was too busy just trying to stay afloat. But when I realized that the real respect came by becoming an old lady, I took a look at my options. There were really only a few.

I knew right away that there was no way in hell I would get Louie locked down. I wasn't stupid enough to think I could secure Mack with him being the president. Toby seemed like a better option, so I put all my effort into seducing him.

I started out small—being there for him whenever he needed anything, even a cold beer. I still slept with some of the other brothers because, well, I'm a club whore. I didn't really have a choice, but it's not like it was all that bad. Most of the brothers are good to me.

Then that cunt showed up and fucked everything all to hell.

I did everything I could to keep Toby interested in me, but once he had her, he didn't need a whore anymore.

After the showdown with Sara a couple months ago, I was even going to try and forget about Toby and find someone else to claim me. Of course I was pissed that years of work went to shit, but I wanted to be an old lady. I wanted the respect, the power it would bring. I was done being a club whore.

I fucked up one day when I was having a particularly bad day. I tried to steer Toby away from his bitch. To say I was threatened within an inch of my life is putting it very mildly. I was actually scared for the first time in years.

I was prepared to just pack up and leave, or just get used to my fate as a club whore for life, but then I got the break I had been looking for.

Sara's ex had been looking for her, I knew, but never thought I would meet him myself and be given the chance for revenge against all these assholes and that stupid bitch, all in one go.

Rick came by the club I worked at on the side of Club Sin about a month ago, trying to find people to help him with his plan of showing that bitch once and for all who she belonged to and teach her a lesson for leaving him.

I overheard him talking to a guy that I had seen a time or two, but didn't really know who he was. Deciding to introduce myself, I walked up to him and told him that I'd give him a free lap dance.

He was hesitant at first, but then when he got a look at all my goods he agreed. When we got into a private room, I told him I could get him close enough to Sara to take her, but I wanted something in return.

So we came up with the perfect plan, and I have a little something up my sleeve that will help me tremendously, blowing them all out of the water. They almost made this too easy for me to pull off. With the help of Rick too, of course. I can't fucking wait. Finally I'll have everything that should have been mine years ago.

CHAPTER 17

Rick

Today is the day, I can feel it. I can practically taste it. Today is the day I make Sara regret ever fucking leaving me. She is going to pay for the trouble she caused and for ruining what I've been working on for years. It should have never taken this long to begin with, but she was stronger than I originally thought when I spotted her all those years ago.

I had just moved to New York from Montana. I had been moving almost every few years, but it didn't bother me. It was a necessity for what I needed.

I was planning on taking a break once I got to New York. When I left Montana, there were a few suspicious authorities watching me, so it would probably be best if I laid low for a little bit, give everything time to cool down. But when I was at a bar after I finished unpacking my things into a shit apartment, I spotted Sara. She was sitting alone in a corner booth. I was instantly drawn to her, but I tried to stay away because I didn't need any heat on me at the time.

I followed her home that night, telling myself I was just curious, but I knew deep down she was going to be next. It might not be right away, but it would happen.

A couple of weeks later, I still couldn't get her out of my mind, so I decided to have a little fun. I approached her that day on the street, asking her out for coffee. She of course agreed, not being able to refuse my charm.

It didn't take me long to get her to become dependent on me, but I found I wanted more; I wanted to *own* her. I was no longer satisfied with my old schemes. I wanted to keep her a little longer, maybe even forever. There was just something about her. It was so much fun to have so much power over her. The way she would shrink back from me made me feel like I was her Master. The way it felt when my fist would connect with her flesh made me feel like I was her God. I didn't want to give that up, not yet.

So I gave myself a timeline. I would give myself five years to have her as my plaything. After that, I would carry out my plan, but then the bitch left me. She actually fucking left me. I don't know who the fuck she thought she was messing with, but if she thought I was just going to let her go, she was wrong—*dead wrong.*

It took me a while to find where she went, but once I had her location, I came for her. I didn't expect her to have friends already, thinking the way

I broke her down over the years would play in my favor. She had found a job and friends. A stupid friend who stood in my way of taking back what was mine.

After the run in at her work, I had to drop back for a while to consider my options and come up with a new plan. It wasn't going to be as easy as I thought to get her back in my possession, but it just made the game more thrilling for me. Sure, I was irritated and pissed off, but in the long run, this is the most fun I've had with a mark in a long time. She's making me work for it. I'll make her pay for all that hard work, of course, but no one ever said there wasn't thrill in the chase.

I was able to recruit a guy that has a grudge against the club that's protecting Sara. It was a lot harder than I thought possible to find willing participants to help me, but this guy actually came to me. He heard I was looking to move against the club and he wanted in. Of course, I'm not necessarily going against the club per se, but in his eyes, taking something or someone that the club feels belongs to them is enough of an act of war for him. Fine by me. He'll be the one to deal with the aftermath, not me, so it works out perfectly.

Then when that bitch Trixie pulled me into a private room at the strip club where I was meeting him, it turned out that I had more luck than I thought. She would provide the perfect way to get inside the club and get my hands on Sara, but she wanted something in return. She wanted her own revenge, but that also worked out perfectly for me. I was definitely game for what she offered.

We worked out a plan and have been waiting for the perfect time to execute it. Turns out, that may be sooner than I thought possible.

My burner phone vibrates in my pants.

Trixie: They just arrived at the club.

I'm so excited that this was really happening that I have to take a minute to calm myself before replying.

Me: Watch them. Wait until they are comfortable, then we'll put the plan into motion. Keep me posted.

She doesn't reply back, but I wasn't expecting her to. Now I just have to wait until I get word that everything is in place.

Soon, I'll have Sara back and be able to finish what I started when I first got to New York.

A couple of hours later, I finally got the text I'd been waiting months for.

Trixie: It's time...

***

Toby

Today couldn't have been better. There's nothing like hanging out with all my brothers and my woman at the club. Beer, BBQ, and brownies. Perfect fucking day if you ask me.

SHELLY MORGAN

When we first showed up at the clubhouse, I was a little worried about how the day would progress. I knew it was going to be more than just my brothers with Dani and Sara. Of course the club whores and a couple hang arounds would be there as well.

It's funny that hardly any of the brothers have an old lady. There's Blaze with Dani. Me with Sara. Lyle has a wife, but he barely brings her around the club. He likes to keep her separate, which is fine. We still go over and visit with her a couple times a month. She knows who we are and has never had a problem with the club or that Lyle is a part of it, but since she's a little older, like Lyle, they both just decided it's how they wanted it. That's really about it as far as permanent woman. It's never really been a problem. Not that it is now, but I just never thought about it before. To each their own, I guess. If a brother wants to take on an old lady, that's his business.

When I saw Trixie sitting at the bar when we pulled up, I stiffened, hoping she wouldn't start anything. I really wanted today to be a fun and relaxing day for Sara and I. Well, for everyone, really. Surprisingly, she kept her distance, and when she was close by, she was actually either quiet or friendly. Maybe my threat worked better than I thought it would. It's amazing how a few words can change things—for the good or bad. Thankfully, this time it was good for me.

Sara's been laughing and smiling all day. Not once have I seen her look uncomfortable, sad, or upset. It's so good to see her like this, unhindered by her past.

The past month has been kind of a struggle with us trying to adjust to having Ollie and her completely forgiving me for the way I acted that night I found her at the lookout, but I think we are finally on solid ground. The only thing that could make everything better is for us to find and take care of her ex, then things really would be perfect.

Mack walks up to me while I'm leaning against the back wall, just watching Sara interact with Dani and Louie. I'm actually surprised Louie has taken such a liking to Sara. "Looks good on ya," Mack says once he takes the same position I have against the wall.

Knowing exactly what he's talking about, I nod. "Yeah, feels good too." Feels too fucking good sometimes that I worry it will all get ripped away from me.

"She's a good girl. Fits in with everyone real nice too. Sometimes it's hard to find a woman that can handle our kind of life, but when you do, she's worth moving Heaven and Hell to keep her." I couldn't agree more. I would do more than just move Heaven and Hell, I'd tear them apart if that was what was keeping me from my girl.

After a couple minutes of silence, I see Lyle walk into the back of the clubhouse with a somber look on his face. Not liking that one bit, I head over to him with Mack hot on my heels.

Once I reach him, I ask, "Is there a problem?" I'm not sure what's going on. If it was something at the club or that we needed to act on, he would have just called.

"No, I just don't feel right leaving the club while

that dickhead is still out there," Lyle says. I'd laugh at the way his face is screwed up like he's constipated, but since he's genuinely worried, it's not a laughing matter, but he deserves some down time too. "The prospect's there, man. He'll let us know if there's any trouble, so don't worry about it. Go get yourself a beer and relax. We'll worry about everything else tomorrow," I say while I clasp my hand on his shoulder, hoping to relieve his worry a bit.

He hesitates for a couple of seconds, but then takes off toward the coolers we have set up by the picnic tables. Within five minutes, he seems to forget all his worry and is now laughing and talking with Dani, Louie, and Sara.

Needing to be close to her, I break away from where Mack and I were standing quietly and make my way over to them. "Hey, doll, miss me?" I say in her ear. I feel her shudder and know that all it takes is my voice to turn her into a shivering ball of need.

When she finally answers, it's barely a whisper. "Always," she breathes. I chuckle lightly at her response, but it's only to hide an almost giddy response to her reply. Fuck, I love this woman.

"Good answer."

We get caught up in good company and even better conversation. We talk about anything and nothing at all. Louie tells jokes, Dani gives smart-ass answers, Lyle laughs loudly, and Sara and I just stand quietly together, content with watching everyone else around us.

It's hard to believe six months ago I would have

been brooding at the bar while everyone else was outside having a good time. I hated being around a lot of people, especially when they were all happy go lucky. It's not that I wasn't happy for them, because I was, it was just that I didn't want to drag them all down with my cold attitude. I acted indifferent and distant, but really, I think I was just jealous and wishing I had what they had. Now I do and I couldn't be happier.

"Foods up!" Blaze yells across the yard. He's been manning the grill, cooking everything from brats and burgers to steak and chicken.

Dani instantly takes off toward the grill, but I can hear her clearly when she says, "It's about fucking time. I was about to wither away." We all laugh after her. She's definitely not shy about her need for food. She says it's because of the baby, but we all know better. She's never been one to turn away from a good meal. Shit, sometimes she could put away more food than one of the guys. She was the same way with her liquor, but at least now, she's stuck only eating the men under the table, which is fine by me. It's never fun having a small woman who's able to drink more than you. I should know, she's outdrank me a time or two.

We all give Dani free rein of getting her food first—no one wants to deal with a hungry pregnant chick—before we all line up and gather our own.

Sara and I sit with Dani and Louie at one of the picnic tables, and before long, Blaze joins us. "Did you get enough food, Baby Girl?" Blaze jokes to Dani. She levels him with a glare, but Blaze just smirks and digs into his food.

"Damn, Sara! These brownies are the shit!" Louie says through a mouthful of brownies. Sara laughs and pats him on the back.

"Careful there, Tiger. Don't want you to choke on it." She's taken to calling each of us different pet names. She's called me Bubba a few times. Louie is Tiger, Lyle is her Teddy Bear, Mack is Papa Bear, but Blaze is still Blaze. I asked her why once, and her reply was simple, "Because I can't think of a name that fits him yet."

When Louie is able to swallow his bite, he leans over and pulls Sara into his arms. "Marry me. Leave Toby and be with me. We can be happy together; you supply the brownies and I'll supply the laughter. We'll be the perfect couple. What do ya say?" I growl at him as Sara laughs.

"Sorry, Tiger, but I don't think that would work."

"And why the hell not?" Louie asks, looking sincerely upset over her answer. The fuck?

"Well, it would be kind of hard for you to supply the laughs and enjoy my brownies if you were dead, wouldn't it?" She's dead serious, which has me laughing loudly. Damn, this woman is something else.

Louie finally laughs and nods. "Yeah, you're right, but I expect brownies at least once a week at the shop. No arguments." Once she's able to settle down, she agrees.

"Anything you want. Just as long as you never suggest I leave Toby for you again." I've been quiet through most of this weird conversation, but decide now is the time to speak up.

"She can bring you brownies once a *month*, and if you ever ask her to marry you again, or suggest she be with you instead of me, I fucking promise you won't be able to walk for a long time. Got me?" I growl, but make sure they know I'm joking by smiling. Well, I'm mostly joking.

Through the laughter and cheery voices, a cell phone rings out. It's Lyle's. He steps away from the table to answer it and for some reason, I just know it's not good news. I watch him talking and I can tell I'm right by his rigid stance and the hard look on his face.

He's on the phone for less than a minute, but watching him, it feels longer.

When he makes it back to the table, he looks at Mack, Blaze, Louie, and me. "We need to talk," he says in a hard voice. We all stand up and head into the clubhouse. The rest of the brothers that were at different tables or standing around, notice and follow suit. Once we are all in the chapel, Lyle speaks. "That was Ryan. Rick is at the club. He's got him detained in the office."

"All right, everyone load up. We ride out in five." All my brothers start to file out of the room, but I stop Mack, Skinner, Louie, and Blaze before they leave. "I'm taking lead once we get to the club. I'm sorry, Mack, I mean no disrespect or anything, but this is my fight. When we have that fucker in our grasp, he's mine," I say in a hard voice.

I look only at Mack, but I can see out of the corner of my eye that Blaze and Louie are looking back and forth between us. I'm sure they're surprised by what I said, but this is about my woman, so it's my responsibility to take care of it. I'm sure if it were Dani, Blaze would be doing the same thing. I appreciate and am grateful to have my brothers behind me in this, but when that piece of shit takes his last breath, it will be because I made it happen. I'm going to make him pay for every word that cut like a knife, every touch that broke her skin, and every vile thought he had about my girl.

Mack finally speaks up. "All right, when we get to the club, Toby, it's your call on how we go about doing this, but you can bet your ass I'm pulling you out if your head's not right in this. You got me?" He looks me straight in the eyes. A lesser man would have shrunk back, but not me. I nod my head, even though I will do anything in my power to make sure it's my hand that delivers the blow that takes his life.

Next, he looks to Louie. "Louie, I want you here with the girls, just in case. We'll keep in touch with what's going on at the club. If you see any sign of trouble here, call." Everyone nods and we all head out to where the girls are outside.

I take Sara off to the side and pull her into my arms. "I gotta go, doll. Be good and listen to Louie, okay?" She looks worried but she doesn't question me.

"Okay. Be safe." With that, I kiss her hard on the lips, then walk toward my bike.

This ends tonight. Either way, I'm ending this. If that means I have to beat everyone in that club within an inch of their lives to get the information I need, so be it, but I'm hoping the dipshit is just fucking stupid and thought with us all at the clubhouse, he could just waltz into our strip club and not be caught.

Starting tomorrow, Sara will no longer have to worry about her ex coming for her. Starting tomorrow, we can begin a new chapter in our lives. Starting tomorrow, there will be no one or anything that will stand in the way of our happiness.

Seeing all my brothers saddled up and ready to ride, I nod to each of them, firm in the knowledge that each of them will stand beside me through anything, even if it's to the end. I love each of my brothers, and it makes me so thankful I have a family that will do whatever it takes to make sure my woman is safe from harm.

Revving our bikes up, we file out one by one, each of us following our president. I hope that by the end of this night, we'll be back at the clubhouse for one hell of a celebration, but for now, it's fucking game time.

CHAPTER 18

Sara

After Toby and the boys left, Louie came over and told us he wanted us all inside. I spot Ollie running around the yard, and since he's not hurting anything or anyone, I decide to leave him outside. I'll grab him after Toby gets back.

The only people who are really left are Dani, Louie, Trixie, and a couple other women that I'm assuming are also club whores, and myself, of course.

Dani and I get comfortable on a couch and just sit quietly. I can't help but have a bad feeling about what's going on. I know it has something to do with Rick, but I was too scared to confirm that with Toby, but what else would they be doing? As far as I know, they don't really have a lot of problems that would force them all to ride out like that. The expression on all the men's faces looked like they were all riding off to war. It was a scary sight.

I'm really glad Louie is the one to stay with us,

though. He and I have gotten close these past couple of weeks. After realizing he wasn't going to give up, I finally let my guard down and as it turns out, he's a really great guy. He's almost like big kid with his goofball ways and stupid jokes. He's always making me laugh and feel carefree, but protected and cared for at the same time. He's come to mean a lot to me.

Louie comes into the bar and yells out, "If you don't have a viable reason to be here, you need to get the fuck out now." He's all business now, which is a little scary. He's the life of the party when it's all fun and games, but as soon as shit gets real, he's like a completely different person. I know that if danger comes here, we'll be okay. Louie will do whatever it takes to make sure we're safe.

Five minutes later, the only people left are Louie, Dani, myself, and Trixie. I don't understand why she's still here, but I don't say anything. I figure if it was a problem, then Louie would say something about her still being here and make her leave.

I can feel the tension coming off of Louie, but I don't say anything to him and he doesn't say anything to any of us. Suddenly, there's a loud crash from the kitchen. Louie takes out his gun and walks quietly, but quickly over toward the kitchen door.

He must realize that we're out in the open because he swears softly and comes over to where Dani and I are still on the couch. He waves Trixie over as well, who looks more scared than either myself or Dani. "I need you girls to go into Mack's room, lock the door behind you, and don't come out until I come get you. Be quiet and don't do anything stupid." Dani and I nod our heads.

"What about me?" Trixie asks nervously, probably not understanding why he didn't tell her not to come with us.

"I need you with me. Watch my back and let me know if there's anything that I don't see, but stay the fuck outta my way. Can you do that?" he says in a mean voice. I'm so glad he's not talking that way to me because the way I'm feeling right now, I'd probably break down and cry.

Trixie looks at him like he's crazy, for which I don't blame her. Why the hell would he want her as back-up? "Look, I need the girls safe and out of the way, but I also need someone with me, so that leaves you. I won't let anything happen to you, I promise, but two is better than one. So, can you do this?" He levels her with a serious look, but he's also looking at her like he's sympathetic too.

"O-okay…yeah," she chokes out, then clears her throat. "Y-yes, I can do this. Just tell me what you want me to do."

Louie gives Dani and I a look that says "get your asses moving" before walking back over to the door with Trixie right behind me. Dani and I don't waste any more time as we hightail it out of the main room and find Mack's door. Closing it softly behind us, Dani locks it, then we back up into the room and look around. For what, I have no idea.

"What are you looking for?" I whisper to her. She's currently pulling out drawers and rifling around through the contents.

"I don't have my purse with me so I need to find

us a weapon in case shit goes bad," she says steadily. If shit goes bad? How is she so calm right now?

"Is that really a possibility?" I ask, starting to freak out now.

Hearing the fear in my voice, she stops what she's doing and comes over to sit beside me on the bed. I didn't even realize I sat down in the first place. "Calm down, Sara. We're going to be fine. I just want to have something, just in case, but there's only a small chance that we'll even need it. However, I'd rather be safe than sorry." Knowing I need to toughen up, I nod and straighten my back. I need to be strong.

Seeing the change in my demeanor, Dani gets back up and starts searching for any type of weapon she can find. I get up and open a door that I thought was a closet, but see that it's a bathroom. Figuring I may as well look just to be sure there's nothing useful in there, I walk in and search all the cabinets.

Under the sink, I find a small knife. Figuring we could use it, I grab it and look through the rest of the drawers, but don't find anything else.

When I walk back into the bedroom, I see Dani's found a small handgun. It's smaller than the one I saw her carry that day at the shop when Rick tried to take me, but hopefully it will do the job if needed.

"Find anything?" she asks without looking up. I think she's loading the gun. I've never even touched a gun before, even though Toby has been trying to get me to go to the shooting range. I now wish I had taken him up on that offer.

"Just this," I say. Once she has the gun loaded, she stands up and tucks it in the back of her pants, then pulls her shirt down to cover it up. I guess we're going for stealth mode.

Dani takes the knife from me and turns it over, examining it. "This is actually perfect," she says, then looks around the room again for something. Whatever she was looking for, she must have found it because she comes up to me and tells me to sit down on the bed. I follow her instructions, not understanding what she's doing, but just going with it.

Once I'm sitting down, she moves to push up my dress. "Whoa, what the hell," I say, but she holds up her hand to stop me.

"Look, when the only weapon you have is a knife and you're a woman, you need to hide it in a place that is easily accessible, but not seen. Since you're wearing a dress, this is actually perfect. I'm going to make a holster for the knife out of the elastic I cut out of a pair of sweatpants. We'll tie it to the inside of your thigh. Your dress will cover it, but if you need it, you'll be able to make a grab for it." I just nod, even though I'm reeling inside from what she just said. I can't even imagine having to use a knife to protect myself. I almost want to ask her for the gun, but since I wouldn't even know how to use it, I'm kind of shit out of luck and stuck with what I've got.

She takes the elastic and wraps it around my thigh. I feel weird having her up my dress, but if this is what it takes to make sure we're both safe, then I'll deal with it.

When she's done, she sits back on her heels. "Okay, so it's already in a sheath so you won't have to worry about it cutting you. I've placed it upside down on the inside of your right leg. You're right handed, right?" I'm so confused, but when I nod, she continues. "Good. So, the way it's placed, it will be hidden, but easier for you to grab if you need it. Whether you're sitting or standing, if you need it, just reach your right hand under your dress and pull down. The Velcro holds the knife in place, but when you pull down, the knife will come out."

I shake my head, trying to digest everything she just said. "Wait, wouldn't it be better to have it on my other leg if I'm right handed?" I ask. This is so new to me, but I would think that if I was going to grab a weapon, I'd want to grab across my body, right?

"No. It will be easier to grab it from the same side of the hand that you'll be using. Just think of it this way; if you were grabbing a gun from a hip holster, you'd have it on the same side of the hand you're going to shoot with, right?" Oh, I guess she has a point. Oh my God, I don't think I can do this! She must see the doubt on my face. "Sara, look at me. We're going to be fine. This is only a precaution. Just remember, if something happens, look at me. I'll help you through this." I nod, but don't feel so confident.

"How are you so calm? And where the hell did you learn how to hide a knife like that?" I always knew Dani was a badass, but now I know for sure. She's got the looks, the attitude, and the knowledge and skills that make up a total badass. I'm glad she's on my side.

She gives me a shy smile. "Well, after what happened to me, I made sure I knew how to take care of myself and make whoever tried to hurt me again pay with their life. I know that sounds wrong, but sometimes that's what it takes." I look at her in shock. She almost seems like she's talking from experience.

"Have you ever had to use these skills?" I'm not sure if I really want to know, but I think right now I need to. Maybe knowing if she's been in a similar situation will make me feel better.

At first, she seems unsure if she should answer me, but she must come to the same conclusion I just did. I need to know. "Yes. A couple of months ago, just after Zane came back into my life, I was taken by a guy that had gotten a little handsy with me one night when we were at a bar down the street from the shop. That night, I beat his ass, but when he came back for me, he was prepared," she says quietly.

"What happened when he took you? Was Blaze able to find you in time before something happened?" This time, she looks directly in my eyes when she answers.

"He got there before anything bad could happen, yes, but I had to do it myself. You have to understand, Sara, I was raped years ago, before I came here." I gasp at her confession, but don't have a chance to say anything before she's talking again. "I felt like I was back there for a minute and I wanted him to pay. I knew that he could just do it to someone else and I wasn't going to let him do that.

He had to pay."

"Did you hurt him?" Surprisingly, I'm angry for her. I hope she did something that would teach him a lesson. I never knew she was raped before she came to California, but I think I always knew from the way she talked that it happened, or something just as bad. Hearing that someone else took her and tried to do the same thing—I would do the same thing, I think.

"I didn't just hurt him, Sara. I killed him." I'm shocked, but it makes me happy and I feel so much better knowing that she was able to make him pay for what he wanted to do, what someone else did do to her.

I pull her toward me and give her a hug, even though she doesn't seem upset. Shit, maybe I'm the one who needed the hug. "I'm glad you were able to protect yourself, Dani, and I'm proud of you too." She seems surprised, but then she smiles.

"Thanks, Sara. I was a little worried you would look at me differently if you knew about my past," she says almost sadly.

"I could never think badly of you. You're a fighter, Dani. You went through something that I don't think if it happened to me, I would have been able to come back from. You fought and you survived. I'm honored to call you my friend."

She almost looks like she's going to cry, but then we hear a knock on the door. We look at each other, not sure of what we should do.

"Dani? Sara? Open up, it's me," Trixie says through the door. Dani looks at me with confusion, but she walks to the door anyway. "Where's

Louie?" she asks Trixie, still not opening the door.

"He's tying up the guy who tried to break in. He told me to tell you that it's safe, but that he wanted us all to stay in Mack's room until he can get the others back here." Dani reluctantly opens the door for her.

Trixie walks past Dani, visibly shaking.

"What happened?" Dani says as she closes the door behind her and locks it again, then looks to where Trixie is standing in the middle of the room. I'm still sitting on the bed. We almost look like we're playing a bad game of Pickle or Keep Away, except we aren't trying to keep anything away from her.

I see Trixie wrap her arms around herself, trying to stop the shaking, but I don't move to get closer. I guess I'm still having a hard time being nice to her, even in a situation like this. Dani seems to be thinking the same thing, but knowing her, she'll take point since she seems to have a better understanding of bad things going down around her.

"I was so scared. Louie had me stay behind him, but I couldn't stop shaking. I wanted to ask if I could just come back here with you guys, but I knew if there was anything I could do to help him, I needed to do it. It was the right thing to do," Trixie says, looking down at the ground, acting almost shy or something about what she just revealed. "We could hear the guy in the kitchen. It sounded like he was searching for something, maybe a weapon, I don't know. Louie told me to be ready and handed me a gun. I tried to relay through my eyes that I had no idea what to do with a gun, but I don't think he understood, because the next thing I knew, he was barging into the kitchen." She pauses for a second and I can tell when she continues that she's crying, though she's looking at Dani and completely ignoring me. Fine by me. "Louie sprang into action, but the guy was fast. He was able to knock the gun out of Louie's hand and knock him to the ground. That's when he spotted me. I just froze. I was holding the gun out but I couldn't move," she's crying harder now. Dani moves a little closer to her and puts her hand on her shoulder.

"Hey, it's okay. It's over now," she says soothingly to Trixie.

Trixie nods, but can't seem to stop the tears. "I know, I know. I just can't get the look in that guy's eyes out of my head. He was going to kill me, I just knew it, and I couldn't do anything about it." She's almost hysterical now, so Dani takes another step before pulling Trixie in to hug her tightly. Before I know it, Trixie pushes Dani away. I'm stunned. Why would she do that? But I don't have to question it for long. Dani suddenly holds her hands up in surrender and that's when I see that Trixie has a gun and is pointing it at Dani. What the fuck? Did she take that from her?

"Don't fucking move, bitch," Trixie snarls at Dani. I stand up out of shock, but that only causes Trixie to turn so she can see Dani and me at the same time. I look at Dani, not sure what's going on and what we should do. What the fuck is Trixie doing?

Dani gives me a look and shakes her head slightly, but it's enough that I see it. She doesn't want me to do anything. Fuck! I completely forgot I had that knife! Why didn't I do something when I had the chance, when Trixie was facing Dani with her back to me? Stupid, Sara.

"Move," Trixie says as she waves the gun between Dani and me.

Dani laughs. "But you just told me not to move. Make up your mind, would ya?" She slowly moves toward me, but when she gets close enough, Trixie lashes out by hitting Dani on the head with the gun.

"NO!" I yell, moving forward to catch Dani as she falls forward, but Trixie points the gun at me.

"Uh uh," she says.

I look on in horror as Dani falls to the ground, unconscious.

Trixie just stands there, smiling evilly down at Dani's unconscious body on the floor, then looks at me. "Bitch had it coming."

I hear a knock at the door and watch Trixie stiffen. Louie! Thank God, but then I see Trixie relax as she goes to answer it. Why would she open the door after what she just did to Dani? Louie's going to kill her. It's not like I'm not happy about that, but is she fucking stupid?

When the door opens, the small bit of hope I had dies a quick death. A man I've never seen before and a man I wish I'd never see again walks in. "Miss me, sweetheart?" Rick says.

I can't fucking believe this. I look from him to Trixie, then briefly look at the mystery guy. I still don't know who he is, but I suppose that doesn't really matter right now. Swinging my gaze back to Trixie, I ask, "You were working with him this whole time?" I'm scared of what is going to happen now. Dani's passed out, Toby is gone, and Louie…God, Louie! I don't even know if he's okay. Did Rick kill him or just hurt him enough so he wouldn't be able to stop him?

"For someone who thinks she's smart, you are pretty fucking stupid," Trixie sneers at me. Is this bitch for real? Does she even hear herself right now?

Rick walks further into the room, closer to me, so I back up as far as I can. When I feel the bed behind me, I fall back. "What's the matter, Sara? Surprised that I was able to get past your new boy toy?" Rick asks with a sickly sweet smile on his face. I look from him to Trixie, then to Dani. What the fuck am I supposed to do?

"What? Now that you don't have that bitch to fight your battles for you, you got nothing to say?" he says as he walks closer. I stay quiet. I can't afford to say anything right now. In the past, whenever he was like this, if I said anything at all, he'd lash out. I need to be conscious if I'm going to get Dani and myself out of this mess.

Then a thought comes to me. Maybe if I can stall him long enough, either Louie will wake up and be able to come to our rescue, or the rest of the guys will know it was just a ruse and come back to make sure everything is all right, but before I can try to put this plan in action, Rick takes my chance away.

"That's okay, I like you better quiet anyway," he says, then he takes the gun I didn't even see him holding and brings it hard across my face. I feel a sharp pain in my eye socket, then everything goes

251

black.

CHAPTER 19

Toby

When we pull up outside the club, I know something's not right. No one is waiting for us outside, and that's not unusual, but for some reason, I thought for sure with Ryan, the prospect, inside holding a hostage, there would be someone outside. There aren't even any cars in the parking lot. The only thing that stood out was not one motorcycle, but two, parked around the club; one by the side door, and one in a lone parking spot within the parking lot.

Killing the engines, we all get off our bikes and cautiously head toward the front door. I pull out my gun, not wanting to be surprised by anything, when suddenly the front door to the club opens.

I point my gun at the guy. At first, I don't recognize him. I only know it's not Ryan. Then, when we get closer, I realize it's a brother who is a nomad that must have come in to help us out with the situation. "Tyke, what the hell are you doing here?" Mack asks, recognizing him as well.

When we get right in front of him, Mack extends his hand for a handshake, then engulfs him in a one shoulder hug. "Mack, good to see ya, brother. I was just getting ready to call you. Seems we have a situation here," Tyke says before motioning us inside.

"Yeah, that's why we're here. One of our prospects called to inform us that the guy we've been looking for was here. He's supposed to be holding him for us inside." It takes me a while for my eyes to adjust to the low lighting inside, but once I do, I see a man tied to a chair in the middle of the empty room.

Thinking it's Rick in the chair, I move to step forward, but Tyke puts his hand on my shoulder, stopping me. "That's not who you think it is." I look at him, trying to figure out what's going on.

"Why don't we go sit down and I'll explain," he says, then leads us to a table off to the side. We're at a better angle now and can see clearly that the man tied to the chair is indeed not Rick, but instead, our prospect, Ryan.

"What the fuck is going on?" Mack growls, obviously seeing our own prospect tied up.

Tyke lets out a long sigh before telling us what happened. "I just got into town, thought I'd stop in for a beer before making my way to the clubhouse. I was coming out of the bathroom when I noticed your prospect walking down the hall looking nervous as shit. I was going to ask what was going on and offer my help, but I could tell there something going on that wasn't right, so I followed him. I stayed in the shadows so he couldn't see me, but I had a clear view of him and could hear him. He kept looking at his phone, almost like he was waiting for something. It wasn't long before his phone went off. After looking at his phone for a couple seconds, I assume looking at a message, he put his phone to his ear, making a call to who I now assume was one of your men. I heard him say that the guy you were looking for was here and that he'd hold him until you got here. Since I didn't see him with anyone and was pretty sure he was lying, I decided to approach him once he was off the phone." I look at Lyle, who's glaring at Ryan like he's going to kill him with just his eyes. Well, he'll have to wait till I'm done with him first.

"What happened when you approached him? I assume since he's gagged and tied up that you were able to detain him for us, but did you figure anything out about that prick he was supposed to be holding?" Mack asks Tyke.

"I followed him outside where he went directly to his bike, like he was going to bail, so I called out to him. He saw my cut and by that point, I think he was scared shitless that he was caught. I played it cool like I hadn't heard him on the phone and I asked what he was doing and he told me that he just got a call from you, Mack," Tyke says as he looks to Mack, "and that he had to get back to the clubhouse. Right then I knew he was up to something, so I jumped him, knocked his ass out, and dragged him inside. I told the manager to get everyone out of the club, then tied your man to the chair. I was just getting ready to call you when you showed up."

I stand up quickly and charge toward Ryan. "You motherfucking son-of-a-bitch!" I yell right before I hit him square in the nose. Blood instantly gushes out and down his face.

I hit him again and again, wanting to kill the fucker, but Mack pulls me back. "Toby, back the fuck off." He's able to pull me back, but just barely. "You'll have your chance, but for now, we need him alive to tell us who put him up to this and what the plan was." I know Mack's right, but I can't stop myself from hitting him once more. Fucker deserves it and so much more.

Stepping back, I take deep breaths to calm myself. Lyle is beside Mack and I can hear them discussing the best way to go about getting the information. Ryan isn't knocked out, but he looks close to passing out any minute.

Lyle steps in front of Ryan and slaps his cheeks to keep him awake. "Wakey, wakey." It's almost funny hearing Lyle say those words, but I don't have it in me to laugh, not until I know what game he's playing and what the plan was.

Tyke walks up to Ryan and pulls the gag out of his mouth. "Care to share why you fucked over the club you pledged your life to?" he says through clenched teeth. One of the worst things a brother, or prospect, could do, is move against their club. It's the ultimate betrayal and is punishable by death. What type of death and how quick it will be depends on the crime, but I'm thinking this prick deserves a lot of pain and a slow death.

When Ryan doesn't answer right away, I push

forward to have another shot at him, but Mack holds me back. "If you don't start talking soon, I'm just gonna start cutting digits off, one by one until you find the words I want to hear," I seethe at him. I don't have time to fuck around. My woman is sitting at the club barely protected, so if shit is going to go down, I need to fucking know what it is. I'm half tempted to let my brothers deal with this traitor and speed back to the clubhouse, but I know Louie can handle himself if anything happens. It's more important right now that I know what their plan was and who's involved so I can come up with a plan of my own. Heads are going to fucking roll and people are going to be put to ground tonight, that I'm fucking sure of.

My threat must finally seep into his brain because he says, "I'll talk, just please don't kill me."

"Oh, you'll talk? The only choice you have now is to how much pain you want to feel before you do," I leave out the part about me killing him after he spills his guts. Ryan looks at me, almost hopeful, thinking I won't actually kill him if he gives me what I want, then he tells us what the plan was and who he's working with.

"I was only supposed to make the call saying that that Rick guy you've been looking for was here at the club. I was told once Lyle left and got to the club, I'd get a text message telling me to call. That's it. I swear, man," Ryan says, like what he did wasn't a big deal. He must not have been paying attention at all during the past six months he's been a prospect or any of the time he spent with us before that. It doesn't fucking matter what you do, how small, or who it's fucking over. You go against the club in any way, you're a fucking dead man. It's that fucking simple.

Mack comes up beside me and asks, "Who told you to make the call?" I'm trying to figure out how Rick got to one of our prospects. I know he has something to do with this, but how? Then I get my answer.

"Trixie. She told me that no one would find out. She said that after I made the call, to just take off for a day and she'd call me back when the smoke cleared. Said after it was done, there would be no fall back on me."

Turning around, I head for the door with my cell phone already at my ear.

The phone just rings and rings, "Come on, Louie, pick up the fucking phone," I yell. Where the fuck is he? Fuck it, I'm heading back to the clubhouse and taking care of the bitch myself.

Mack, Skinner, Blaze, and Lyle make it to me just as I'm heading out the door. "You call Louie?" Blaze asks.

"He's not answering. Something's wrong. I'm heading back there now."

None of them say anything as they follow me out to the bikes. "Mack! You want me to take care of things here?" Tyke yells out just as I start up my bike. Not even waiting to hear what Mack says, I take off at a fast clip toward the club. Please fucking be there. Please God, let my girl be all right.

I make it back to the clubhouse in record time.

I'm the first to pull in, but the rest of my brothers aren't far behind.

If I already didn't know there was something wrong with Louie not answering his phone, I would know by the look of the clubhouse. All the windows are busted in, the doors are wide fucking open, and I can smell gas.

Jumping off my bike, I take off inside, searching for everyone.

The main room is trashed, but there is no one visible here, so I take off toward the back hall that leads to the rooms. I check them all, but come up empty. Heading back into the main room, I see Mack and Blaze come out of the kitchen, carrying a limp Louie. "Fuck!" I yell as I run over to them. "What the fuck happened to him?"

"I can only guess that he was knocked out from behind. He's got a good size gash on the back of his head that's bleeding like a motherfucker. Where are the girls?" Blaze asks.

"I searched the back rooms. They're not here," I get out, then all of a sudden there's an explosion that comes from inside the kitchen. "We need to get outta here now. The gas lines were cut. This place is gonna burn to the fucking ground with us inside if we don't fucking move!" Mack yells.

I can see flames coming from inside the kitchen, and they're spreading fast. Lyle and Blaze grab hold of Louie's feet while Mack and I take his arms, then we haul ass outside. "Where's Skinner?" I yell to Mack, not seeing him anywhere.

"He's at the club with Tyke," Mack replies and we run outside.

We barely get out the door before the whole place blows.

The force of the blast kicks us up a few feet before dropping us onto the hard gravel of the parking lot. My ears are ringing, but I try to shake it off to make sure everyone's okay.

I see Mack gingerly getting to his feet, wiping blood off his eyebrow. Other than that, he looks fine.

Blaze is hunched over Louie, checking him over, but as far as I can tell, Blaze isn't hurt and Louie isn't any worse than what he was when we found him.

I turn slightly and see Lyle still lying on the ground, not moving, and I can see a lot of blood. I try to rush over to him, but on my first step, pain shoots up my right leg. Fuck, that hurts! Looking down, I see a piece of debris sticking out of my calf. Well, that's not fucking good.

Mack is instantly by my side. "Are you hurt?" I shake my head and point toward Lyle. "I'll be fine, but we need to check on Lyle. He's not moving," I say, my voice laced with pain and worry for Lyle and the girls. We still have no idea where the fuck they are, but I'm confident they weren't inside.

I watch as Mack runs over to where Lyle's lying face down on the ground with blood everywhere. He rolls him over and starts looking for injuries. I limp on my bad leg over to them and kneel down by his head while Mack is feverishly patting down his body for where the blood is coming from. He's covered with it. I reach a shaky hand out and check for his pulse, praying that I'm not right, but there's nothing.

Falling back onto my ass, I say, "He's gone." Even though I'm not speaking to anyone in particular, Mack's hands instantly stop searching and I can see Blaze stiffen out of the corner of my eye. "He's gone," I say again, not really believing it, but knowing it's true.

We're each quiet for a moment, then Mack stands up and yells, "GOD FUCKING DAMMIT!" He looks down at Lyle, running his hands through his short hair, then glances toward the clubhouse. The flames look like they are licking the sky.

I don't know how long we stay like that, but we snap out of it when we hear a groan coming from Louie.

"Yo, Louie? You with us, man?" Blaze says to him over the noise of the flames. Louie coughs a little and tries to sit up, but Blaze pushes him back down. "Just stay still, brother. You've had a pretty good fucking hit to the head."

Mack and I make our way over to where our brothers are at and drop down beside them. "Dani...Sara..." Louie's finally able to say. None of us say anything because really, we have no idea where they are or if they're even okay.

"We've gotta fucking find them. Someone broke into the clubhouse and—" He looks over Blaze's shoulder as he's talking and must finally notice the clubhouse in flames. His eyes get big and then he starts freaking out. "*No!* Dani! Sara!" He starts struggling against Blaze when he tries to keep him still. "Let me fucking go! We've got to get them out of there!"

We finally get a hold of him and keep him down. "They're not in there, man. They're fucking gone. Just settle the fuck down before you hurt yourself even more," Mack says. Louie looks at him with confusion and anger.

"What the fuck do you mean they're not in there? Where the hell are they?" he asks as he looks around the parking lot. That's when he notices Lyle and comes to the conclusion that I did.

"No," he says.

A few seconds later, we hear a motorcycle pull in next to where we're still sitting on the gravel. "What the fuck? Are you guys okay?" Tyke asks as he jumps off his bike and runs toward us. Next, Slayer skids to a stop and jumps off his bike.

"What the fuck happened?" Slayer yells out, looking first at the clubhouse, then at Mack, Blaze, Louie, and I, before his eyes finally land on Lyle.

Slayer rushes over to him and checks his pulse, but when he doesn't find it, he stands up stiffly and runs his hands through his hair, spewing every curse word he can think of.

Tyke speaks over his ranting, "Mack, I was able to get more information out of your guy. He said that Trixie was supposed to meet him in ten minutes at some lookout."

I cut my eyes instantly to Mack. He must be able to read my thoughts because he says, "Toby, head out and get the location of the girls. Do whatever you have to do to get her to fucking talk, then get rid of the bitch. We need to get Louie to Doc to get checked out and we've gotta take care of Lyle." I nod, but look over toward Lyle once more. I'll have time to say my piece to my fallen brother when we end this shit. Standing up, I stumble to my bike, but remember my leg.

Tyke rushes over to his bike and removes a first aid kit from his saddlebags. When he makes it back over to me, he pulls up my pant leg and quickly removes the piece of metal that's sticking out of my calf. After he wraps it, he pulls my pant leg back down and stands back. "You're good to go," he says.

"Thanks, brother," I say as I jump onto my bike and tear outta there like a bat outta hell toward the lookout Tyke said Trixie would be at. Bitch is gonna find out what it means to play games with the big dogs.

***

A couple minutes later, I'm coming up to the lookout point. Parking a little ways away so she doesn't hear me coming, I get off my bike and limp up the hill.

I spot her right away. She's leaning against the guard rail, looking out over the city.

When she hears me come up behind her, she turning around. "About fucking time, you laz—" she starts to say but she's cut off when I reach out and grab her by her throat. Her eyes are as big as saucers and her mouth is gaping open, gasping for air that she's not going to get.

"Thought you were smart, huh, bitch?" I growl, my face only inches from hers. She struggles, so I push my body against hers, trapping her between me and the guard rail. "This is what's going to happen. I'm going to ask you one time where that fucker took Dani and Sara, and you're going to tell me," I spit. I'm leaning into her, forcing her body half over the railing.

Trixie nods her head as much as she can with my hand wrapped around her neck. Letting up just a little, but keeping her in my grasp, I wait for her to speak.

She takes in a few shallow breaths, but she's taking too fucking long. "You've got three fucking seconds before I really get pissed," I say between clenched teeth.

"Please," she pleads.

"Talk now!"

"The old mill. He's taking them to the old mill," she says, her voice low and cracking from the limited air and my hand holding her throat.

"Does he have anyone else helping him?" I ask, needing this to be done with so I can get to my girl.

She nods her head, but when she doesn't speak, I tighten my grip on her neck. She gasps, but pushes out the words I want to hear. "One...guy. He's got...one guy with him." I loosen my grip again so she can tell me who it is. "I've only met the guy a few times, when he came into the strip club I worked at on the side. But he said he has beef with the club, a debt that needed to be repaid."

I release her neck completely and take a few steps back, which allows her to hunch over and take in large gulps of air. She looks up at me with tears running down her cheeks. "What are you going to do to me?" she asks weakly. I don't answer, not

264

wanting to waste any more time on her. Instead, I kick out my leg and connect with her stomach, then watch as she's forced backwards, tumbling head first over the railing from the force. I turn around, not even bothering to watch her fall to the ground hundreds of feet below. Bitch isn't worth my fucking time.

As I hurry down toward my bike, I call Blaze, knowing he'll want to be with me when we get the girls back. "They're being held at the old mill. Rick has another guy with him, but I'm uncertain who it is. Trixie only knew he has something against the club. Meet me down the road in five," I say, then hang up without waiting for him to answer. It's time to get our fucking girls back.

CHAPTER 20

Sara

When I wake up, my head and the right side of my face is killing me. I feel like I went twelve rounds with Mike Tyson, though if that were true, I'm sure the only pain he's feeling is in his hand from beating my head in.

I try to open my eyes, but only one is working. Reaching up, I run my finger lightly along the eye that's shut and realize it won't open because it's swollen. What the hell happened? Then I remember—the clubhouse. Trixie, Rick, Dani…shit, Dani!

Frantically searching around me, I see her a few feet away, lying on her side. "Dani," I whisper yell at her. Please be okay. When she doesn't answer, I gingerly crawl over to her. "Dani, wake up." I lightly shake her, not wanting to hurt her more than what she might already be. Oh God, this is all my fault.

Dani finally starts coming to, groaning as she

reaches behind her head. "Shit, my head fucking kills." When she opens her eyes and looks at me, she flinches. "What the fuck happened to you?" She reaches up and feels around my face. When she hits just below my eye socket, I flinch away from her touch. "What happened?" she asks. I let out a deep sigh and lean back against the wall beside her as she slowly sits up.

"Trixie stole your gun and knocked you out, then Rick, my ex, came in with a guy I don't know and Trixie. She helped him. I don't even know how she even knew about him, but they were working together." I try to remember what was said, but can't really think of anything specific. "He hit me with his gun, then I woke up here. That's all I know."

"Did they say anything about Louie?" Louie? Oh my God, I forgot he was at the club with us. Did they hurt him?

"I don't know. They didn't say anything about him and I was out of it when they took us from the club," I say when I look at her worried eyes. Louie is her best friend, and he's become mine too. Please don't let him be dead because of me.

"Stay calm. Louie will be fine. He's tough, and he's dealt with worse shit than this." I shake my head, not understanding how she can be so calm.

"How do you know? What if they shot him? What if they shot him because they were trying to get to me?"

"Knock it off. He's fine, do you hear me? We can't think like that. We need to figure out where the fuck we are so we can get out of here," she yells.

I stare into her eyes and see that she really believes Louie is okay. If she believes that, then I need to as well. I nod, but I'm not able to say anything because the door suddenly slams open.

Rick stands in the doorway with a sick smile on his face. "Well, look who's finally awake?" he says as he steps into the room and closes the door behind him.

He walks in halfway and stops, looking from me to Dani, then back at me. "I've really missed you, sweetheart. I haven't had anyone to soothe my frustrations and anger out on for a long time, but that's okay. We have some time to make up for before we leave here and head back home." I open my mouth to say something, but the look on his face silences me. I'm back in New York, back at his house, and feeling the pain from his hand across my face or the leather from his belt.

"You're not going to fucking touch her, asshole," Dani seethes. I look to her and try to get her to stop talking with a look, but she doesn't take her eyes off Rick, looking at him like she wants to kill him. Fuck, she probably does, but she doesn't have a gun this time. We're stuck in a room. We have no idea where we are, and the guys might not even know we're missing. How are we supposed to get out of here?

The smile on Rick's face disappears and is replaced with a snarl directed at Dani. "You talk awfully big for a bitch who doesn't have her gun with her anymore."

Dani laughs. She fucking laughs at him.

"You think I need a gun to kill you? You are one stupid motherfucker," Dani says while she continues to laugh. "You on the other hand seem to need a lot of help to wrangle two helpless girls. Maybe you should call him in here before we prove that you're not man enough to handle us."

Rick, having enough of Dani and her words, rushes forward. Before I can stop him, he punches her in the face so hard that she falls to the side from the force of the hit. "I don't need help with either of you bitches, even if that pussy hadn't run scared," Rick says, then straightens before kicking her in the stomach. God dammit, the baby! I'm going to kill him.

I jump up, hitting him with my fists anywhere I can connect on his body, but he easily pushes me away. I don't back down though. I won't let him touch Dani again. This is my fight, and it's time I stand up for myself.

When he turns his back to me to face Dani again, I jump up and wrap my arms around his throat. Maybe if I can hold on long enough, I'll be able to choke him close to the point he passes out, then I can grab Dani and we can get the fuck out of here.

He struggles against my hold, but I don't let up. I wrap my legs around his waist and feel something poke the inside of my thigh. The knife. I try to maneuver him so I can reach down with one hand and grab it, but before I can get a strong enough hold on his neck to reach, I feel him move us backwards and my back hits the concrete wall. I'm stunned, but I'm able to tighten my hold around his neck. I'm afraid that if I let go, it will be the end of both Dani and I.

Rick takes a few quick steps forward before ramming us into the wall again. This time, the back of my head hits the wall so hard I see black dots in my vision.

When he feels me loosen my hold a little, he takes full advantage by removing my arms and legs from around him. Once he's out of my reach, he looks at me and says, "First I'll take care of your friend, then you and I are gonna have some fun." My eyes go to Dani, who's awake, but clutching her stomach. She looks like she's in pain, but more than that, she actually looks afraid. I've never seen her afraid, but after everything she's told me about her past and everything she's done, I know it's not for herself. She's afraid for her baby.

Fuck this.

Pushing off the wall, I charge Rick again, but this time, he expects it. He turns around before I can even reach him and slams me into the wall again. My head hits harder than last time, but I don't allow myself time to think of the pain.

Rick pushes his forearm into my neck, blocking my airway. "You stupid fucking whore. When are you going to learn your place?" he screams in my face.

I use my left hand to try and distract him by clawing at the arm that's holding me against the wall, but with my right hand, I reach down and pull the knife free from its spot. I spare a quick glance at Dani to satisfy myself that she's okay, then I look Rick in the eyes. "As soon…as you…learn where yours…is," I gasp out as my vision starts to fade.

He laughs. "And where's that?" I smile as much as my face will allow.

"Six feet in the ground." Then I ram the knife into his side and twist, watching as shock takes over his face.

He releases me enough that I can push his arm off my neck and take a few quick breaths. "You stupid fucking bitch!" he yells as he holds his side and looks down to see blood soaking through his shirt and fingers. Before he can regain any type of control, I rush forward and stab him in the chest.

I step back and watch in amazement while he struggles to remove the knife. He falls to his knees and looks up at me right before he falls face first onto the ground.

I vaguely hear Dani saying my name, but I can't remove my eyes from Rick's now lifeless body. I killed him. I actually killed him. He will never be able to scare or hurt me again because I *killed* him.

I don't know how long I stand there and stare, but it had to have been only a few seconds when the door is suddenly kicked in.

When I finally drag my gaze up, I see Toby standing in the doorway. I have to tell him that Dani needs him, but when I look over to her, I see Blaze crouching down to pick her up. She's crying and clinging to him, but she's looking at me.

"Look at me, doll," Toby says quietly. I move my head slowly back to him. He's standing so close to me now, but not close enough for me to touch him. I just need him to hold me. I feel so weak and wrong.

Lifting my leg to move toward him, the last thing

I remember is falling as my world starts to fade out.

"*Sara!*" The pain in my head goes away and the numbness takes over, right before it all goes black.

***

Toby

"*Sara!*" I yell out as I see her collapse. I rush forward and catch her before she can hit the ground. "Sara, wake up, doll. Please."

Out of the corner of my eye, I see Blaze holding Dani, engulfing her in his arms as she cries and holds her belly. I hear him ask if she's all right, but I can't hear her answer because I'm focusing all my attention on Sara.

Bringing a shaky finger up to her neck, I check for her pulse, praying she's still alive. When I finally find it, I let out a sigh of relief. Though it's slow, it's there. Thank fuck!

I pick Sara up. "Let's go. We need to get to the hospital." Both of the girls need to be checked out. I just pray to God neither of them are seriously hurt and Dani's baby is all right. I have no idea what happened to her or how her stomach was hurt, but I can guess. She's still holding her belly, and that scares me as much as Sara being unconscious.

I follow Blaze out of the room and watch as he holds Dani with one arm and lifts his phone to his ear with the other. "Mack! We need the truck. We've got the girls, but they need to get to the hospital."

"Dani, do you know where the other guy is?" I

ask as we make our way outside.

"I don't know. Rick said he ran."

Dani reaches down and runs her hand across Sara's face. "She saved me, Toby. Rick was coming toward me, said he was going to kill me, but she stopped him," Dani whispers to me, but she doesn't look away from Sara.

"Do you know where she's hurt or what could have happened to make her pass out like that?" I ask, running my hands over Sara to see if I can find the source of why she's not waking up. Her eye is swollen and there's a good gash, but I don't think that's the reason why she passed out.

"She jumped on his back and was choking him. He slammed them backwards into the wall and I saw her head bounce off the wall twice. He was choking her too," Dani cries. "She can't die, Toby."

Seconds later, I hear a truck pull up and slamming doors. Then I feel someone at my side. "Let's get her to the hospital. She's gonna be all right," Mack says calmly, but I can tell by the tone of his voice that he's not so sure.

Picking her up, I get into the backseat of the truck and lay her down across my lap. Mack jumps in the driver's seat while Blaze and Dani get in the passenger side. "Let's go," I say. Stroking Sara's face, I whisper, "It's gonna be okay, doll. You're safe now." I feel the truck speed off down the road, but the only thing I focus on is Sara.

***

It's been five hours since we arrived at the

hospital. Sara was taken into surgery as soon as we got here. She had swelling on her brain and some fluid build-up, so they needed to relieve the pressure it was causing. They aren't sure if there will be permanent damage or not, though. They said we'd have to wait till she wakes up.

They gave her some medicine that will make her sleep for a while, and help her head heal faster, at least that's what they said, but I just want her to wake up. I need to look into her eyes and know she's going to be fine.

"Any change?" Blaze says as he quietly walks into the room. Rubbing my hands across my face, I shake my head.

"No. Doc said that it could be a few days before she wakes up…maybe more."

He sits on the other side of the bed, opposite me, and looks at Sara sleeping.

"How's Dani doing?" I ask after a few minutes of silence. When we arrived, Dani just wanted to make sure that Sara was okay, but we finally got her to let a doctor check her out. She said that Trixie hit her upside the head with a gun and that she was fine, but when she stood up and grabbed her ribs, we knew it was more than that.

Turns out Rick kicked her in the stomach, which caused her ribs to bruise. Thankfully, the baby wasn't harmed in any way, but it will take a few weeks for Dani to heal. "She's sleeping now. Was raising all kinds of hell, yelling at everyone that if we didn't take her to see Sara, she was gonna start breaking shit," he says, laughing at the end.

I crack a small smile, but can't find it in myself

to laugh with him. "Yeah, that sounds like her."

We're quiet again, neither of us really knowing what to say, but it's a comfortable silence, and it's his form of support, which is very much appreciated.

"Any word on the mystery guy Rick had helping him?" Blaze asks after a few minutes.

Blowing out a long breath, I say, "No." Getting up, I start pacing the room. "I have no idea who this guy is, how to find him, or what he has against the club. I'm going insane, brother. What if he comes back, tries to finish what Rick started? I can't live without her, man. I can't."

Thinking of even a minute without Sara in my life, knowing she is no longer of this world, breathing the same air as me, makes me crazy.

"Look, I get it. I feel it too, but we'll find him. I have a feeling this beef he has with us won't keep him away for long." Blaze says. A part of me hopes he's right so we can eliminate the threat and keep the girls safe. But the other part fears that in the process, one or both of them will be hurt.

"Mack has been putting feelers out, calling in more favors. We'll get him and the girls will be protected. Nothing will happen to either of them. You have my word." I look in his eyes and know he's telling the truth. He'll protect Sara with his life, just like he would Dani. He feels he owes her for what she did to protect Dani and the baby. Nodding my head, I sit back down and take Sara's hand in mine.

About an hour later, Mack comes into the room. "Dani's awake. She's asking for you," he says as he looks at me. Not wanting to leave Sara's side in case she wakes up, I just shake my head.

"I'll sit here with her. If she wakes up, I'll send for you right away," Blaze says. I realize that if I don't go, Dani will most likely go against everyone and make her way up here. Not wanting that, I stand up, then lean over Sara to kiss her on her forehead. "I'll be right back, doll," I whisper, then hesitantly walk out of the room.

Mack leads me to Dani's room, but doesn't come in with me.

I open the door and can't help but laugh when I see Dani charging around her room, throwing shit everywhere. "Redecorating, I see."

As soon as she hears my voice, she stops and turns to me. When she sees the smile on my face, she lets out a laugh. "Yeah, well, this place looks like shit so I thought I'd help them with that."

After a few moments of silence, she finally asks, "How is she?" I walk over to a chair that's on the side of the bed and she follows.

Letting out a sigh, I rub my hand back and forth across my shaved head. "She's still unconscious, but the doctor said that she'll wake up in a day or so. They removed the fluid from her brain, so they said the swelling should start to go down now." I feel her reach out and grab my hand.

"She's gonna be okay. We just have to give her time to heal, then we can yell at her for being the hero. That's your job," she says seriously.

I look at her in surprise, never thinking she'd ever say something like that. Usually, it's about her saving the day or that women can do anything a man can. She sees my surprise and says, "I think I finally understand that sometimes we need to just let you men take care of things for us."

I nod, afraid that if I comment, she'll change her mind and that wouldn't be good.

I sit with her for a few more minutes, but when she can see me itching to get back to Sara, she tells me to go. I kiss her head and walk out the door, heading back upstairs to sit with my girl.

When I push the door open, I hear Blaze talking softly. "Thank you. You saved my girl and our baby with what you did. Even though it was fucking stupid and you put yourself at risk, you saved them. I can never repay you for that, but I promise you, it will not be forgotten," he says, taking a deep breath and letting it out. "I'm sorry about the way I've been treating you. I can't promise that when you wake up I'll say that so you can hear me, but I can promise that it won't happen again. I owe you everything. Thank you, Sara."

I wait a minute before walking back into the room, not wanting him to know I heard him talking just now.

He looks up when I get close to the bed. "You might want to get back to your woman. She was redecorating her room when I got there. She was in bed when I left, but who knows how long that will last if you don't get there soon," I say as I sit back down in the same chair I've been in for the past couple of hours.

Blaze laughs and stands up. "Jesus, that fucking woman. Even bruised ribs can't keep her down." I nod in agreement because Dani is definitely one

277

strong woman.

After he leaves, I grab hold of Sara's hand and bring it to my lips. "Hurry up and come back to me. I love you," I say, then lay my head down on the bed beside her hand and close my eyes. Please God, let her wake up soon and be my Sara again.

CHAPTER 21

Sara

I open my eyes and pain explodes in my head. At first, I think I'm back in that room with Rick, but then I remember stabbing him in the chest and Toby coming to save me. I don't remember anything after that, though.

Glancing around the room, I realize I'm in the hospital. I feel pressure on my hand, like someone is squeezing it. Slowly, I turn my head to look down, but have to shut my eyes for a minute until the pain subsides a little.

When I'm able to open them again, one just barely, I look to my left and see Toby in a chair beside my bed, leaning back, not looking comfortable at all. He's at an odd angle, trying to hold my hand while he's reclining back.

Movement catches my attention to the side. Instead of moving my head, I decide to just try moving my eyes to see who's come into my room. Hopefully, that won't hurt so much.

279

It works and I see Dani quietly walking into the room. She's not really paying attention. She glances around the room, then at Toby before she actually sees that I'm awake. She gasps, then rushes to the other side of the bed, taking my other hand in hers. "You're awake," she breathes out. I try to speak, but my throat is dry and sore. Noticing the trouble I'm having, she looks around her and sees a glass of water on the bedside table. Lifting it to my lips, I take a small sip before swallowing. It hurts a little, but feels good too. "Better?" she asks as she sets the glass back down.

"Yeah," I croak, my voice sounding raspy and unused.

"How are you feeling? Fuck, that was a stupid question. I'm sorry." She looks sheepish, which makes me laugh, causing me to wince in pain from both my head and my throat. Well, guess I won't do that again.

Finally, I say, "My head hurts a little bit, but other than that, I think I'm good."

"Do you want me to call the nurse? She can probably give you something for the pain." I try to shake my head, but when I feel the pain in my head again, I stop.

"No, not yet." I pause for a moment before continuing. "What happened?" I ask, needing to know if what I remember actually happened, and what I missed after passing out.

She sits down in the chair and gets comfortable. "Well, when Rick came at me, you stopped him. Thank you, by the way. You saved my life." Not wanting any thanks, I ask about her and the baby, needing to know. I pray to God that she didn't lose the baby.

"The baby is fine. Perfect, actually," she says with a big smile. "I've got a few bruised ribs, but nothing that a little rest and time won't heal. It could have been a lot worse if it weren't for you." I weakly hold up my hand.

"Please, don't thank me. You wouldn't have been in that situation to begin with if it weren't for me." I feel horrible that she could have been hurt and lost the baby, all because of me.

I look away from her, up at the ceiling, not wanting to see the gratitude in her eyes. I don't deserve it. "Sara, look at me," she says with an edge in her voice. When I turn my eyes back to her, she says, "This was not your fault. Do you hear me? What happened was not your fault, so stop blaming yourself." I wish I could believe that.

"It is my fault. Rick came after me and ended up taking you too because you were with me," I say, disgusted with myself.

"No, he took you because he wanted to break you, but he didn't. He couldn't because you are so much stronger than you were when you were with him. And he took me because he was working with Trixie and she wanted me out of the way. She thought if we were both gone, she'd be queen bitch." I knew Trixie was working with Rick, but I didn't know the reason why. Was that really why she helped him? To get rid of Dani? I guess it makes sense considering the way she talked about her that night at the clubhouse.

Deciding to let that part go, I ask the next

pressing question. "Louie? Please tell me that he's okay." Rick never said anything about him either way.

"He's fine. He was here, but was released already. I'm sure he'll be back soon to check in on you." She says this hesitantly, like there's more, but she's afraid to tell me. Maybe he was hurt worse than she's letting on.

"What aren't you telling me?" I ask, getting right to the point. Another thing I learned about Dani—if you're blunt and direct with her, she'll do the same. I need that from her right now. I need to know what's going on.

"I'm not sure if now is the right time to say anything," she says sadly. So it's really bad, whatever it is.

"Dani, please just tell me. I need to know," I say with patience I don't have.

"When the boys got to the strip club where Ryan, the prospect, was supposedly holding Rick, they figured out it was a ruse. After interrogating him, they found out that Trixie was in on it, so they rushed back to the clubhouse, but we were already gone." She's quiet for a minute, maybe judging my reaction, but I mostly knew all of this already, except that Ryan was in on it too. "When they got into the club, they knew we were gone, but found Louie knocked out in the kitchen. As they were getting him outside though, there was an explosion in the clubhouse. They got out, but the clubhouse is gone."

"Is everyone okay? No one got injured, did they?" The only people I've seen since then has been Toby, and of course, Dani. Wait, Blaze was with Toby when they found us, so I know he's fine too.

I see a tear fall and know that someone was hurt, or worse. "Louie, Mack, Toby, and Blaze came out of it with little to no injuries, but Lyle wasn't so lucky," she says. *No, not Lyle!*

"How bad was he hurt?" I finally choke out over tears I don't remember crying. Dani just shakes her head and I know. He didn't make it.

We both cry silently for a while, each quietly mourning the life and death of a great man. Lyle was like an uncle to me. He was my Teddy Bear, and now he's gone.

Once our tears have dried, I get angry. "Did Trixie get away?" When I find that bitch, she's going to pay for her part in all this. "And what about that other guy?"

Dani laughs sadistically. "Oh no, they got her. They found out from Ryan where she was going to be. That's also how they knew where to find us. Toby met her there instead of Ryan and got it out of her, then he took care of her. I don't know how because they won't tell me, but they said we don't have to worry about her anymore. In club speak, that means she's dead." Instead of being horrified with the news, I'm happy. Ecstatic, actually. I never thought hearing about someone's death would make me happy, but hearing that Trixie is no longer able to cause anyone else to be hurt or killed, I'm almost giddy with joy.

"Good," I say and leave it at that.

"As far as the other guy…I don't know anything

about him. I never saw him when they took us or after I woke up where they were holding us. The only thing I know about him is from what Rick said—that he fled. The guys haven't said much about him, but I know they are looking for him. And they'll find him and make him pay for his part. You can count on that." The way Dani speaks, it's with certainty.

Hearing a groan come from the other side of me, I slowly roll my head over to see Toby waking up. He scrubs his hands across his face before opening his eyes.

When he notices that I'm awake, he shoots up and runs his hands over my face and down my shoulders. "Thank fuck, you're awake!" he says frantically. I give him a small smile.

"I'm awake," I confirm.

Toby looks over and for the first time notices Dani sitting beside me. "What are you doing down here? You're not supposed to be out of bed," he says with concern. Hmm, if I would have known she wasn't supposed to be up, I would have told her to go back to her room and rest. What the fuck am I saying? Dani wouldn't listen to me anyway.

I give him a hard glare, but I can see the love in it. "I wanted to see my friend, thank you very fucking much. I'll get out of bed any time I want, so fuck off," she practically growls at him.

I laugh a little, which has Toby looking back at me with a small smile of his own face. "You have no idea how much I missed that laugh, doll," he says happily.

"Yeah, well, I missed your face more." That has

him laughing, then he leans down and kisses me softly on the lips. "I love you," he whispers.

"I love you too," I whisper back, never looking away from his eyes.

***

It's been a week since I was released from the hospital. I've been staying at Toby's house since he refused to let me out of his sight for even a second.

After I woke up and he told me again what happened, I remember that we had Ollie at the club. Toby made a call right away to Mack and asked if he could look around for him in what was left of the clubhouse. I remember I left him outside after the guys left, so I'm praying he was far enough away when the clubhouse burned down.

It didn't take Mack long to call back and say that he found him and he was safe. He said he would keep him at his place until I was released and feeling better.

He kept Ollie with him after I was released because I didn't really have the energy to play with him. I feel bad, but I know he'll understand. Or he would if he could.

We're going over to Mack's today to pick him up and talk about the reconstruction of the clubhouse. Then, later tonight, we're going to have a service for Lyle. Even though he already had a funeral, the club always holds a special service that's just for club members, or people associated with the club. Thankfully, everyone agreed to wait till I recovered a bit before doing it. I didn't get to go to the actual funeral service, so I didn't want to miss this one.

We take the truck to Mack's house because Toby doesn't want me on his bike just yet. Also, we can't bring Ollie home without the truck.

When we pull up outside his house, everyone is here already. Toby comes around to my side and helps me out. I haven't had a headache since we left the hospital, but he's still so careful with me. It's actually starting to piss me off. Now I know what Dani feels like when Blaze is all over her and acting like an overprotective dad.

I see Ollie barreling out of the house and making a beeline straight to me. Looks like someone missed his mama.

Kneeling down, I pet him from his head to his tail. "Hey, boy. Mama missed you," I say, then lean forward and give him kisses on his nose.

After a couple seconds of Ollie licking my face, Toby growls at him. "Okay, Ollie, that's enough. You need to back up off my woman." Is he seriously jealous of a dog? Wow, Toby takes alpha male to a whole new level.

Toby pulls me up to my feet, then we walk over to where Mack and the rest of the club are gathered around in a circle.

"I decided that since you all are a part of this club, not just the men, that we would all discuss building the new clubhouse. Hope that's all right with all of you," Mack says, looking at each of us before moving on to the next person.

It only takes about an hour to come up with a plan and set it into motion. The guys are going to do most of the work, but they will need help building the frame for the building. Dani said she heard of a company an hour away that would be perfect for the job. She gave them a call and they're coming next week to start the re-build.

With that out of the way, we all head inside and grab some food Mack had delivered and have a couple of drinks.

I spot Blaze looking at me funny, but try to ignore him. I haven't spoken to him much since everything went down, and frankly, I'm a little afraid to. I don't want him to blame me for Dani being taken and again, her and the baby put into danger. I blame myself enough as it is, though Dani says that it could have happened anyway with Trixie involved. I still can't believe she helped Rick. Her reasoning is really beyond me. She could never be Dani, so she obviously had delusions of grandeur.

I make my way back outside so we can start the service for Lyle, but Blaze reaches out his hand to stop me. "Can I talk to you for a minute?" he asks without emotion, so I have no idea what's coming. I almost wish he'd look pissed instead of indifferent, so I knew what to expect.

"S-sure," I finally get out, then follow him into a room in the back of the house. Now, I'm really nervous. No witnesses.

Once we are both in the room, he looks at me with a small smile on his face. "No reason to be nervous, Sara." He laughs.

"Easy for you to say," I murmur to myself.

"I just wanted to say thank you for what you did

for Dani. She told me that it would have been a lot worse if you hadn't done something. So, thank you," he says like it's almost painful. I guess for him, it probably is. I doubt he ever really says thank you to anyone, and I know for a fact he never says sorry. That would mean he did something wrong, and to him, I don't think he ever does anything wrong—at least in his eyes.

"O-oh, uh, sure?" I phrase it as a question because I have no idea what else to say to that. Surely saying you're welcome is uncalled for in this situation, especially since I don't feel like I deserve thanks. It was my fault to begin with.

I'm not sure what he was looking for out of this conversation, but he must be just as uncomfortable, or maybe it did go the way he wanted, because he nods his head and finally relaxes a bit. "Okay. Well, let's get back out there before Toby starts tearing this house apart looking for you," he says, which has me laughing because he's not that far off from the truth.

When we get back outside, everyone is there and waiting. Mack starts a fire in the fire ring and everyone goes quiet for a moment of silence. Then, we all go around sharing stories of the times we've had with Lyle. When it's my turn, I wipe my eyes.

"I hadn't known Lyle as long all of you, but I considered him like an uncle. When I first met him at the strip club, I knew instantly that he was a good man. He always made me feel safe, could always make me laugh, and was always there to offer a hug when I needed it. He was my Teddy Bear, of course," I say, which has everyone laughing. "I know you all have told me numerous times that it wasn't my fault that people were hurt or that Lyle died last week. And though I may never agree with you, I've come to terms that regardless of fault, we all lost a great and wonderful man. He was a brother and a friend. He was a guardian angel. So here's to Lyle; may he rest in peace and always look over us." I raise my beer above my head and watch everyone else do the same.

Taking a long drink, I look up into the sky and can almost feel Lyle looking down upon me. "I'll miss you, Teddy Bear, and I will always think of you and keep your memory alive," I whisper to myself.

EPILOGUE

Sara

When we finally make it back to Toby's house that night, it's past one in the morning. I'm still recovering a bit, so I feel completely drained.

"Let's get you to bed, doll," Toby whispers in my ear, leaning against my back as we walk in the door. Not having enough energy to argue, or say anything, really, I nod my head and let him lead me to his bedroom.

Once inside, I let him undress me before he picks me up and carries me to bed. Placing me in the middle, I watch as he removes his shirt, then his pants and boxers. Damn, I'll never get tired of seeing this man naked. "See something you like?" he asks with a cocky smile.

Feeling suddenly energized, I reach out to him and pull him on top of me. "As a matter of fact, I do," I say right before I lean up and touch my lips to his.

He growls, reaching his hands up to cradle my

face and take control of the kiss, deepening it. I moan into his mouth and pull on his shoulders, needing him closer—so much closer. I don't want to be able to tell where I end and he begins. I want to be one with him.

Sensing what I need, he reaches down and pulls my right leg up around his waist, grinding his cock against me. He eases inside of me, taking his time. It's been a while since we last connected like this, since before the whole episode with Trixie and Rick. Toby was concerned that he would hurt me if we moved too fast, too soon.

"Yes," I moan into his ear, loving the feel of him inside of me. If we could stay like this forever, I would gladly give up anything.

"Fuck, you feel so fucking good wrapped around my cock," Toby growls out. The way he talks to me while fucking me is enough to make me come with his words alone.

Feeling that I'm close to exploding, he slows his thrusts down a little. Even though the rhythm is slower, when he does thrust inside of me, it's harder and deeper. It's amazing. He reaches his hand between us and starts rubbing fast circles on my clit. "Oh my God, yes," I yell, so close to reaching my orgasm, I'm seeing stars.

"That's right, doll, come all over my cock," he says in his low, sexy voice, and I instantly explode, screaming out his name.

When I come down from my high and open my eyes, I see him staring at me with wonder. He's barely moving, so wanting him to finish, I grab onto his ass with both hands and pull him into me.

"Please fuck me, Toby. I want to feel you come inside of me."

"Fuck, Sara," he groans, then starts up a punishing rhythm, pounding me into the mattress.

"Yes! Right there," I scream, feeling another orgasm coming.

Pumping into me a few more times, I feel him stiffen before I feel the warmth of his cum fill me.

I rub my hands up and down his back while both of us try to catch our breath.

I don't know how long we lay here like this, but I'm almost asleep when I hear him whisper, "Marry me." I'm shocked and not sure if I heard him right. I don't say anything or even move a muscle.

After a few silent seconds pass, he props himself up on his elbows and looks down at me. My eyes are open, but I'm afraid to look into his. If I was hearing things and he didn't actually say that, I'm afraid I'll be disappointed. But also, if he did say it, maybe he didn't mean it. Maybe it was a heat of the moment kind of thing.

"Look at me, doll," he says, grabbing my chin and forcing my eyes on his.

When I finally comply, all I see is love. "I think I've loved you from the moment I saw you walk into the gym. You were everything I didn't know I wanted, everything I wasn't looking for, but as soon as I saw you, I knew you were mine. I love you more than anything in this world, Sara. I'd lay down my life for you, and do anything to make you smile. You make me want to be a better man. I don't have a ring yet, but will you please say you'll marry me? Tomorrow, a month from now, or even a year? Just say that you'll marry me. Be mine, Sara."

I'm full-on crying by the time he finishes, but I manage to get out a weak "yes" before he takes my mouth in a passionate kiss. This man loves me and wants to spend the rest of his life with me. I no longer have to fight this world alone.

**

Toby

Long after Sara falls asleep, I continue to watch her. I was so scared when I found out Rick had gotten her, but I didn't want to think she was lost to me forever. I don't know what I would have done if I lost her. She's like the air I need to live.

I wasn't planning on asking her to marry me tonight. I wanted to plan something special, get a ring and do it right, but lying here with her after making love, I just couldn't wait. I needed her to know that she was it for me and that I wanted to spend the rest of my life with her by my side.

I know she was shocked and maybe even a little scared, but when she said yes, my world felt right.

For so long, I had nothing until I became a part of the club. The only thing that really made me happy, that helped me get through the day, was knowing I had a family of sorts, and my fighting career. Now, my family is complete with her in my life, and I no longer need the cage to feel whole or grounded.

While I waited for her to wake up in the hospital, I had already decided that I would no longer fight.

I'm going to start training new fighters at the gym. I also want to set up more classes for women, to teach them how to protect themselves. We're going to make it free to those that are currently in shelters, trying to start their lives over after walking away from their abusive pasts. I haven't told Sara about it yet, but my hope is that she'll help. Maybe not with the classes, but with talking to the women—telling them her story about how she was able to move on and make a better life for herself. Maybe Dani can help too.

Finally closing my eyes, I fall asleep, knowing that today marks the start of the rest of my life. With Sara in my arms, loving me, I know we can make it through anything life throws our way. It will be her and I against the world, fighting destiny.

ACKNOWLEDGMENTS

I want to take this time to thank everyone who has stood beside me through this journey. I never thought I'd be able to get one book written and published, let alone another one. I hope you all enjoyed Toby and Sara's story. I put a lot a blood, sweat, and tears into the book and I hope it's everything you wanted it to be.

To everyone who read *Rewriting Destiny* and posted a review, thank you for your kind words and encouragements, and for all the criticism about what could have been better. I tried to do you all proud and use those words of advice to make *Fighting Destiny* better. I hope you like it and are just as excited for the next books. I know I am!

I also want to give a few shout outs to a couple of people that really helped make this book what it is.

Of course, my beta readers. You girls freaking rock and I love you three dearly.

Limitless Publishing, thank you for taking me on. My dream is be a writer. Thank you for helping me achieve me dream. Everyone on the LP Team, thank you for all your hard work to make this book shine.

All my Facebook friends that have stood behind me as a new author and supported everything I'm trying to do. Thank you for helping me get the word out and sharing all my teasers. I wouldn't be where I am today without you all, so thank you all so much!

My friends and family, you all are amazing. Thank you for bearing with me through the last couple of months and allowing me to accomplish my dream of writing. I know it's been a long road, but thank you for allowing me time to write and complete this book. Now…onto another one!

And everyone else that has supported or helped me along the way, I can never repay you for what you've done for me, no matter how small.

I love you all! Thank you for everything!

Keep an eye out for more books in the series!

Rewriting Destiny; Book 1–Prequel to the Forsaken Sinners MC Series

Born into Destiny; Book 2.5–Forsaken Sinners MC Novella

Defying Destiny: Book 3–Forsaken Sinners MC Series

Owning Destiny: Book 4–Forsaken Sinners MC Series

ABOUT THE AUTHOR

I grew up in a small town in Iowa. I have 2 older sisters and amazing parents. Growing up, I was always a daddy's girl, hanging out with him in the garage, fishing, and building stuff. I loved to play softball and swimming, but reading, telling stories, and writing were my passion, even at a young age. I took a break from writing for a while, but you could always find me with a book in my hand.

I have three children–two boys and a girl. They are my whole world. Even when I'm having the worst day ever, they brighten up my day and make me smile.

A few years ago, there was this story that would always play out in my head and no matter how many times I went through it, from beginning to end, it would never fade. So I decided to put it on paper. I didn't plan on publishing it, but when it was almost done, a friend asked to read it. She said it was a story that needed to be shared. And that's what started my writing career.

I love all genres of books, and even though I started with writing MC Romance, I have a whole book of ideas, so you can expect more from me than just MC, though romance is in my blood.

Even though I currently work two jobs, my ultimate dream is to become a full time author. I want to be able to spend my days filling pages with stories. I want to be the reason people find a reason to smile or laugh from lines on a page. Reading a book allows me to live in someone else's shoes, even if only for a few minutes. It's a way to leave my life and troubles behind and I want to be help others do that as well.

Facebook:
https://www.facebook.com/pages/Author-Shelly-Morgan/809266812448318

Twitter:
https://twitter.com/Shelly_Morgan34

Website:
https://www.goodreads.com/author/show/10914599.Shelly_Morgan

Join my fan group on Facebook:
https://www.facebook.com/groups/866725876706109/